'*Bueno, gracias,*' [illegible] but remained where he was. 'Y[illegible] wondering who the Sam Hill I am?'

'On the – um – contrary,' Mr. Reeder replied, applying the manual safety catch and returning his pistol to its holster, 'Your name is Alvin Dustine Fog. It is said that, in addition to being the most competent – um – gun-fighter of your generation, you are the youngest man ever to attain the rank of captain in the Texas Rangers and, because of this, you have acquired the sobriquet – um – "Cap".'

'I'd tell a man you know *all* about me,' the still concealed Southron chuckled.

'Not – um – all,' the detective corrected apologetically. 'I did not know you were in this country. Nor, I imagine, did Colonel Besgrove-Woodstole. Or he might have offered to – um – "trade", I believe is the term you American gentlemen employ, the information for something I know and in which he is *very* interested.'

'Whee-doggie!' "Cap" Fog ejaculated, leaning against the window's ledge and studying Mr. Reeder, who had walked over while speaking, with interest. 'Is whatever old Mad John Flack's setting up likely to get the Colonel and his boys from British Military Intelligence on their trail?'

'Nothing so – um – dramatic, as far as I'm aware,' Mr. Reeder said mildly. 'He would have made the exchange to obtain the names of the – um – chickens we are entering for the National Poultry Show.'

Also by J. T. Edson, in chronological order

Ole Devil Hardin series:
YOUNG OLE DEVIL
OLE DEVIL AND THE CAPLOCKS
OLE DEVIL AND THE MULE TRAIN
OLE DEVIL AT SAN JACINTO
GET URREA

Civil War Series:
COMANCHE
YOU'RE IN COMMAND NOW, MR. FOG
THE BIG GUN
UNDER THE STARS AND BARS
THE FASTEST GUN IN TEXAS
KILL DUSTY FOG!
THE DEVIL GUN
THE COLT AND THE SABRE
THE REBEL SPY
THE BLOODY BORDER
BACK TO THE BLOODY BORDER

The Floating Outfit Series:
THE YSABEL KID
.44 CALIBRE MAN
A HORSE CALLED MOGOLLON
GOODNIGHT'S DREAM
FROM HIDE AND HORN
SET TEXAS BACK ON HER FEET
THE HIDE AND TALLOW MEN
THE HOODED RIDERS
QUIET TOWN
TRAIL BOSS
WAGONS TO BACKSIGHT
TROUBLED RANGE
SIDEWINDER
RANGELAND HERCULES
MCGRAW'S INHERITANCE
THE HALF BREED
THE WILDCATS
THE BAD BUNCH
THE FAST GUN
CUCHILO
A TOWN CALLED YELLOWDOG
TRIGGER FAST
THE MAKING OF A LAWMAN
THE TROUBLE BUSTERS
THE LAW OF THE GUN
THE PEACEMAKERS
TO ARMS, TO ARMS, IN DIXIE!
HELL IN THE PALO DURO
GO BACK TO HELL
THE SOUTH WILL RISE AGAIN
SET A-FOOT†
THE RUSHERS
THE QUEST FOR BOWIE'S BLADE
THE FORTUNE HUNTERS
THE HARD RIDERS
THE RIO HONDO KID
WACO'S DEBT
THE TEXAN
THE FLOATING OUTFIT
APACHE RAMPAGE
RIO GUNS
RIO HONDO WAR
GUNSMOKE THUNDER
THE MAN FROM TEXAS
GUN WIZARD

The Floating Outfit Series, contd:
THE SMALL TEXAN
THE TOWN TAMERS
RETURN TO BACKSIGHT
TERROR VALLEY
GUNS IN THE NIGHT

The Waco Series:
SAGEBRUSH SLEUTH
ARIZONA RANGER
WACO RIDES IN
THE DRIFTER
DOC LEROY, M.D.
HOUND DOG MAN

The Calamity Jane Series:
COLD DECK, HOT LEAD
CALAMITY SPELLS TROUBLE
TROUBLE TRAIL
THE BULL WHIP BREED
THE COW THIEVES
WHITE STALLION, RED MARE
THE WHIP AND THE WAR LANCE*
THE BIG HUNT

The John Slaughter Series:
SLAUGHTER'S WAY
SLAUGHTER'S NEIGHBOURS†

The Brady Anchor And Jefferson Trade series:
TWO MILES TO THE BORDER
WHO DO YOU TRUST, UNCLE BRADY†

The Waxahachie Smith series:
NO FINGER ON THE TRIGGER†
SLIP GUN
WAXAHACHIE SMITH†
CURE THE TEXAS FEVER†

The 'Cap' Fog series:
'CAP' FOG MEET MR. J. G. REEDER

The Rockabye County Series:
SIXTEEN DOLLAR SHOOTER
THE SHERIFF OF ROCKABYE COUNTY†
THE PROFESSIONAL KILLERS
THE $\frac{1}{4}$ SECOND DRAW
THE DEPUTIES
POINT OF CONTACT
THE OWLHOOT
RUN FOR THE BORDER
BAD HOMBRE
THEY CALL IT PROGRESS†

The Bunduki series:
BUNDUKI
BUNDUKI AND DAWN
SACRIFICE FOR THE QUAGGA GOD

The School Swot series,
written in collaboration with Peter Clawson:
BLONDE GENIUS

* Awaiting Publication.
† In preparation.

J. T. Edson

'Cap' Fog, Texas Ranger, Meet Mr. J. G. Reeder

CORGI BOOKS
A DIVISION OF TRANSWORLD PUBLISHERS LTD

'CAP' FOG, TEXAS RANGER,
MEET MR. J. G. REEDER

A CORGI BOOK 0 552 10578 3

First publication in Great Britain

PRINTING HISTORY
Corgi edition published 1977

Corgi Books are published by
Transworld Publishers Ltd.,
Century House, 61–63 Uxbridge Road,
Ealing, London W5 5SA
Made and printed in Great Britain by
Cox & Wyman Ltd., London, Reading and Fakenham

This book is dedicated to the memory of a truly great writer whose stories have provided me with many hours of most enjoyable and entertaining reading:

EDGAR WALLACE

The author wishes to thank Penelope Wallace for allowing him to present further details regarding the career of her father's famous detective, Mr. J. G. Reeder.

'CAP' FOG, TEXAS RANGER, MEET MR. J. G. REEDER

IN EXPLANATION

WHILE attending the 21st Annual Convention of Western Writers of America at Fort Worth, Texas, in 1974, I was fortunate enough to meet several members of the Hardin, Fog and Blaze clan with whom I had previously only been in written contact. At that time, I was chiefly engaged in learning the facts pertaining to the early career of General Jackson Baines 'Ole Devil' Hardin, C.S.A.,[1] about how Marvin Eldridge 'Doc' Leroy finally qualified as a doctor[2] and why Belle, 'the Rebel Spy' Boyd[3] required the assistance of Martha 'Calamity Jane' Canary[4] on one of her assignments for the United States' Secret Service.[5]

When the first of the General's series of biographies appeared in print, several members of the J. T. EDSON APPRECIATION SOCIETY wrote asking why a fully trained Japanese *samurai*[6] like Tommy Okasi – this, incidentally was not his real name, but an Americanized corruption of the one he had given when rescued from a derelict vessel in the China Sea by a ship under the command of the General's father – had to leave his home land and could not return. So, following the 22nd Convention, held in Carson City, Nevada, I returned to Forth Worth in search of the information. Unfortunately, I have never learned to drive,[7] so I am indebted to my good friends Ellen and Chuck Kurtzman of that city. They not only put me up and put up with my horrible 'Swiss' jokes, but also supplied me with the 'wheels' which are so vitally necessary when one wishes to travel around in Texas.

My quest for information on the subject of Tommy Okasi

came to nothing. I was told that, because of the circumstances and the high social standing of the various families involved – all of whom have descendants holding positions of influence and importance in Japan at the time of writing – it was inadvisable even at this late date to make the facts of his departure public.

However, in the course of a conversation with Alvin Dustine 'Cap' Fog – formerly captain commanding Company 'J' of the Texas Rangers[8] – about his grandfather, Captain Dustine Edward Marsden 'Dusty' Fog, C.S.A., the legendary Rio Hondo gun wizard – for whom I have the honour to be biographer[9] – he mentioned that, early in his career, he had been to England and was involved in a case with the celebrated British detective, Mr. J. G. Reeder.

Instantly, my disappointment over the failure of my mission with respect to Tommy Okasi was forgotten. I had, of course, read all the volumes of biography which dealt with the known career of Mr. J. G. Reeder;[10] but I could not recollect seeing any mention of his association with 'Cap' Fog. Reading 'Cap's' official report and his other records removed all doubts. Regrettably, while thorough in their coverage of his part in the affair, they left a number of unanswered points where Mr. Reeder's participation was concerned.

On my return to England, I contacted Penelope Wallace, daughter of Mr. Reeder's biographer and organizer of THE EDGAR WALLACE SOCIETY, requesting corroboration of my information. Ms. Wallace kindly placed at my disposal all of her father's notes and the relevant case-book he had received from Mr. Reeder, but had not worked upon. Not only did these allow me to fill in the gaps of 'Cap's' story, but they cleared up several hitherto puzzling aspects relating to Mr. Reeder. The latter, in fact, proved to be as intriguing and interesting as the story itself. They enlarged upon the suggestions put forth by John A. Hogan, A.M.I.M.I. – arguably the world's foremost *serious* student and researcher of Edgar Wallace – in his excellent article AUREUS HARUNDUM.[11]

Finally, Ms. Wallace had kindly allowed me to set down

the facts and here they are:

J. T. Edson,
Active Member, Western Writers of America.
Melton Mowbray,
Leics. England.

1. *Details of General Jackson Baines Hardin's early career are given in the 'Ole Devil' series of biographies by J. T. Edson. His nickname arose in part from the way in which he deliberately enhanced the Mephistophelian aspect of his face, but mainly through the reputation he gained among his contemporaries as being a 'lil ole devil for a fight.'*
2. *Told in:* DOC LEROY, M.D., *by J. T. Edson.*
3. *Details of Belle Boyd's background and career are given in:* THE COLT AND THE SABRE; THE REBEL SPY; THE BLOODY BORDER; BACK TO THE BLOODY BORDER; THE HOODED RIDERS; THE BAD BUNCH; TO ARMS, TO ARMS, IN DIXIE!; THE SOUTH WILL RISE AGAIN *and* THE QUEST FOR BOWIE'S BLADE *by J. T. Edson.*
4. *Details of Martha Jane Canary's background and career are given in the 'Calamity Jane' series of biographies by J. T. Edson. She also makes 'guest' appearances in various of the 'Floating Outfit' series by the same author.*
5. *Details of the assignment are given by J. T. Edson in:* THE WHIP AND THE WAR LANCE.
6. Samurai: *a member of the Japanese lower nobility's élite warrior class, usually acting as a retainer of the* Daimyos, *the hereditary feudal barons. A masterless* samurai *who became a mercenary was known as a* roñin. *During the mid-19th century, shortly after Tommy Okasi's departure, an increasing contact with the Western World was bringing an ever growing realization that the retention of an hereditary and privileged warrior class was not compatible with the formation of a modern and industrialized society. Various edicts issued by the Emperor between 1873 and '76 abolished the special rights of the* samurai *and, although some of their traditions and concepts were retained, they ceased to exist. J.T.E.*

7. *The author is too modest to suggest that, during his twelve and a half years' service with the Royal Army Veterinary Corps, he was too valuable as a dog trainer to be spared for long enough to be taught to drive. However, anybody who wishes to believe this was the case is at liberty to do so. J.T.E.*
8. *The Texas Rangers were to all practical purposes abolished – their functions being absorbed by the more prosaic Department of Public Safety and the Highway Patrol – on October the 17th, 1935, almost one hundred years to the day after their formation. Details of modern Texas law enforcement techniques are given in J. T. Edson's 'Rockabye County' series of biographies.*
9. *Details of Captain Dustine Edward Marsden 'Dusty' Fog, C.S.A.'s career and background are given in the 'Civil War' and 'Floating Outfit',* q.v., *series of biographies by J. T. Edson.*
10. *Other details of Mr. J. G. Reeder's career and cases are covered in:* ROOM 13; THE MIND OF MR. J. G. REEDER; RED ACES; MR. J. G. REEDER RETURNS *and* TERROR KEEP *by Edgar Wallace. J.T.E.*
11. Aureus Harundum: *to quote John A. Hogan, 'It is the nearest I can get with my memories of Latin to "Golden Reeder", which seemed rather apt in this case.' J.T.E.*

CHAPTER ONE

I NEVER EXPECTED TO MEET A YANKEE

IN consideration of subsequent events, although some of the participants who were to become involved might have disagreed with such a viewpoint, quite a number of people – not excluding the young lady in question – had good cause to be grateful that Beryl Snowhill was a very competent driver and that her silver-grey 1925 MG Super Sports two-seater tourer was equipped with well maintained vacuum servo-operated brakes.

All in all, Beryl presented an attractive picture as she sat in the swiftly moving vehicle and guided it with deft assurance around a fairly sharp and blind curve. Not quite five foot four inches in height, she would be twenty on her next birthday. Her boyishly short and shingled platinum blonde hair framed a radiantly beautiful face which showed strength of will and intelligence in its lines. Even being clad in a thick white woollen roll-neck pullover and jodhpurs could not entirely conceal the contours of a body fast ripening into womanhood. In fact, although until recently she had been regarded as something of a tomboy, several eligible young bachelors had begun to grow increasingly aware of the change. They – and their mothers, as she was well connected and wealthy in her own right – began to consider her in a more intimate light than that of a companion who could ride, shoot, fish, play golf and drive a sports car with the best of them. However, as yet none of the potential suitors had found favour in her eyes.

Having been asked rather belatedly to take a package into Swindon so that it could be dispatched to London on the one forty-five train, Beryl was driving somewhat faster than was advisable when traversing the narrow and winding country lane which joined the main road at Little Venner. In exculpation, as she was neither reckless nor irresponsible by nature, she was confident that she would have the lane to herself. The second Sunday in May was traditionally celebrated by a free lunch and garden fête at the village's vicarage. The remarkably pleasant weather could be counted upon to ensure a large attendance of visitors, all of whom – as the vicar frowned on late-comers – would already be there. Nor was she given the slightest indication or warning of the highly dramatic situation in which she was to become involved on emerging from the curve.

The field that the girl was passing belonged to Charles Wagon, one of her uncle's neighbours. Having previously been concealed by its high and thick hedge, a man came into her range of vision without her receiving any previous notice of his presence in the vicinity. Erupted into her view would have been a much more apt description of his appearance. Impelled by some motive which was not apparent to her, he vaulted over a five-barred gate with such vigour that the momentum prevented him from coming to an immediate halt on landing. Instead, he advanced from the right side into the middle of the lane about thirty yards ahead of the MG.

As she frequently took part in various sporting activities, some of which were not considered suitable for a well-bred young lady, Beryl's natural aptitude for rapid thought and action was greatly improved. She had dire need for quick responses at that moment. A glance at the speedometer warned her that she was travelling at just over forty miles per hour. Experience with the little tourer had taught her that, at such a speed, she could not stop in less than ninety feet.

The man who had confronted her so unexpectedly was much closer than that!

Even as Beryl was drawing her conclusions, almost without the need for conscious thought her driver's reflexes assumed control and started to cope with the emergency. Before she had completed the depression of the foot brake and clutch, she realized that they were unlikely to prove sufficient for her needs. So she applied the hand brake as an additional aid in the hope of halting before she reached the man. Flying back to the steering wheel, her right hand sought to attempt to swing the tourer away from him.

It was to no avail!

In spite of all Beryl's efforts, as if being drawn towards its victim by a magnet, the vehicle continued to slide onwards to the accompaniment of a screeching protest from its tyres and the stench of burning rubber.

Much to the girl's horror, although there was a noticeable deceleration, she could do nothing further to prevent the MG from converging with the man.

Under less trying circumstances, Beryl would have found the man to be of considerable interest. Not, however, because he was of an imposing and impressive appearance. Rather the opposite, in fact. At most, although sturdily built and – as had been proven by the way he had bounded over the high gate – remarkably agile, he was only two inches taller than herself. Bare headed, with an unusual broad brimmed, low crowned white hat dangling by a fancy leather chinstrap on to his wide shoulders, he had curly black hair and a tanned, fairly handsome, but not eye-catching young face. Like his hat, the rest of his garments were not of a kind one would have expected to see being worn in Wiltshire during 1928. He had on a waist long brown leather jacket and an open necked grey worsted shirt with an attached collar. Held up by a wide brown leather belt with a floral pattern carved into it, his peculiar trousers had faded to a very light shade of blue. Their narrow legs were turned up at the bottoms to form cuffs almost three inches deep and were hanging outside sharp-toed, somewhat high heeled, riding boots of foreign origin.

Unimpressive and, apart from his attire, unnoticeable as the young man might seem, he showed himself to be capable of thinking and acting with great rapidity. At the last moment, when it seemed to the distraught girl that a collision was imminent and inescapable, he averted it. Swinging to face the tourer, instead of trying to throw himself either forward or to the rear – neither of which would have saved him at such a close proximity – he launched himself into the air and spread his legs wide apart. Bringing down his hands on either side of the radiator cap's rearing horse mascot, he thrust with them as if playing leapfrog and landed astride the rounded, Morris-style 'bullnose' bonnet.

Even as the young man was rising into the air, the tourer was being brought to a stop. For all that, his evasive actions had been necessary and he would have been run down if he had not taken them. What was more, despite – or because of – the alacrity with which he had moved, if Beryl had been dilatory in her response and the car's brakes less effective, he would still have been in danger. The vehicle's momentum would not have been sufficiently reduced to prevent a disaster. As it was, instead of being thrown against, or even through, the windshield, he came to rest without having reached it.

Some thirty seconds went by in silence. It was disturbed only by the purring of the tourer's engine, which had not stalled in spite of the stresses imposed by the emergency halt. Beryl was sitting as if turned to stone. All the colour was drained from her face and she clutched at the steering wheel so hard that her knuckles had turned white.

Considering that he had had such a narrow escape, the young man was showing neither distress nor alarm. Instead, after throwing a quick glance in the direction from which he had come, he thrust back his left leg and quit his perch on the car's bonnet as if he was dismounting from a horse.

'I'm right sorry to have come out on you-all that way, ma'am,' the young man said, in an almost casually conversational tone, stepping to the passenger's door. 'And I surely hope I didn't spook you too much.'

'Spook—!' the girl yelped, jolted out of her state of shock by the quiet words and, despite her nerves being in a jangled condition, realizing what the final sentence must mean. Relaxing her grasp on the steering wheel and sinking from the braced position she had assumed, but keeping the foot brake and clutch held down, she glared at the speaker for a moment before bursting out angrily, 'Do you know that I might have killed you, running in front of me the way you did?'

'Might say's how I'd got right good cause for doing it, ma'am, even though I didn't aim to,' the young man answered and Beryl suddenly became aware that his drawling accent was not English. Looking past her, he went on in the same matter-of-fact manner, 'And, happen you'd oblige, ma'am, I'd take it right neighbourly to get a ride the he— right away from here.'

Much to her surprise, as the tension caused by the narrowly averted accident began to ebb away, the girl identified the young man's accent. It was that of a person who had his origins somewhere south of the Mason-Dixon line[1] in the United States of America.

The drumming of hooves came to the girl's ears before she could comment upon her discovery. Turning her head, she saw three horsemen galloping across the field from which the stranger had emerged so precipitously. The rider in the lead was the owner of the property and she could think of a very excellent reason for the young man having made such a hasty departure.

Close to six foot tall and broad in proportion, attired in the kind of clothing a well-to-do country gentleman might wear if he was not too selective in his choice of a tailor, Charles Cuthbert Horace Wagon had a surly face even his mother might have been excused for disliking.

Although they shared a mutual interest in horse racing – he owned a small training stable adjacent to General Snowhill's larger establishment – Beryl had never met Wagon socially. She had heard that he was a bad tempered bully, heartily disliked by most people with whom he came into contact and not noted for scrupulous – or even partial – honesty. In fact, her uncle and others in a position to know claimed that he was – using the parlance of the Sport of Kings – 'hot' and more than once had been on the verge of being 'warned off' by the Stewards of the Jockey Club for suspected malpractices.

1. Mason-Dixon line: sometimes erroneously called the 'Mason-Dixie' line. The boundary between Pennsylvania and Maryland, as surveyed in 1763–67 by the Englishmen Charles Mason and Jeremiah Dixon, which came to be regarded as the dividing line separating the Southern 'Slave' and Northern 'Free' States of America. J.T.E.

Being the kind of person he was, Wagon had an understandable – if not commendable – antipathy towards anybody showing an uninvited interest in his activities and took grave exception to trespassers upon his property. From the stories that the girl had heard, he did not restrict himself to merely invoking the due processes of the law when dealing with interlopers. Instead, he was said to inflict corporal punishment of some severity upon them.

Almost matching the trainer in size, not so elegantly – or flashily, depending upon one's tastes in sartorial matters – dressed, but with – if possible – even more unprepossessing features, the other two riders were his employees. While they were listed upon the returns he reluctantly rendered to the Inland Revenue authorities as 'stablehands', it was rumoured in Little Venner's two public houses that their duties were less concerned with such basic tasks as mucking out stalls and filling hay-nets than in ensuring that his desire for privacy was respected.

Although Beryl had grown up around racing stables and derived a good proportion of her income from the breeding and training of thoroughbred horses, she considered that there were distinct limits to how far the discouragement of touts should be taken. As Wagon was alleged to far exceed these bounds and nothing of the little she had seen of him caused her to believe otherwise, she reached a decision. In her opinion, such a diminutive intruder as the escaping stranger would have no chance of defending himself against a man of the trainer's size, much less with the two bulky 'stablehands' present.

'Get in!' the girl snapped.

'*Gracias,* ma'am,' answered the stranger, obeying with alacrity. Then, realizing that his rescuer probably did not speak Spanish, he repeated his expression of gratitude in his own brand of English. 'Why thank you 'most to death, ma'am. I surely appreciate it.'

Even as her unexpected passenger was speaking, ignoring the trainer's bellow of furious protest, Beryl released the hand brake. The riders were almost at the gate, but she knew there would be ample time for her to take the young man to safety. Changing into first gear, she let out the clutch and, removing the pressure she had been exerting on the foot brake, set the little tourer into motion.

Once the vehicle was moving and picking up speed, the girl found herself consumed by curiosity.

What had brought the young American to England?

And why had he found himeslf engaged in the precarious, hardly lucrative, occupation of racehorse tout?

A sense of compassion, and a distaste for the kind of bullying which could bring training into disrepute, would have made Beryl save anybody, particularly such a small and harmless looking a person, from Wagon's wrath. However, after covering about half a mile in silence and knowing they were safe from pursuit, she could not restrain her curiosity any longer.

'Life's funny,' the girl remarked, glancing sideways. 'I never expected to meet a Yankee when I left home this afternoon.'

'Where'd you come across one, ma'am?' the young man inquired, swinging his gaze around from watching the lane behind them.

'Why you, of course,' Beryl explained, but the winding nature of the lane prevented her from looking at her passenger. 'You're one, aren't you?'

'No, ma'am, I'm *not*!' the stranger declared and his lazy sounding drawl contrived to sound very emphatic. 'And, was I you-all, I wouldn't go calling anybody else from Texas a Yankee.' The words came out as 'ah', 'yawl', 'Taixsus' and 'Yonkee'. 'It's all right by me, mind, I've been raised tolerable broadminded. But most folks back home to Texas'd rather you said's they'd voted Republican than for you-all to go accusing them of being Yankees.'

Something in her passenger's voice caused the girl to turn her head in his direction without regard for the winding state of the lane. She found a pair of grey eyes which were twinkling with merriment. They seemed out of place in the tanned and otherwise expressionless face which was focussed upon her.

Suddenly Beryl had an uneasy suspicion that she might have been mistaken about the young man who was sitting by her side. One of her reasons for helping him had been because she had assumed he was slightly younger than herself. On making a closer examination, she decided that there was vastly more to him than had been suggested by her original and, of necessity, hurried glance. Various details began to impress themselves upon her. There was, she observed, an aura of controlled self-assurance about him that was not in accord with callow youth. He certainly was somewhat older than she had imagined, in his mid-twenties at least and with far more worldly wisdom than his appearance implied. What was more, he was far from puny. The spread of his shoulders, trimming down to a lean waist, and the play of the thigh muscles which stretched tight the upper legs of his peculiar trousers suggested a physical strength well above average for his height.

'Wouldn't want to sound pushy, ma'am, being your guest and all,' the young man commented, with a note of strangely unhurried urgency coming into his voice although his general demeanour did not change. 'Only I reckon's it'd happen be better was you to watch the trail.'

'I don't know how it is in the United States,' Beryl said, after a piece of skilful manipulation on her part had taken the speeding tourer around the fairly sharp bend that had provoked her passenger's advice. 'Or should I say how it is in *Texas*—'

'Shucks, ma'am,' the young man replied, still with the faintly sardonic timbre to his voice which the girl was finding increasingly annoying. 'Us Texans let the United States join up with us back in 'Forty-Six.[2] We'n's don't mind folks figuring we're a part of it, just so long's they don't forget we're the biggest and dad-blasted best State of all.'

'I'll be sure to remember!' Beryl promised, practically spitting the words out and seeking for a way to disturb the calm composure of the man by her side. 'I don't know how it is in *Texas*, but you shouldn't let yourself be talked into

2. On February the 16th, 1846, after protracted negotiations, the United States of America annexed what was then the independent Republic of Texas. The Texans had won their freedom from Mexican domination in a campaign which culminated on April the 21st, with the decisive Battle of San Jacinto, see OLE DEVIL AT SAN JACINTO by J. T. Edson. It was supplanted as the largest State of the Union by Alaska in 1959. J.T.E.

touting race-horses in this country. Particularly where somebody like Charlie Wagon is concerned. If he'd caught you—'

'Likely, ma'am,' the young man replied, as the girl allowed her words to trail away in what she regarded as a dramatically warning manner. 'Happen thishere "touting" means what I reckon it does, it's not took kindly to back home to Texas neither. Only I wasn't on his range trying to see how fast his horses can run.'

'Then why were you—?' the girl began, before she could prevent herself.

'Thishere's a right smart lil old jalopy you've got, ma'am,' the Texan drawled, after his politely prohibitive gaze and the girl's innate good manners had brought the question to a halt. 'It doesn't handle *too* bad at all, but give me my Kissel Eight Seventy-Five most any ole time. Now *there's* a gas-buggy with what I'd call *real* good road-handling and performance.'

Belonging to a generation with an inborn sense of purpose and with no need to try and boost a realization of personal inadequacy, Beryl was infuriated at the young foreigner's somewhat condescending reference to her highly prized vehicle. While its manufacturers were already developing more powerful and sophisticated models to supersede it, the little MG Super Sports Tourer had built up a good reputation, even in comparison with various more expensive overseas' competitors. Certainly she did not accept that it deserved to be dismissed as nothing more than a 'lil ole jalopy', 'right smart' or otherwise. So she decided to show her passenger that he was riding in a car which possessed qualities that left nothing to be desired.

Causing the tourer to go faster, the girl guided it along the lane in a way which she felt sure was displaying it to the very best advantage. Although she managed an occasional swift sideways glance in the hope of discovering if the Texan was impressed by the demonstration, driving required her complete attention and precluded the possibility of continuing the conversation.

Beryl had reached Little Venner and the Texan was asking to be put down before she realized that she had not satisfied her curiosity about him. As she drove away, leaving him standing at the edge of the village green and looking towards the front door of the Starter's Hack public house, she wondered if that was the reason he had made the provocative comment.

CHAPTER TWO

GET DOWN, QUICKLY

'PERSONALLY, although I can't dispute that in general their egg-laying capacity is inferior, I've always found Minorcas to be far less excitable than either Brown or White Leghorns,' remarked the slightly shorter of the two gentlemen who were strolling in a leisurely fashion across the front lawn of Daffodil House. He watched his companion as if searching for a reaction to his words as he continued, 'But none of them stand out as well as Buff Cochins when it comes to catching the judges' eye and, from what I hear, Cochins are what old Barraclough's putting his faith in for Crystal Palace this year.'

'I've heard rumours to that – um – effect too, Colonel,' admitted the second stroller, his mild tones almost apologetic in their timbre. He gave no sign that he was aware of the other's scrutiny.

'They stand out even better than – Wyandottes – shall we say,' the first speaker remarked in a somewhat challenging fashion.

'That is, of course and with – um – respect, a matter of opinion,' the second man answered, but his attitude suggested that he would not think of arguing with the other's point of view.

Despite each being a person of some considerable importance in his own right, there was nothing out of the ordinary in the pair's appearance apart from the taller's rather archaic attire. In fact, they blended harmoniously with the early Sunday afternoon's peace and tranquillity which pervaded Brockley Road.

The first speaker was a little above medium height, spare

of build and had close cropped, iron grey hair. There was a firm, disciplined hardness about his tanned and clean shaven face which, taken with his ramrod straight carriage was suggestive of a military background. He had on a smartly tailored Harris tweed suit, a white shirt and a Rifle Brigade's diagonally striped black and dark green regimental tie such as a serving, or retired, officer in *mufti*[1] might be expected to wear.

Almost six foot tall, the second of the gentlemen did not exude any such martial aura and, apart from a mutual interest in domestic chickens, he seemed to have little in common with his companion. His clothing was of a style which had been practically *de rigueur* for the bailiff of a County Court, or a coroner's officer, in an earlier decade. In spite of being on his own property, he sported the kind of high and flat crowned black bowler hat which had ceased to be fashionable several years ago. Nor was his black frock coat, buttoned tightly around him as if to emphasize his slender frame, any more modern in its cut. Furthermore, a ready-made cravat of the broad 'chest protector' pattern – buckled under a white 'Gladstonian' shirt collar – combined with the coat, somewhat narrow legged striped trousers and a pair of black, square-toed boots to imply that their wearer was no longer in the first flush of youth. For all his sprightly movements, his sandy side-whiskers, rather outstanding ears, mournful cast of features and fairly prominent nose – upon which, secured to his lapel with a silk cord, steel rimmed *pince-nez* perched so far down that it would be impossible for him to see through them – failed to do anything to correct a general impression of advanced middle age.

'I haven't made up my mind what to enter,' the military-looking visitor remarked, coming to a halt at the front gate.

'Neither have we,' his host replied.

'You wouldn't have any difficulty in making your selection if Curly Toes was still alive,' the visitor commented, referring to the other's champion Blue-Laced Wyandotte hen which – in addition to its almost perfect physical conformation – had been celebrated for its predilection towards

1. *Mufti:* civilian clothing, especially when it is the attire of a person who normally wears a uniform. J.T.E.

eating fruit cake.[2] 'We're not likely to see her equal for a long time.'

'Hardly, Colonel, hardly,' agreed the elderly seeming owner of Daffodil House, his whole bearing redolent of sorrow at the reminder of the superlative Curly Toes' demise. 'Regrettably as yet, none of her – um – progeny have attained such high standards.'

'Then you won't be showing any of them?' the visitor inquired, with a guileless air that begged to inspire confidence.

'As I – um – said, Colonel,' the host sighed, as if regretting having to impart such negative information. 'As yet, we haven't reached any definite decision about which birds to enter.'

Mr. J. G. Reeder always derived considerable enjoyment from discussing his hobby with such an eminent authority – albeit, also a friendly rival – as Colonel Brian Besgrove-Woodstole, D.S.O., M.C. and Bar. That afternoon, the conversation was being given the added fillip of parrying the visitor's attempt to discover which of his birds would be exhibited at the forthcoming National Poultry Show at the Crystal Palace. However, he did not forgo his habit of constant – if far from obvious or noticeable – all round observation. Even before he had succeeded to the post of Chief Investigative Officer for the Director of Public Prosecutions, he had learned the value of unceasing vigilance as a means of avoiding the attentions of persons who had reasons to be evilly disposed towards him.

On the face of it, there was not much for Mr. Reeder to see and certainly nothing to cause him concern.

At that hour on a Sunday, especially such a pleasant one, those residents of Brockley Road who were not paying visits to the sea-side, the Zoological Gardens in Regent's Park, or other areas of pleasurable and cultural relaxation, were seated around the tables of their respective dining rooms and partaking of that most sacrosanct of British institutions, Sunday lunch. In fact, if there had not been some minor contretemps in the kitchen of Daffodil House, Mr. Reeder and his guest would have been conforming with the tradi-

2. See Chapter VIII, RED ACES, by Edgar Wallace. J.T.E.

tion. So, except for a police constable who was approaching along the opposite pavement from the direction of Tanners Hill and a car that had turned out of Lewisham High Road, the detective and the Colonel were the only signs of life.

Big and heavily built, the constable was walking with his hands behind his back and using the slow, measured stride which seemed to epitomize the reassuring solidarity of a legal system that still had a bite to ensure that its authority was respected. However, even as Mr. Reeder's gaze turned upon him, he came to a halt and stared ahead. Although a good hundred yards separated them, to the detective it seemed that the officer's attitude was suggestive of his having seen something unexpected. Yet there was no apparent reason for his behaviour. Certainly it had not been caused by the sight of Mr. Reeder and his guest. It was common knowledge, particularly to the local constabulary, that the former was the owner of Daffodil House and might be seen in its grounds, but the Colonel was not sufficiently famous in his official capacity to arouse interest.

Nor, at first sight, did the car appear worthy of the constable's attention. It was a dark blue 1926 Clyno Royal four door sedan and had the comfortably solid look becoming a competitor with the Ford, Austin, or Morris ranges of vehicles which were aimed at the suburban family market. Driven by a thickset, black bearded man of middle height who had on a black bowler, respectable brown suit, white shirt with a sedate blue tie and thick rimmed dark glasses, it was carrying two just as soberly attired but bare headed passengers seated one behind the other. It was cruising in a decorous manner to which even the most officious police officer could not take exception.

In spite of the constable's behaviour, to most people the scene would have been one of orderly suburban peace and serenity. However, as Mr. Reeder not infrequently mentioned, he was possessed of what he described as a 'criminal mind'. It caused him to look behind the exterior of everything which came to his notice. He could examine the most innocuous seeming sights and activities, considering how they might be converted to the purposes of evil and wrong doing. When, for example, his views had been made public on how the harmless and generally accepted practice of leaving deliveries of milk on doorsteps in the early hours of the morning might become an adjunct to mass murder,[3] they were said to have caused great consternation in the dairy industry.

Whether the sensation was due to the potentially criminal inclinations of his mind, or because his brain had been trained to function as an orderly and efficient card-index file, Mr. Reeder began to feel perturbed. It had often been claimed that he was the best informed man in England. To a great extent, that was true. Details gathered from a multitude of sources were brought to his attention and, once absorbed, he never forgot them.

In conjunction with what Mr. Reeder had observed and was deducing, two such items came crowding to the fore.

They were alarming in their implications!

'In a way, it's a deuced pity that we can't make line-breeding an exact science,' Besgrove-Woodstole went on, oblivious of the disturbing thoughts which were assailing his host and still hoping to gain some idea of the kind of competition his prize Barred Plymouth Rock cocks and hens would have to contend with in the dual-purpose – egg-laying and table meat producing – classes at the Crystal Palace. 'But if we did, there'd be no pleasure and anticipation, nor any real purpose even, in holding the National Poultry Show.'

'That is very true, Colonel,' Mr. Reeder conceded.

Even as the detective was speaking, although the Clyno's occupants were unaware of the fact, he kept his attention directed towards it and could now make out certain highly significant details. The driver, for all his bushy beard, was undoubtedly British, but – in spite of their attire having been purchased in England – the passengers had the swarthy features distinctive of Latin certainly and probably Italian parentage.

Although Mr. Reeder had drawn his conclusions from the appearance of the man behind the steering wheel and the possible nationality of the passengers, he realized that the constable was too far away to have been able to duplicate it. Nor, at that distance, would the two letters and three

3. See Chapter IX, TERROR KEEP, by Edgar Wallace. J.T.E.

numbers of the vehicle's London and May 1926 registered license plates be readable. So none of those details could have supplied the officer with a suggestion that something was wrong.

Yet a further item for Mr. Reeder to add to the puzzle was that he did not recognize the constable. While he could not claim to be acquainted with every member of the Metropolitan Police Force, he had had dealings – even if only to the extent of supplying a surreptitious cup of tea on a cold and wet night – with those officers who were generally assigned to the beat which incorporated Brockley Road. Of course, there were a number of completely innocent reasons why an unfamiliar man should have been assigned to the duty.

But, as has been mentioned, Mr. Reeder had a 'criminal mind'.

All of which suggested—;

Yet there had been no warning that—;

While Mr. Reeder was trying to reconcile the lack of information to his fund of alarming conjecture, he noticed that the man in the front passenger seat was saying something in the brisk manner of one who was giving an order. Instantly, the Clyno's leisurely pace was accelerated and, to add to his suspicions Mr. Reeder observed that both of the left hand windows had been wound down until fully open.

In itself, the latter discovery ought to have meant little or nothing.

However, if Mr. Reeder's theory was correct, the windows were open for more than letting the occupants take advantage of the exceptionally clement weather.

They were posing a very serious and terrible threat to the lives of the detective and his guest!

'Get down, quickly!' Mr. Reeder snapped and, while the words were exploding from his lips, he wondered if his appreciation of the situation had come too late.

Already, despite there having been nothing to give a warning that they had such devices in their possession, each of the passengers brought into view a wicked looking double barrelled, sawed-off shotgun. Working with the deft motions which were indicative of considerable training, they started to thrust the yawning .729 of an inch calibre muzzles through their respective windows. Instead of placing the butts to their shoulders, the pair were aiming by rough alignment. They were confident that the nine buckshot balls in each of the four chambers' shells would spread upon being discharged and encompass the two victims standing by the front gate of Daffodil House.

Without the need for conscious guidance, two right forefingers tightened on triggers. To the accompaniment of an almost simultaneous quadruple roar, so expertly had the weapons' mechanisms been adjusted, white smoke gushed from first the right and then the left barrel of each shotgun. It followed in the wake of the invisible to the naked eye, but nevertheless potentially lethal, sprays of .32 calibre lead balls which were being emitted.

CHAPTER THREE

WHICH OF US WERE THEY AFTER

COLONEL BRIAN BESGROVE-WOODSTOLE, D.S.O., M.C. AND BAR, might have considered himself fortunate in that he had gone against his family's tradition and taken his commission in the 95th Regiment of Foot instead of following his three older brothers and several other predecessors into the Brigade of Guards. Being arguably the British Army's finest light infantry regiment, the Rifle Brigade did not march at the generally accepted one hundred and twenty paces a minute. Performing drill movements at a lively one hundred and eighty paces' timing trained a man to think and act with great rapidity. Although the Colonel had been seconded to duty away from his regiment, he retained the swiftness of reaction which had been instilled in him.

Hearing his host's command – the words, spat out in a vastly different fashion to that of Mr. J. G. Reeder's normally hesitant delivery – the Colonel did not waste time asking questions. A quick glance at the Clyno Royal sedan, which was rushing nearer at an ever increasing pace, indicated why the warning had been given. For some reason that was as yet far from obvious, the detective believed the occupants of the vehicle were up to no good. Nor, in spite of his much vaunted 'criminal mind', was Mr. Reeder an alarmist given to over-dramatic flights of fancy.

Even if Besgrove-Woodstole had thought otherwise, the sight of the two Latin-featured passengers producing the sawed-off shotguns would have removed all his doubts that the peril was genuine. So, acting with commendable speed, he twisted and flung himself down behind the thick privet hedge at the right side of the garden gate.

Satisfied that his guest not only appreciated the danger, but was taking the correct measures to counter it, Mr. Reeder gave thought to his own welfare. Nor, from what he could see happening, had his realization of their precarious situation come a moment too soon. In fact, he wondered if he might have delayed his plunging dive in the opposite direction to the Colonel too late to save himself.

Consternation showed briefly on the two would-be assassins' swarthy faces as they watched their prospective victims disappearing behind the dense masses of dark green foliage on either side of the gate. The understanding that their sinister purpose had been detected came just an instant too late. Try though each might, neither could prevent his right forefinger from completing the necessary pressure on the trigger and causing the twin barrels' charges to fire. Experts in their line, they both knew that their victims stood a better than even chance of passing beyond the spread of the disgorged buckshot balls.

Realizing that his companions' plot was miscarrying and knowing against whom they were contending, the driver's only thought was to get as far away from Brockley Road in the shortest possible time. With that in mind, he thrust his foot down even harder upon the accelerator. Ignoring a demand from the passenger at his left side – delivered in the harsh and snarling dialect peculiar to a certain type of Italian-born citizen of the United States – for him to stop so that they could return and finish the job, he kept the Clyno's speed increasing.

Conscious of the swishing caused by lead passing through the foliage above him, Besgrove-Woodstole alighted on his hands and knees without injury. Listening to the car speeding onwards and wishing he had a weapon with which to defend himself if the attackers should return, he glanced over his shoulder to find out how his host had fared.

What the Colonel saw caused him to feel considerable alarm.

Although the *pince-nez* had been dislodged by the violence of Mr. Reeder's evasive action, he still retained his hat and had clearly come through the attack unscathed.

However, much to Besgrove-Woodstole's consternation, he was already starting to rise with remarkable agility for one who seemed to be so ancient and fragile. Knowing his host, the agility was not the cause of the Colonel's emotion. Rather it was produced by what he regarded as the other's incautious behaviour. While the Clyno sounded as if it was continuing to depart, it could still return, giving its occupants a chance at a second attempt. Yet, despite the fact that he too was unarmed, Mr. Reeder showed no indication that he was contemplating a dash for the safety and shelter of Daffodil House.

Oblivious of the apprehension experienced by his guest, the detective peered over the hedge. He was equally aware that there could still be danger, but he had snatched a quick glance at his front door. What he had seen told him that it was reasonably safe for him to carry out an observation of their attackers.

Even as Mr. Reeder attained a position from which he could gaze along Brockley Road, the Clyno had come almost level with the constable. Showing no hesitation, which was remarkable under the circumstances, he darted forward. Instead of keeping up its speed, the vehicle slowed down and he threw himself on the running board. Almost as soon as he had done so, the driver accelerated once more. Nor, strangely enough, did the other occupants make any attempt to dislodge what one might have assumed to be an undesirable burden to their flight. Instead, with the blue clad figure clinging to it, the car sped down Tanners Hill. It passed out of sight beneath the railway bridge and disappeared into Deptford.

'Just as I suspected,' Mr. Reeder said quietly, and with an air of gloomy satisfaction. Replacing his *pince-nez,* he turned his gaze to where his guest was rising. 'I trust you aren't hurt, Colonel?'

'I managed to dodge them, too,' Besgrove-Woodstole replied. Having risen just in time to catch a glimpse of the Clyno as it went out of sight, he looked around and decided that, as none of the neighbours were making an appearance to investigate, the sound of the shots had gone unnoticed or had not been recognized as such by them. Then he remembered something else. 'Where's that policeman?'

'He was carried off by the vehicle,' Mr. Reeder answered.

'Carried *off*!' repeated the Colonel. 'Gad! It might have been foolhardy of him, but he was a brave man to try and tackle those thugs.'

'I'm afraid you have – um – over charitable regard for his motives,' Mr. Reeder contradicted, if his hesitant correction could be described by such a strong term. 'In fact, Colonel, I regret that you are in – er – something of an error when you refer to him as a policeman.'

'Gad!' Besgrove-Woodstole barked, swinging around to glare at his host. 'Do you mean that he wasn't a constable?'

'I do,' Mr. Reeder confirmed dismally. 'While he certainly passed muster as far as his attire and deportment – I believe that is the correct theatrical term – went, he has no connection with the Metropolitan Police Force other than a possible – um – reference to him in the Records Office at Scotland Yard.'

'Come on,' Besgrove-Woodstole growled, turning away from the gate. 'We'd better go and put the police on their track.'

'Mrs. Grible is just going to attend to it,' Mr. Reeder replied, nodding towards his house. 'But, of course, there are certain – um – details which she will be unable to supply and we will be able to do so.'

Turning his gaze in the same direction, the Colonel realized why his host had not been concerned over the possibility of their attackers returning. Holding a double barrelled shotgun of similar calibre but more conventional dimensions than the pair's weapons (which he had not been aware was on the premises) the lady in question was stepping back through the front door.

Almost six foot tall and weighing in the region of two hundred pounds, none of which was flabby fat, Mrs. Jane Amelia Grible had been in Mr. Reeder's service, ostensibly as a housekeeper, for a number of years.[1] Although the neighbours found her to be dour and uncommunicative where her famous employer's affairs were concerned, they could not find fault with the manner in which she performed her household duties. Only a select few people knew just how competent she was in other, more exacting, fields.[2]

'Which of us were they after, Mr. Reeder?' Besgrove-Woodstole inquired, as he accompanied his host along the garden path. He guessed that, having come to the front door to announce that lunch was ready, Mrs. Grible had seen the attack being launched. Realizing that neither of them had the means to defend themselves, she had armed herself ready to do so if necessary. However, his question prevented him from wondering from whence she had obtained the shotgun. It also took precedence over his interest in the matter of the man in the constable's uniform. 'Was it you, or I?'

Considering that the Colonel was the head of M.I.5, British Military Intelligence – which at that time was the supreme force in the field of international espionage – the query was no mean tribute to the high esteem and regard he had for the man to whom it had been put.

'That – um – point had occurred to me too, Colonel,' Mr. Reeder admitted. 'As this is my home, it suggests I was the intended victim. As against that, however, the nature of your – er – appointment presupposes you are required to keep

1. The author realizes that his description of Mr. Reeder's housekeeper is not in accord with the references made to her in earlier biographies. The most stringent condition imposed when Edgar Wallace received permission to write them was that there would be nothing to expose Mr. Reeder's security arrangements, nor to identify his employees. The restrictions have now been lifted and the late Mrs. Jane Amelia Grible can be given the credit she deserves. The closest Mr. Wallace was allowed to come to doing this at first hand was on Page 53 of RED ACES, quote: 'This lady is Mrs. Grible of my Department,' he – Mr. Reeder – said gravely. J.T.E.

2. Edgar Wallace was allowed to pay an indirect tribute to Mrs. Grible by recording the part she played in the case which he called: THE TRAITOR'S GATE. However, he referred to her as Mrs. Jane Ollorby and, omitting all reference to her connection with Mr. Reeder, claimed she held a post at Scotland Yard. He also altered her description slightly. While her face was big, with three chins and a somewhat masculine nose, her eyes only twinkled with amusement on very rare occasions and her expression was not often genial. J.T.E.

your Department informed of your whereabouts. If – and I hesitate to suggest such an – um – unpalatable contingency – some member of your staff should be disloyal, the miscreants could have learned that you are paying a visit to me.'

'They couldn't have known we'd be out in the garden,' Besgrove-Woodstole objected. 'If lunch hadn't been delayed, we'd have been inside, eating it.'

'In the dining room, at the front of the building and with a large bay window commanding an excellent view of Brockley Road,' Mr. Reeder pointed out, almost apologetically. 'I'm afraid that they were prepared for just such an – er – eventuality, Colonel.'

'Blast it!' Besgrove-Woodstole ejaculated. 'If you knew it was going to happen—.'

'Good gracious, Colonel!' Mr. Reeder protested, sounding aghast over the imputation that he would have deliberately placed a visitor to his home in a position of jeopardy. 'If I had had the slightest – um – inkling that such a thing was even contemplated, I would have taken steps to prevent it.'

The comment gave rise to other questions, but Besgrove-Woodstole was diverted from uttering them. Arriving at the front door as he finished his protest, Mr. Reeder allowed his guest to precede him into the house. On doing so, the Colonel found out how Mrs. Grible came to have a weapon available so fortuitously. The discovery momentarily drove all other considerations from his head.

The housekeeper was not to be seen, but her voice could be heard through the open door of Mr. Reeder's study as she was speaking over the telephone. However, instead of putting away the shotgun before going to inform the authorities, she had left it leaning against the wall. There was no doubt from whence it had come.

To the right of the front door, within easy reach of anybody who was standing on the threshold, was a particularly unattractive bust of Napoleon set on a sturdy wooden pedestal. For the first time, Besgrove-Woodstole learned that it was more than a mere ornament. Opening a secret panel in the pedestal gave access to a well-equipped arsenal which he had not known was in his host's possession.[3]

Held in clamps on the wall of the pedestal facing the front door were a .303 Lee Enfield No. 1 Short Magazine Mark V rifle[4] equipped with a telescopic sight and a Moran silencer,[5] one of the powerful .177 Webley & Scott Mark 1 air rifles that had come on to the market in 1926 and a Winchester Model of 1897 twelve gauge trench gun with a bayonet in its scabbard attached to its muzzle.[6] A dozen assorted revolvers and automatic pistols – the latter with their magazines removed and placed on shelves which also held boxes of ammunition for the various weapons – hung by their triggerguards on hooks.

To a man of the Colonel's military background, it was obvious why Mrs. Grible had selected the double barrelled shotgun instead of the more accurate rifle, or the trench gun which would have allowed her to fire five times instead of only twice. It was, to his way of thinking, further proof of her clear thinking competence. Leaving the springs of the firearms' magazines, or the mechanism of the air rifle, under compression for long periods could weaken and render them ineffective. So the Lee Enfield, Winchester, Webley & Scott and the automatics were only charged when they would be required. While the revolvers could be – and were – left loaded without detriment to their functioning, they were essentially short range *defensive* arms. So, appreciating that the distance was beyond their capacity, the housekeeper had

3. Ms. Wallace informed me that, as her father did not learn of the arsenal until long after he had published the last of Mr. Reeder's biographies, he had never seen any reason to mention the presence of the bust and its pedestal. J.T.E.

4. First issued in 1922, the Lee Enfield No. 1 Short Magazine Mark V rifle differed from its predecessors in having the rear sight mounted on the receiver bridge and an additional stock band fitted behind the nose cap. J.T.E.

5. Moran silencer: designed by bank manager–financier, Leopold Moran, but never manufactured commercially: see THE CLUE OF THE SILVER KEY by Edgar Wallace. J.T.E.

6. Trench gun: a five shot, tubular magazine, pump action shotgun designed for use in the trench warfare of World War 1. The twenty inch barrel has a radiating cooling sleeve and is equipped to take a bayonet. An extremely effective close quarters arm, particularly when loaded with buckshot. J.T.E.

wisely chosen the other type of weapon which could be kept ready for immediate use.

'With the exception of the air rifle,[7] we've never had to put any of the shoulder arms to use, Colonel,' Mr. Reeder remarked, noticing his guest's unconcealed interest in the arsenal. 'But it is a matter of some considerable – um – comfort to know they are available if the need for them should – as today – arise.'

'Excuse me, sir,' Mrs. Grible said, coming to the door of the study and speaking with a note of asperity. 'I've just called Lewisham Police Station. Inspector Mudgkin says he'll come round straight away and take charge personally.'

'Most – um – reassuring,' Mr. Reeder answered, in tones which – on the surface at any rate – held not a trace of sarcasm. For all that, his visitor suspected he shared the housekeeper's obvious dislike for the police officer she had mentioned. 'I trust you warned him—.'

'I didn't have a chance, sir,' Mrs. Gribble put in, oozing indignation. 'He just said you were to wait until he got here and hung up before I could ask you if that was all right with you.'

'*Botheration!*' Mr. Reeder ejaculated, in what – for him – was an outburst of great profanity. Inspector Mudgkin was one of those members of the Metropolitan Police Force who regarded him as an interloper and an outsider. 'Very well, Mrs. Grible. In that case, call Scotland Yard, please, and have them send half a dozen men to Camden High Street. Ask whoever is in charge if he will await my – um – arrival near, but out of sight of, Carrington Mews—.'

'*Carrington* Mews!' Mrs. Grible growled, before her employer could complete his instructions, and an expression of incredulity came to her face. 'That couldn't have been Bert the Jump-Up driving!'

'I'm afraid it not only – um – could have been, but was,' Mr. Reeder confirmed. 'And please tell the officer in charge

7. Mr. Reeder's reticence where the arsenal was concerned caused his previous biographer to assume that he had used an air pistol and not, as was the case, the Webley & Scott rifle to frighten away a pair of criminals who were lurking outside Daffodil House: see the 'Kennedy The Con Man' case recorded in: RED ACES by Edgar Wallace. J.T.E.

that I consider it would be most – um – judicious for he and his men to be armed.'

'Yes, sir,' Mrs. Grible assented and disappeared into the study once more.

'Who is this "Bert the Jump-Up" chap?' Besgrove-Woodstole demanded, watching his host returning the shotgun to its place in the arsenal.

'His full name is Albert Henry Fredricks,' Mr. Reeder explained, closing the secret panel to leave no sign of the pedestal's second function and glancing out of the front door. 'Shall we wait in my study until the Inspector arrives to – um – take charge.' Leading the way as his guest nodded agreement, he went on, ' "Jump-Up" is the archaic term given to the formerly lucrative practice of – um waiting, suitably attired, until a carter left his horse drawn vehicle, then climbing – or jumping – aboard and driving off with the load. The current name employed by what the more – um – sensational newspapers refer to as the "underworld" is "dragging"—.'

'Stealing cars,' the Colonel translated.

'Chief Inspector Gaylor says he'll do as you ask, sir,' Mrs. Grible reported, hanging up the telephone as the men entered.

'Very well,' the detective replied. 'If you would be so kind as to make the rest of the – um – calls from your room, please—?'

'Certainly sir,' the housekeeper agreed.

'As you say, Colonel, stealing – um – motor vehicles,' Mr. Reeder agreed, going to the desk as Mrs. Grible left the room. From it, he extracted a Colt Government Model .45 automatic pistol, three empty magazines, a box of fat, rimless[8] cartridges and a special type of holster. He continued talking while feeding seven bullets into each of the magazines. 'Fredricks is considered one of the finest – um – exponents. However, as his father and grandfather were

8. Revolver cartridges have a protruding rim to hold them in the chambers of the cylinder. With the exception of .22 Long rifle calibre, those designed for use in automatic pistols are level – apart from having a groove at the base of the case allowing the jaws of the extractor to obtain a grip and eject it after firing – to facilitate being fed from the lips of the magazine in to the barrel's chamber. J.T.E.

equally capable as "jump-up" men, he used the title as a – er – tribute to their memories.'

'You're sure it was him?'

'In this day and – um – age, Colonel, one can rarely be sure of – um – anything. However, while I can't claim any personal acquaintance, I have been informed that Bert the Jump-Up invariably "disguises" himself by wearing a black bowler hat, respectable raiment, dark glasses and a false black beard when – um – perpetrating a theft, or whilst driving a stolen vehicle during some form of criminal activity.'[9]

'So he's a habitual then?' Besgrove-Woodstole inquired, realizing what had provoked Mrs. Grible's response on learning who had been driving the car.

Very sensibly, at that time the courts of Great Britain dealt severely with crimes of violence. Having no desire to invoke the exceptionally painful consequences, the majority of habitual criminals were chary of being involved in the use of firearms during illegal enterprises.

'As he has had six – or is it *seven*? – convictions for stealing cars, or being in possession of a vehicle used in the commission of a crime, I believe one could say he *is* a – um – habitual criminal,' Mr. Reeder conceded, pushing a charged magazine into the butt of the pistol. Drawing back and releasing the cocking slide, he caused it to feed the uppermost round into the chamber. Without the need for conscious thought, he eased up the safety catch before slipping the weapon into the compact holster.

'Yet he was driving the Clyno,' Besgrove-Woodstole pointed out, as the detective unbuttoned his jacket. 'And he *must* have known what was going to happen.'

Designed to carry the eight and a half inches long, thirty-nine ounce automatic as inconspicuously as possible while still allowing it to be withdrawn swiftly when necessary, the holster was not meant to be attached to a belt. Instead, Mr. Reeder slipped it inside the waistband on the left side of his

9. The tradition, but not the 'disguise' which acted as a trademark and was responsible for at least four of Albert Henry 'Bert the Jump-Up' Fredricks' convictions – was continued by his son, Harry; see the 'Ace of the Jump-Ups' episode of UNDERWORLD NIGHTS by Charles Raven Hulton Press, London, 1956. J.T.E.

trousers, with the pistol's butt pointing forward so as to be accessible to either hand. It was held securely in place by its steel spring retaining clip around the top of the trousers. When he had refastened his jacket, only by looking very carefully could his guest detect that he was armed with an extremely potent weapon.

'I too am puzzled by *that*, Colonel,' the detective admitted, dropping a spare magazine into each of his jacket's pockets. 'And I wonder how *they* induced him to participate? They, of course, would require somebody who is fully cognizant with the geography of London and the different – um – regulations pertaining to the driving of a motor vehicle in this country. Oh well. *When* Inspector Mudgkin condescends to put in an – um – appearance, we – if I may make so bold as to assume that you will accompany me, Colonel – will endeavour to discover the – um – answers.'

CHAPTER FOUR

GOT YOU, YOU LITTLE BAS—!

CHARLES CUTHBERT HORACE WAGON was in an even viler and more unpleasant frame of mind than was usual for him as he cantered into Little Venner on his big bay hunter. A light rider for all his bulk, capable of taking much less out of his mount than would a smaller but not so skilful person, he invariably exerted his control with far more force than was necessary. Sensing his evil mood, the horse moved warily and was alert to respond to his slightest signal less worse should befall it. Scowling along the village's main street, he rode past the Royal Colours Hotel without giving it a glance and made for the second, smaller licensed establishment, the Starter's Hack.

Everything, the trainer told himself and not for the first time, was going wrong on what ought to have been a pleasant and relaxing Sunday.

It was bad enough having *Him* on the premises, in addition to all the foreigners *He* had been sending since *His* proposition had been put to and accepted by Wagon. Now two more damned guests – if one could call them that – were arriving. The thought of having a woman – especially *that* particular woman – in the house was anything but conducive to a sense of contentment and well being for the trainer.

Not that Wagon had mentioned his misgivings.

One did not argue against *His* requirements and demands!

Not twice, anyway!

Wagon felt as if he had been touched by a cold hand at the recollection of the tantrum *He* had thrown when *He* had learned that the only car at the training stable, on *His* own insistence to avoid attracting unwanted attention, had broken down and would not be able to collect *Her* from the railway station at Swindon. As if the failure of the car had not been sufficient of a misfortune, the only vehicle for hire locally was already taken and unobtainable before Monday morning.

Remembering *His* rage and the fear displayed by *His* attendants, who had not previously appeared to the trainer to be men who were easily frightened, Wagon wished that *He* had chosen somebody else to help implement *His* remarkable scheme.

Or that Wagon had refused it in the first place.

Yet there had been nothing else the trainer could do except accede to the circumstances. Already in dire financial straits as a result of making several unfortunate selections when betting on other people's racehorses, he had recently suffered a very serious business reversal. A certain little gentleman[1] of a tipster – one Educated Evans of Bayham Mews, Camden Town – had ruined a carefully prepared coup by giving out the name of the animal with which Wagon had planned to win the Braxted Selling Welter at Birmingham.[2] Although Little Buttercup had romped home an easy winner, helped by a certain noxious potion administered shortly before the race commenced, the volume of wagering induced by Evans' communiqué had caused the odds to shorten from a healthy thirty-five to one as far as a decidedly unadvantageous and hardly acceptable eight to one *on*[3]. The result was that, instead of the anticipated solvency – and the possibility of another call to appear before the Stewards of the Meeting to explain the remarkable improvement in his entry's erstwhile uninspiring performance, which did not worry him as much as one might imagine, due to his having survived similar ordeals on three previous oc-

1. Wagon's exact description was *not* '*little gentlemen*', rather it cast slanderous doubts on the marital status of Educated Evans' parents at the time of his birth. J.T.E.

2. Told in Chapter Ten 'The Goods', EDUCATED EVANS by Edgar Wallace. J.T.E.

3. For the benefit of readers who are unfamiliar with the terminology of wagering, 'eight to one on' means the better must stake eight units to win one. J.T.E.

casions – he had found himself too close to bankruptcy to turn down *His* potentially lucrative proposition.

As if wishing to prove that it never rains but what it pours, as the old saying claims, there had been the discovery of the something-or-other, so-and-so trespasser coming towards the Orchard Meadow to add to Wagon's misfortunes. Of course, providing that the two 'stablehands' carried out their instructions and said nothing about the incident, *He* would not have heard what had happened.

Thinking about the affair, the trainer scowled in puzzlement. He wondered what the strangely dressed young man had been up to. While smallish, he was somewhat too large to have been a jockey in search of employment. Or, if that was all he had been, he would have come straight along the front drive to the house and made his request. Anybody so deeply connected with the business of horseracing would have known better than to be found wandering around unbidden on Charlie Wagon's property.

On the other hand, while shortly after noon on Sunday might appear a poor time to gather unauthorized information, Wagon was notorious for working his horses at peculiar hours when more reputable stables were resting. So the visitor could have been a tout. However, Wagon had never seen one of that detestable fraternity clad in such strange attire. Generally, having no desire to draw unwanted attention to themselves or be easily identifiable, they tended to wear garments which would blend with the clothing of the local population.

The garb of the intruder had been unlike anything the trainer had ever come across locally or even during visits to London.

Considering the latter aspect opened up a whole new line of conjecture for Wagon.

The trespasser must be a foreigner. In fact, his attire seemed similar to that worn in 'cowboy' motion pictures which the trainer had seen at cinemas.

One thing was certain!

The small young man had not come at *His* bidding. Several of *His* employees had been brought from the United States of America, but they wore much the same kind of clothing as the English occupants of the stables. Furthermore, they and the other foreigners had arrived, if unconventionally, in the means pre-arranged by *Him*. None of them had put in an appearance by sneaking furtively across the fields.

Once again, Wagon experienced a chilling sensation!

What if *He* had instructed the intruder as a means of testing the way in which the property was being guarded?

There was some slight consolation for the trainer in the latter thought. The prevention of unwanted observers was the responsibility of *His* second-in-command. What was more important, although Wagon had failed to capture the stranger, he had been driven off before he could come into visual distance of the stables.

Giving consideration to how the intruder had escaped, Wagon did not care for some of the possibilities that opened up. He had recognized the rescuer as General Snowhill's niece and he knew his neighbour to be one of that exclusive coterie who supplied the Stewards for every major race course in the United Kingdom.

Had some hint of *His* scheme leaked out?

If so, the Jockey Club was certain to investigate!

After some earnest and worried thought, Wagon decided against the assumption. From what he knew of them, that august body would employ more subtle tactics. Perhaps the Snowhill girl had been acting on her own initiative, attempting to find out if he was up to something in his normal line of suspected malpractice. Or she and the young man could merely have been trying to win one of the stupid kind of bets in which members of the pampered Upper Class frequently indulged. Or, remembering the squealing of her car's brakes just after the intruder had vaulted the gate, she might not have been connected with him and merely helped him out of a misguided sense of compassion.

In which case, what had the interloper been hoping to do?

Reaching the front of the Starter's Hack public house caused Wagon to bring an end to his cogitations. He looked at the deserted pavement, then dismounted. There was a large, enclosed yard with an exit at the rear of the building where horses could be left. It was a facility of which many of the customers, wishing to avoid letting it be known they were on the premises, frequently availed themselves. Having no need for such a subterfuge, in fact being one of the reasons for it, he tied the hunter's reins to a ring on one of the hitching posts which were necessitated by the area's main industry.

Crossing the pavement, Wagon opened the front door and stepped into the tap-room of the Starter's Hack. As might be expected, with the proprietor once having been a noted jockey, the *leitmotif* had to do with the Sport of Kings. There were framed photographs of the owner seated on his most successful mounts, or pictures of celebrated racehorses, around the walls. Sets of the special horseshoes known as 'racing plates', bits and stirrup irons formed the other decorations. The only reading matter in evidence was copies of *The Calendar*, or other journals equally devoted to training, racing and wagering on horses.

'Good morning, Mr. Haggerty,' the trainer greeted, directing a look of what – for him – passed as cordiality at the small, wizened, bow-legged and grey-haired man who was standing behind the bar counter. He hated to employ the honorific when addressing one whom he regarded as a social inferior, but had come to ask a favour. 'Nice weather.'

'Aye, it's not bad,' agreed the proprietor, with less cordiality than might have been expected in view of the fact that he was alone in the room and addressing a potential customer. 'I haven't seen any of your lads this morning.'

There was a good reason for the second comment. The inborn British trait of an unwillingness to mingle with people outside one's kind and social level had caused the Starter's Hack to become the province of the local racing fraternity's lower echelons. As a further subdivision, while apprentices and stable-lads mingled freely in the tap-room, jockeys and head lads would only be found in the adjoining lounge. However, except upon Christmas and Boxing Days, or New Year's Eve, when the barriers were traditionally relaxed by common consent, such exalted personages as trainers and owners gave their custom to the more elegant Royal Colours Hotel. When one of them came in to the Starter's Hack at other than those festive occasions, particularly when it was Charlie Wagon, Mr. Haggerty was usually suspicious and wondered if the arrival was to check up on his normal clientele.

'I wasn't looking for them,' the trainer replied, knowing what had been meant, but still trying to retain his air of amiability. 'My car's broken down and—'

Before Wagon could complete his explanation and request the loan of the proprietor's vehicle, the opening of the back door drew his gaze in that direction. Although the person who had been about to enter changed his mind and retreated hurriedly, the trainer had caught a glimpse of him.

A low growl of rage burst from the trainer and he darted across the room. In spite of only having been granted a brief sight, he had identified the newcomer as the smallish trespasser who had evaded his wrath earlier. There could hardly be two men in a village the size of Little Venner, nor the whole of Wiltshire for that matter, who dressed in such an outlandish fashion.

Watching Wagon dashing towards the back door, Mr. Haggerty gave vent to a startled and profane exclamation. He did not know what the trainer might have against the short, strangely dressed and funny sounding young man who had taken room in his premises. However, it was obvious something was wrong and he was aware of Wagon's reputation where people who crossed him were concerned.

Wishing to prevent any unpleasantness in his house, the proprietor started to walk from behind the counter. A serious injury to his leg, which had caused him to give up his career as a jockey and also precluded him from taking employment as a stable's head lad, restricted the speed at which he could move. So, by the time he was approaching the door, Wagon and the small stranger had already left the building. Nor was he able to see them as the exit to the back yard was almost closed. All he could hear from outside increased his sense of perturbation.

'Got you, you little bas—!' Wagon's voice bellowed, beginning to employ one of his favourite terms for anybody who earned his disapproval.

The word went unfinished!

There sounded a rapid scuffling noise, followed by a

startled wail something like, 'Augh!' from the trainer. It was followed by a thud similar to that of a bale of hay being dropped to the ground.

Limping the remaining few feet as swiftly as he could manage, Mr. Haggerty hardly knew what to expect as he opened the back door. Stepping through, he found that there was no sign of the small stranger. Not that the proprietor gave much consideration to his absence, nor where he might have gone. Instead, the publican stared at Wagon, sprawling supine on the ground.

'What happened?' Mr. Haggerty demanded, approaching as the trainer sat up.

'Wh – Where is—?' Wagon gasped, glaring around in a dazed fashion. Then he shook his head. When he continued speaking, it was obvious that he had recovered his wits if not his composure. 'I – tripped over your something-or-other, so-and-so yard brush, that's what!'

There were, Mr. Haggerty decided, certain objections – although he had no intention of mentioning them, unless he was given cause – to the explanation. For one thing, Wagon had been lying on his back and with his feet pointing towards the gate in the yard's wall. He should not have attained such a position if he had arrived there from the kind of accident he had described.

However, the chief argument against the trainer's statement was that there was no brush anywhere in the yard.

CHAPTER FIVE

I HAVE THIS PECULIAR PERVERSION

'AMERICAN *gangsters*?' challenged Inspector Mudgkin, heavily built in his blue uniform, his harsh voice redolent of disbelief as he interrupted Mr. J. G. Reeder's explanation of the would be assassination.

On his arrival, accompanied by a detective sergeant and two other cars filled with officers, Mudgkin had listened to Mr. Reeder's description of the attackers and their vehicle. On learning that the Clyno Royal sedan had gone in the direction of Deptford, without waiting to hear anything further, he had ordered the men in the two cars to go and institute a search. What was more, he had brushed aside Mr. Reeder's warning of how dangerous the party they were seeking would be. Having dispatched his small force, he had requested that he was given a full report of the incident. So Mr. Reeder had suggested he and the detective sergeant went into Daffodil House. Taking them and Colonel Brian Besgrove-Woodstole into the dining room and seating them at the table, he had started to comply.

'Their names are Joseph "Joe the Actor" Steffens, Generoso Rizzito and Giovanni Aiello,' Mr. Reeder supplemented in gentle tones, eyeing the Inspector with what might have passed for benevolence to anybody who knew him less well than either Besgrove-Woodstole or Sergeant Rudge. 'Born in New York, Detroit and Chicago respectively, which suggests they are – um – Americans. As for the rest, a colleague of mine domiciled in the United States, Mr. Eliot Ness – who, in my modest – um – summation, will make a major contribution to the law enforcement of that country[1] – has written and told me sufficient to lead me, possibly erroneously, to conclude that they might also be – um – gangsters.'

Catching the detective sergeant's eye, after seeing the frown that came to Mudgkin's face, Besgrove-Woodstole exchanged a quick smile with him. Mr. Reeder being hesitantly apologetic was capable of producing a tremendous amount of cutting sarcasm.

Apparently oblivious of the Inspector's disapproval, Mr. Reeder continued with his explanation. He spoke concisely, describing the *modus operandi* of the American trio with none of his usual hesitant delivery and sounding far younger than he looked.

When a contract was received to make a kill, Steffens would frequently allow himself to be knocked down by a car carrying Rizzito and Aiello outside wherever their victim was located. In addition to giving a most realistic performance of being struck and thrown over the vehicle's bonnet, using the technique he had perfected as a stuntman in the motion picture industry, he also demonstrated how he acquired the name 'Joe the Actor' by posing as the kind of person most likely to arouse the victim's sympathy. The garb of a Catholic priest had lured an Italian-born gang-boss from the safety of his headquarters and a rabbi's attire had brought a Jewish accountant, who had to be prevented from giving evidence in a criminal case, out of his house and to his death.

One of the trio's precautions was always to hire a driver who had a complete knowledge of the city in which they were working, ensuring there would be no mistakes during their flight from the scene of the crime. That would be more essential than ever, Mr. Reeder pointed out, in London. Not only were they unfamiliar with the geography of the city,

1. Mr. Reeder's assumption proved to be correct. Eliot Ness was at that time forming a special Prohibition Detail from carefully selected agents of the United States' Department of Justice. Earning the title 'The Untouchables', because they could neither be frightened nor bribed from carrying out their duties, they played a major part in causing the downfall of Alphonse 'Scar-Face Al' Capone in Chicago; see THE UNTOUCHABLES by Eliot Ness (with Oscar Fraley). J.T.E.

but they would have been compelled to work under the added disadvantage of remembering the vehicle must be driven on the left and not the right side of the street.

'Whoever arranged for my – um – removal knew that I would be sitting here and having my lunch, with a clear view of the road from my table,' Mr. Reeder went on. 'And, seeing what I took to be a constable struck by a motor car, I would go out to investigate. There is, however, – um – one point which I must confess puzzles me. How they could be sure that the genuine constable would not appear inconveniently. Doubtless they had anticipated and taken care of that contingency.'[2]

'When did you find out those Yankees were over here, Mr. Reeder?' Rudge asked.

'I had no idea that they were, Sergeant,' the detective answered. 'However, because of Bert the Jump-Up's well known predilection for such – um – attire, I recognized him and noticed that the "constable" seemed puzzled when he could not have duplicated my recognition, nor even been able to read the license plate and – um – discover that the vehicle was stolen. As I may have mentioned, I have this peculiar perversion—.'

'Your "criminal mind",' Besgrove-Woodstole supplied with a frosty grin.

'As you so succinctly put it, Colonel, my – um – criminal mind,' Mr. Reeder agreed. 'It is a terrible affliction, but suggested what – um – might be about to happen.'

'Then you knew they were after you?' Mudgkin asked.

'I considered that it might be a – um – distinct possibility,' Mr. Reeder admitted, deciding against causing a further delay to his own investigations by mentioning that his guest could have been the proposed victim. 'However, I may learn

2. Mr. Reeder subsequently discovered that the genuine constable was called into a public house to settle a dispute over a counterfeit half-a-crown piece which the proprietor claimed was passed to him by a customer. The matter was settled amicably and no arrest was made, the customer – a stranger in the district – being allowed to leave on paying with a genuine coin. The name and address he gave proved to be false and he was finally identified as a small time criminal who had been employed to keep the constable occupied and away from Brockley Road while the murder attempt was in progress. J.T.E.

differently when I meet with those detestable fellows from Scotland Yard who are, doubtlessly with great – um – impatience, awaiting my arrival near Bert the Jump-Up's residence.'

'That's not on my manor,' Mudgkin grunted, standing up. 'We'll look for them down here, Sergeant.'

'Exercise extreme care in the event that you come upon them, Inspector,' Mr. Reeder stated, speaking more firmly than was usual. 'They are armed and *very* dangerous. In fact, if I may make so – um – bold, I would advise you *not* to try and arrest them unless you have a superior number of well-armed men available.'

'That's a decision *I'll* have to make for myself,' Mudgkin answered stiffly. 'My superiors have given definite instructions regarding issuing firearms since the Right Honourable Benner, M.P., put a question about it in the House of Parliament. Thank you for your time, Mr. Reeder. Come on, Sergeant.'

'Yes, sir,' Rudge replied and, as he started to follow the Inspector, looked over his shoulder. 'I'll let you know – *if* anything develops, Mr. Reeder.'

'Pompous oaf!' Besgrove-Woodstole snorted, when the sound of the officers' footsteps died away. 'I'd say his sergeant doesn't think they'll do any good.'

'True, Colonel,' Mr. Reeder said gently. 'And, if I thought that there was the *slightest* possibility of him locating the Americans, I would have exercised my – um – official authority to insist he took the appropriate precautions. For his own – um – sake as much as that of his men. Steffens and his – um – associates aren't like any criminals with whom the constables have come into contact.'

'You're right, by gad!' Besgrove-Woodstole admitted, being aware of just how little acquaintance the average British police officer had in dealing with miscreants who would not hesitate to use firearms. 'Shall we go and meet your colleagues from the Yard?'

'I was on the point of – um – suggesting we did so, although it will mean a further delay to our lunch.'

'I doubt if it's the first time, or the last, that will happen to us.'

'Undoubtedly. May I take the – um – liberty of offering you the loan of a weapon?'

'That Socialist M.P. chap might not approve if he heard about it,' Besgrove-Woodstole answered. 'But I think I will, if you feel it's necessary.'

'At the risk of offending Mr. Benner's susceptibilities, assuming he has any,' Mr. Reeder said and, despite his mild – almost bantering – tone when referring to the prominent politician, his guest knew he was in deadly earnest. 'I consider it to be a – um – mandatory precaution. In fact, if I thought we were going to find them, I would feel – um – constrained to brave the Right Hon. Mr. Benner's disapproval and arm us with the sniper's rifle and the trench gun.'

'I'll take a revolver in that case,' Besgrove-Woodstole decided, impressed by his host's attitude. 'Never could get the hang of automatic pistols.'

'While I don't – um – subscribe to it, Colonel, that is a not uncommon prejudice,' Mr. Reeder asserted and looked to where his housekeeper was entering the dining room. 'Would you be good enough to allow the Colonel to – um – select and sign out a revolver and ammunition, please, Mrs. Grible?'

'Yes, sir,' the formidable looking lady replied. 'I've called Mr. Golden and he says he hasn't heard anything. Mr. Grant and Captain Gray are both away on holiday, so I didn't bother them. I tried to get Parker, but there's no reply.'

'Very well,' the detective answered, little about him showing how gravely he regarded the negative information. He looked at his guest and went on, 'Possibly it was *you* they were after, Colonel. Would it be – um – impolitic for me to ask if your Department is involved in any affair of such magnitude that your – er – demise would affect the outcome?'

'Not that I can think of,' Besgrove-Woodstole stated, after a moment's consideration. 'The Russian Secret Police caught a man I've had investigating rumours that they're sending money to British Trade Union agitators, but they'd know killing me won't halt the investigation. My second-in-command would take charge.'

'That was what I – um – assumed,' Mr. Reeder sighed. 'If

only we could lay hands on Bert the Jump-Up, we might learn something. But I– um – fear that it is not to be.'

'But I thought you were going to his home to arrest him,' Besgrove-Woodstole protested.

'Not exactly, Colonel,' Mr. Reeder corrected.

'Do you think that they've already separated?'

'That is most probable.'

'Then he could be there,' Besgrove-Woodstole insisted.

'I have serious doubts as to the – um – likelihood of him being present,' Mr. Reeder confessed in hushed tones. 'My perverted sense of – um – reasoning suggests – and I fear it is all too often correct – that Bert the Jump-Up is already dead and has – um – arguably gone to Heaven.'

CHAPTER SIX

THERE'S NO POINT IN US *BOTH* STAYING

'Good heavens above, man. Do you mean to tell me that there's *nowhere* I can get a taxi, or hire a car even, to take me out to Little Venner?'

The words reached Beryl Snowhill's ears as she was walking from the main entrance of Swindon's Great Western Railway Station, after having arranged for the dispatch of the package, to collect her MG Super Sports two-seater tourer. Although there was a distinct note of asperity, which could be understandable under the circumstances, they were uttered with carefully modulated feminine tones suggesting the speaker was a person of breeding.

Turning her head, the girl had no difficulty in locating the source of the comment. Only two other people were in her immediate vicinity. Confronting a miserable looking old porter, who was setting down the four suitcases with which he was loaded, was a strikingly beautiful woman. About four inches taller than Beryl and in her late twenties, she exuded an aura of wealth. Her slender figure was clad in plain, but elegantly tailored and expensive travelling clothes of the latest mode. A pair of black gloves concealed her marital status. All in all, she seemed to be the kind of person who received invitations to visit at any of the large houses in or around Little Venner.

'I dunno about that, mu'um,' the porter answered, straightening up and refusing to meet the pallid-faced passenger's cold gaze. 'It's Sunday "art-noon" and there bain't many's'd want to go right out there 'n' back.'

'Excuse me,' Beryl said, walking over. 'I couldn't help overhearing. If you're going to Little Venner and don't mind riding in an open car. I'll gladly take you.'

Two dark eyes, looking out of place in such a palely beautiful set of features, swung to study the girl. There was, Beryl decided, something hard and almost hostile in them. They failed to reflect the smile that came to the woman's lips.

'I do have to get there,' the beauty conceded, waving a languid hand towards the luggage. 'But I've all this and a – *friend* – with me.'

'Well,' said Beryl, wondering why there had been a slight pause and a faintly sneering timbre about the way the word "friend" had been uttered. With her attention drawn to them, she could see the suitcases were of two different kinds. 'I could manage the luggage, but—.'

'It's no use, Olga!' announced a male voice, in a whining tone. The accent was similar to that of the young men Beryl had met who, although having received a good education, could not entirely throw off traces of their Cockney upbringing. 'I can't get through on the telephone.'

Glancing over her shoulder, Beryl felt puzzled. Tall, thin, in his mid-thirties, the approaching man's face was sallow, hollow-cheeked, weak chinned, with deep set eyes and a thick lipped, sullen mouth. He wore a rumpled, but costly, brown suit and matching trilby hat, with a grubby white shirt decorated by a red tie, and his brown shoes were unpolished. Everything about him implied that his untidy appearance was voluntary rather than the result of a lengthy train journey.

Recognizing the man from photographs she had seen in newspapers, although his present attire was more expensive than that in which he always went among his constituents – where he invariably wore cheap garments and a flat cap to show that, in spite of his present position of superiority, he was still one of the 'workers' at heart – Beryl knew him to be the Right Hon. Horatio Benner, M.P. Remembering his frequently quoted views on the evils of wealth and social position, he was a Socialist of the most radical kind, she was surprised to find him in the company of such an obviously well-to-do and, apparently, upper class woman.

The girl also wondered which of the local families would be accepting the couple as house guests. Almost without exception, the families had military, or naval, backgrounds.

They would be unlikely to have forgotten that, while their male members were fighting for King and Country in the Great War, Benner had been a conscientious objector. Or that he was now prominent among the Socialist faction in Parliament who were most vocal with objections against any expenditure to help maintain the Armed Forces in a strong enough position to defend Great Britain against foreign aggression.

'This young lady has a car, Horatio,' the woman replied. 'She's offered to help—'

'Has she?' Benner said, turning a gaze at the girl which gave her an uneasy feeling that his eyes were trying to strip her naked. 'That'll save us hanging about—.'

'It's only a two-seater,' the woman pointed out, frowning as she noticed the lascivious manner in which her escort was scrutinizing Beryl. 'We can take the cases, but there won't be any room for you.'

'But—!' Benner began.

'There's no point in us *both* staying here!' the woman interrupted, and her tone was much the same as when she had been addressing the porter. 'If you haven't got something by the time I arrive, I'll make arrangements to have you fetched.'

'Oh hell, Olga—!' Benner protested, scowling furiously.

'There's no other way!' the woman declared and her manner showed she considered the matter was closed. Returning her gaze to Beryl, she went on in a more pleasant manner. 'I'm grateful to you, dear. Take the luggage to the young lady's car, my man.'

'Yes'm,' answered the porter and he regathered the suitcases.

'Your father—!' Benner began, stalking at the woman's side as she accompanied Beryl to the tourer.

'Won't mind when I tell him what's happened,' the beauty said, her voice growing harder. Listening, Beryl formed the impression that she was both amused and pleased by the M.P.'s discomfiture and not sorry to have an excuse to leave him behind. After the luggage had been loaded and she had climbed into the passenger's seat, she looked at him. 'Tip the porter for me, that's a darling. I'll see you when you get there.'

For a person who always professed a great sympathy for the sorry state of the working classes' finances, Benner showed reluctance over carrying out the request. He had the kind of mentality common among his kind. While he wanted conditions improving, he objected to it being done at his personal expense.

'Thankee kindly, sir,' the porter grunted, eyeing the three-penny piece which was handed to him. 'That be *most* generous of you, I'm sure.'

'I'm Beryl Snowhill,' the girl introduced, as she drove the MG away from the station. 'My uncle trains near Little Venner. Perhaps you could pop over and have tea with us if you're staying for a few days in the vicinity.'

'Perhaps,' the woman answered non-committally. Then, clearly as an afterthought, went on, 'I'm Olga Garvin.'

'Pleased to meet you,' Beryl responded automatically, but was just a trifle nettled by her passenger's off-hand attitude. 'Where can I drop you off?'

'In Little Venner.'

'Do you know the area?'

'I've never been there before,' Olga admitted and, although she did not say, 'and wish I wasn't going now', the words were implied by her manner.

'You may have trouble finding and reaching your friends unless they live in the village,' Beryl warned, despite a growing irritation at the other's behaviour.

'I suppose I will,' Olga conceded and, clearly reaching what she regarded as an unpleasant but necessary decision, she continued, 'Do you know Charles Wagon's stables?'

'Yes,' Beryl replied, trying to avoid sounding as puzzled as she felt. If there was one place to which she would *not* have expected the elegant woman to be going, it was Wagon's reputably bachelor establishment. 'It's on the way to my uncle's home. I can drop you off as I go by, if you like.'

'I'd be obliged if you would,' Olga stated, after she had once again paused as if considering whether to accept. 'Look, dear, I had a *very* late night at the Embassy and a tedious journey. I'm sorry I'm not much of a conversationalist today, but – well, *you* know how it is.'

Beryl gave something between a nod and a shrug, but did not make a verbal reply. While young, she was neither naive nor inexperienced. So she had noticed how her passenger had spoken. Unless she was wrong, the final words had been intended to make her feel she was being treated as a woman of the world being addressed by another, although the speaker really considered she was anything but that.

Taking the hint, Beryl concentrated on driving as quickly as possible so as to be rid of her passenger in the shortest time. She did, however, occasionally study the other with the aid of the rear-view mirror. A shrewd judge of character, she felt there was something repellant about the woman. She could not decide exactly what it was, but did not care for it. Not, Beryl told herself, that it mattered. Nothing about Olga Garvin made her eager to make overtures of friendship and, considering the woman's destination, they were unlikely to come into contact after they had parted. The General not only regarded Wagon as socially unacceptable, but also he never referred to the dishonest trainer in terms suitable for mixed company. So he was unlikely to extend an invitation to Wagon's guest.

There was little conversation for the remainder of the journey. Olga sat with her head tilted back and eyes closed, giving the impression that she was sleeping. Nor did Beryl do anything to disturb the other's pose. Instead, she found herself thinking about the young Yankee – no, *Texan* – with whom she had come into contact earlier. She wondered what he had been doing on Wagon's property and if their paths would cross again.

Passing through Little Venner, Olga asked if it was always such a dead hole. She listened, with no great display of interest or enthusiasm, to Beryl's description of the vicarage's garden fête and fell silent again. Although of a friendly disposition and always willing to give anybody a helping hand, the girl felt considerable relief when, a few minutes later, she saw that they would soon be at her passenger's destination and could part company.

Turning the MG through the open gates and along the driveway, the girl realized that she had never been near – nor was even conscious of having looked at – Wagon's premises. Not that now, having the opportunity, there was much for her to see. Either by accident or deliberately, the sprawling and somewhat dilapidated old Georgian house in which the trainer lived hid most of the stables from the view of passers-by on the road. Going closer, Beryl saw a line of loose boxes. These were built of brick, with boarded and slated roofs. As their doors were closed, she could not tell if any of them were occupied. At the far end, facing the house across a large cobble-stoned yard, was a further building. From its appearance, she guessed that it held the feed barn, possibly the trainer's office, certainly the tack- and feed-storage rooms.

Before the tourer had reached the house, its front door opened and two men came out. Neither was Wagon and both were strangers to Beryl. Tall, well dressed in the style of the city rather than country-dwellers, there was a resemblance about their hard and unsmiling faces that suggested they might be brothers.

'Sorry we couldn't get over to Swindon and meet you, Olga,' said the older of the pair, striding forward as the girl brought the MG to a halt.

'Didn't you get Benner to come?' the second man went on, advancing to open the vehicle's passenger door.

'How could I in this – car?' the woman snapped, inserting the final word as a by-product. Climbing out, she waved her hand in a commanding gesture little different to that which she had employed with the porter. 'Take my bags inside. He's still at the railway station, unless he's managed to hire something to come here in.'

Watching the men, Beryl felt that their hard faces were showing a hint of relief at hearing the Socialist M.P. was not too far away. She also felt puzzled by their acceptance of the woman's high handed treatment. Neither looked the kind who would take such behaviour from a member of the 'weaker' sex, yet they appeared to be letting her imperiousness pass.

'Er – thank you for bringing me, dear,' Olga said, looking down at the girl after her luggage had been unloaded.

'The pleasure was all mine,' Beryl answered, trying not to sound too sarcastic.

'I'd ask you in, but—,' Olga went on, making a deprecatory gesture at the house.

'That's all right,' the girl replied. 'I have to be getting home. Good-bye.'

'Good-bye,' Olga responded and, as if making a half-hearted and belated attempt to make amends for her treatment. 'Perhaps we can get together for a drink and a chat some evening?'

'Perhaps,' Beryl admitted, setting the MG into motion.

Reversing, so as to return down the drive, the girl glanced sideways. Much to her amazement, looking across the stable yard and between the gap separating the loose boxes from the other building, she saw a familiar figure approaching from the trees of the Orchard Meadow. The glimpse she received was brief and she could hardly believe her eyes.

For a moment, Beryl was on the verge of stopping the car. Then she decided against it and made her way out of the gate. However, as she drove along the lane towards her home, she wondered if she really had seen the Texan whom she had met so dramatically earlier that afternoon.

CHAPTER SEVEN

HE *WAS* A DECENT AND HARD-WORKING MAN

For a gentleman who as a pedestrian displayed remarkable concern and caution where what he termed as the 'vehicular traffic' was involved,[1] Mr. J. G. Reeder's recently developed taste for possessing his own means of transport was surprising. Certainly Colonel Brian Besgrove-Woodstole, D.S.O., M.C. and Bar found it somewhat amusing to be seated in the passenger seat of the gentle detective's powerful dark blue 1925 Frazer-Nash Fast Tourer. Certainly his host had driven the vehicle from Brockley Road with considerable aplomb. Cruising along Camden High Street, they were approaching two black police cars which were parked near an intersection. A big, burly, quietly dressed man they both identified as Chief Inspector Frank Gaylor of Scotland Yard[2] was standing on the pavement.

'Good afternoon, Mr. Reeder, Colonel,' Gaylor greeted, walking forward as the tourer came to a halt. 'I hear that you've been doing something to liven up Sunday lunch time in Brockley Road.'

'That is – um – correct,' Mr. Reeder replied, deciding that the recently gained well deserved promotion of the man from Scotland Yard had done nothing to remove his painful sense of humour.

'Who's after you?' Gaylor inquired, addressing the question to the gentle detective.

1. See Case 3, 'The Troupe' of THE MIND OF MR. J. G. REEDER by Edgar Wallace. J.T.E.

2. Gaylor's promotion to Chief Inspector took place after 'The Case Of Joe Attymar' which is recorded in RED ACES by Edgar Wallace. J.T.E.

'I've no idea,' Mr. Reeder admitted. 'In fact, as yet, I'm not certain whether the Colonel or I was the intended – um – victim.'

'Hasn't Golden been able to tell you?' Gaylor asked.

'No,' Mr. Reeder answered. 'Excellent as our sources of information usually are, regrettably we aren't – um – omniscient. However, I'm reasonably – er – sanguine that, particularly if I was the intended victim, details will soon be forthcoming.'

'We stayed here and haven't even as much as looked at Bert's place,' Gaylor announced. He had worked with Mr. Reeder on several occasions and had great respect for his judgment. 'What do you want us to do?'

'Are your officers – um – armed?'

'You can bet they are when they're going after somebody who's been taking pot-shots at *you*.'

'Sir!' called one of the detectives, thrusting his head through the front window of the nearer car. 'There's a message for you just come over the radio.'

There was something close to awe in the officer's voice as he referred to the instrument with which the vehicle was equipped. While the Metropolitan Police Force had been experimenting with radios since 1922,[3] they were still regarded by many policemen – especially such a one as the speaker, who had recently transferred from a Force in a less progressive part of the country – as being a new-fangled and, because of the difficulties met with ensuring constant reception, not entirely trustworthy means of communication.

'Well?' barked Gaylor, being too far sighted to share his subordinate's misgivings. He strode forward, followed by the newcomers who had left the Tourer. 'What is it?'

'The River Police have just pulled Bert the Jump-Up's body out of the Thames at Deptford, sir,' the detective constable reported. 'He's been shot in the back of the head. Sergeant Wade, it's his boat, said he hadn't been dead for long.'

3. Radios of that period were only capable of receiving and could not transmit. It would not be until the improved technical developments in the field of communications produced during World War II were made available, that two-way and three-way – respectively, car to transmitting station only, and car to transmitting station and to other cars – were manufactured and fitted to police vehicles. J.T.E.

'You were right,' Besgrove-Woodstole told his host admiringly.

'I frequently am,' Mr. Reeder answered dolefully. 'It's one of the – um – disadvantages of my perverted line of – um – reasoning, due entirely to my – er—.'

'Having the mind of a criminal,' Gaylor finished for the gentle detective. 'Young Johnny Wade's a bit that way, too.[4] And he's seen enough dead 'n's come out of the Thames to make a good guess at the time of death. What do we do now?'

'It would seem judicious – humane even – to go and – um – inform his, I suppose it would be proper for me to say – um – widow,' Mr. Reeder suggested, in a hushed voice that would have been more in keeping with an undertaker discussing a bereaved and wealthy client.

'You know how Annie feels about Bert,' Gaylor remarked. 'Those blokes aren't likely to come back after they've killed him.'

'It's possible they might have,' Mr. Reeder warned. 'If she knows them, they might – um – consider that such knowledge is dangerous to their – um – well being and wish to take steps to ensure it does not continue to be so.'

'They might,' Gaylor admitted, patting his jacket's right hand pocket without realizing he was making the gesture. 'And they'd just about have had time to get here.'

'Would you send one car around the back of the Mews and have the other remain here, please?' Mr. Reeder requested. 'Then, unless you have any objections, the Colonel and I will accompany you and see what – um – eventuates.'

'Whatever you say,' Gaylor assented, knowing that to arrive in vehicles and at full strength would be to attract unwanted attention. Approaching on foot, the three of them might reach their objective undetected. 'Who do I tell the men to watch out for?'

After passing on the required information, the Chief Inspector went with Mr. Reeder and the Colonel. The alley they entered was lined with mews occupied mainly by families who had made the transition from being grooms to

4. Some details of John Wade's career after his promotion to Inspector are given in: THE INDIA RUBBER MEN by Edgar Wallace. J.T.E.

serving as chauffeurs. Externally, there was nothing to distinguish the Fredricks' residence from those of the neighbours.

Climbing the steps with as little noise as possible, their destination being on the first floor, the three men halted. Glancing at Mr. Reeder, who held the tightly rolled umbrella which he had collected from the stand in the hall of Daffodil House – and was as much *his* trademark as Bert the Jump-Up's 'disguise' – in his left hand whilst unbuttoning his jacket with the right, Gaylor stepped forward meaning to knock on the front door.

'*Wait*!' Mr. Reeder hissed with such vehemence that Gaylor froze as if he had been turned to stone. 'Step to one side, please. You too, Colonel. It is a laudable – um – precaution I learned from the American police who have had greater need than we to develop such – um – techniques.'

With that, the detective advanced until he was standing with his back to the wall at the unhinged side of the door. Allowing his companions to adopt similar positions opposite him, he slid the umbrella until he was grasping it by the ferrule. Reaching around, he rapped on the door with the handle.

Glancing across as his right hand went under his jacket, Mr. Reeder observed with satisfaction that his companions were in postures of equal readiness. He also noticed that they were exhibiting to his trained gaze a similar aura of tension to that which he was experiencing. Of the two, he was most concerned with how Gaylor would react if the Americans should be present and if, as they were practically certain to do, they resisted. As he knew, Besgrove-Woodstole had seen active service and killed men in combat. While the chief inspector had considerable courage and was capable of taking care of himself in a roughhouse, he had not been required to face criminals who were carrying and would not hesitate to use firearms.

'Who is it?' called a woman's voice.

'Police, Mrs. Fredricks,' Gaylor replied, after looking for and receiving a nod of confirmation from Mr. Reeder. 'Can we speak with you, please?'

While the man from Scotland Yard was speaking, Mr.

Reeder closed his hand around the butt of the Colt Government Model automatic. He could see that his companions were also grasping their weapons. If the Americans were inside, they would be informed of the fact in no uncertain fashion very shortly.

The door began to open!

None of the men drew his weapon, but each was prepared to do so.

'Oh, it's you, Mr. Gaylor, I didn't think it was the "Miller's"[5] voice,' said the attractive woman who stepped on to the landing. Then she swung her gaze in the other direction, frowned for a moment and continued, 'You're Mr. Reeder, aren't you?'

'I'm – um – he, madam,' the aged-seeming detective confirmed, but more in the manner of one who was making an apology for a regrettable oversight of nature rather than admitting he was a person of some importance.

Watching Mrs. Fredricks' face, Mr. Reeder – who had been trained by Leon Gonzales[6] until he too was as great an authority as Montegazza on the subject of the ravages that emotions created upon the human countenance – could see that she was worried. Yet he felt her concern stemmed from seeing the Chief Inspector rather than out of his own presence. He regarded this factor as being suggestive and informative. While his current appointment in the Public Prosecutor's Office gave him a wider frame of reference than when his organization had worked privately and with an extensive bank practice, her husband's particular legal infractions – stealing cars and driving the vehicles employed in such enterprises as smash-and-grab raids – were more in the province of the man from Scotland Yard.

'Bert's not here!' Mrs. Fredricks declared, returning her

5. The Miller: Detective Sergeant William Arbuthnot Challoner, Criminal Investigation Department, attached to the Camden Town Police Station and whose nickname arose from his habit of chewing on a straw; see EDUCATED EVANS, MORE EDUCATED EVANS and GOOD EVANS by Edgar Wallace for further details of his career. J.T.E.

6. Leon Gonzales: one of the 'Four Just Men', who had gone into retirement following his marriage to Mirabelle Leicester; see THE THREE JUST MEN, also THE FOUR JUST MEN, AGAIN THE THREE, THE COUNCIL OF JUSTICE and THE LAW OF THE FOUR JUST MEN by Edgar Wallace. J.T.E.

attention to Gaylor and displaying such virtuous indignation that many people would have believed her next words could only be the pure and unvarnished truth. 'He's gone down to Chalfont St. Giles to see his poor old mum who's not in the best of health and—.'

There was an interruption before the woman would complete an alibi as traditional as Bert the Jump-Up's 'disguise' and title. Far from living in the sedately respectable town of Chalfont St. Giles, his mother was currently ruling with an iron hand one of the roughest public houses in the less respectable district of London called Hoxton – slap out of the Nile, as its residents said and, according to the Metropolitan Police Force, the toughest 'manor' on Earth bar none – and enjoying exceptionally robust health.

'Ah-humph!' Mr. Reeder coughed. 'We appear to be the object of – um – considerable interest to your neighbours.' He waved his umbrella-filled hand languidly while – although he was growing increasingly sure that the weapon would not be needed – keeping the other on the butt of the big automatic pistol. 'Could I suggest that we carry on our – um – discussion inside?'

'Huh?' Mrs. Fredricks grunted, then glared around and realized why the gently spoken suggestion had been made. 'Yes. Come in. That lot across there don't have nothing better to do than just stand around watching what's none of their business.'

On the point of following the woman and Gaylor into the building, Besgrove-Woodstole discovered the cause of the comments. A number of female faces were pressed against the windows of the rooms in the apartments across the alley. Then he noticed what Mr. Reeder was doing. The gentle detective raised his high crowned hat and, to the Colonel's astonishment, poked out his tongue towards the watchers. They disappeared rapidly from their points of vantage and he went in on Gaylor's heels. Shaking his head in amused admiration, Besgrove-Woodstole brought up the rear.

The Fredricks family occupied a large suite of four rooms. However, there was nothing about the furnishings and other appointments to suggest the owner had a more lucrative means of earning a living than any of his neighbours. Mr.

Reeder, for one, was aware that they maintained a much more luxurious home in the best part of Bournemouth which had been bought by his illicit earnings. They used it frequently, excusing their absence by saying that they were travelling with their mythical employers.

'I don't know what you've come here for, really I don't, Mr. Gaylor,' Mrs. Fredricks stated, having seated her unwelcome guests and received a refusal to her offer that she should get them a cup of tea, or something. 'Oh yes. I know my Bert made a mistake once, but that's all behind him now. He's a decent hard-working—.'

'He *was* a decent, hard-working man,' Mr. Reeder corrected quietly, grateful that the woman did not threaten them with the righteous wrath of the Right Hon. Horatio Benner, M.P., as had become the habit of many criminals recently.

'Wha—?' Mrs. Fredricks began, staring at the elderly-looking detective. Something in his voice and manner sent a shiver through her. 'Here – What's brought you here?'

'I'm afraid that we are the – um – bearers of most distressing – er – news, madam,' Mr. Reeder replied, his demeanour gentle.

'What's wr—?' the woman commenced, then she stiffened. 'Something's happened to my Bert!'

'I'm afraid so, Mrs. Fredricks,' Mr. Reeder agreed. 'I deeply regret having to – um – tell you, but your husband is dead.'

'D – Dead?' the woman gasped and slumped into a chair. There was no faking about the alarm, shock and grief she showed. 'How – What – Wa – Was it an acci—?'

'No, madam, it wasn't an – um – accident,' Mr. Reeder answered. 'He was murdered by his – um – confederates in crime.'

'Mur – Mur—?' Mrs. Fredricks croaked, then a shudder ran through her and she burst into a flood of tears.

Watching Mr. Reeder, Besgrove-Woodstole was impressed. He had men in his Department who were trained and efficient in every form of interrogation methods, but none of them could have handled the distraught woman in a more capable manner. Within a quarter of an hour, she was sufficiently composed to answer questions. Gaylor had used the telephone – fitted and paid for by the 'Duke' for whom Fredricks was supposed to be chauffeur – to inform his mother and ask her to keep his son Harry at the public house for the time being.

'Yes, I knew Bert was on a job,' Mrs. Fredricks admitted, her face reddened and make-up smeared by the tears she had shed, but set in grim and angry lines. 'That's why I sent our Harry to his granny's. But you know him, Mr. Gaylor. He never told me nothing about his work, so's I couldn't get into trouble for knowing.'

'So you've always told me,' the man from Scotland Yard conceded gruffly and, catching the look Mr. Reeder directed at him, hastened to go on, 'And I've *always* believed you.'

'He didn't like this one, though,' Mrs. Fredricks declared, mollified by the acceptance of what was a valid claim, even though Gaylor had always been inclined to disbelieve it. 'I could tell *that*. And he admitted so when I asked, but he said he'd got to go through with it.'

'Do you mean he was afraid to refuse the – um – proposition when Mr. – er – Birkstone put it to him?' Mr. Reeder suggested, naming a prominent leader of the London underworld who had good reason to hate him and had been Fredricks' employer in the past.

'*Him*!' the woman snorted derisively. 'My Bert wouldn't have thought twice about turning down anything he put up. He'd have said "no" to Lou Birkstone, Billy Churgwin, or any other of them if he was so minded. He was independent, my Bert, the best driver of them all. None of *them* scared him.'

'Then who did?' Mr. Reeder asked mildly, for Mrs. Fredricks' statement confirmed what he and Gaylor had heard from other sources.

'I wish I knew! I'd shop him without thinking twice about it!' the woman replied vehemently and none of the men doubted that, either. 'My Bert wasn't scared of nobody – except for old Mad John Flack and *everybody* was scared of him.'

'He's dead,' Gaylor pointed out.

'I saw it in the newspapers,' Mrs. Fredricks answered, then stared at the gentle detective. 'You got him, Mr. Reeder.'

'I'm afraid that I didn't – um – "get" him,' the gentleman in question corrected. 'He met his – um – end when the caves under his – hideout – I believe is the term – caved in.'[7]

'That's as maybe,' Mr. Fredricks said, exuding determination. 'But he was still the only man who could have made my Bert do something he didn't want to do.'

Nothing could shake the woman from her conclusion. Nor did further questioning by Mr. Reeder produce the slightest suggestion of a clue to the identity of the man behind the murder attempt. So, ascertaining that she would be all right until some of the family arrived to look after her, the trio took their deparure.

'Where now?' asked Besgrove-Woodstole, as they left Carrington Mews. 'We didn't learn anything there.'

'Nothing – um – positive,' Mr. Reeder conceded. 'However, Mr. Gaylor, while I would hesitate to presume to proffer a – um – suggestion—.'

'Why?' interrupted the man from Scotland Yard with a grin. 'You've never held back from doing it all the time I've known you.'

'I would suggest that whichever officers you leave to keep – um – watch over the lady are those most competent in the use of their firearms,' Mr. Reeder went on, as if the other had not spoken. 'The killers may not share our summation regarding her dearth of – um – knowledge.'

'I'll attend to it,' Gaylor promised, unhesitatingly taking the advice of a man whom he willingly acknowledged as at the top of their mutual profession. 'What are you going to do?'

'Continue my – um – doubtless ineffectual investigations.'

'Do you need any help?'

'Not at the – um – moment.'

'Have it your way, you always do,' Gaylor grunted, knowing there were few men in London better equipped to take care of themselves than the frail-seeming detective. 'Try not to get killed. Or if you do, leave word who's done it for me.

7. Told in TERROR KEEP by Edgar Wallace. J.T.E.

I've got a lot of work on at the moment and don't want to be tied down to another investigation.'

'I'll do my – um – best to comply,' Mr. Reeder promised, so solemnly that he might have anticipated being killed and able to oblige by supplying the required information. 'Would you care to continue to – um – accompany me, Colonel?'

'Certainly,' Besgrove-Woodstole agreed. 'We still don't know which of us they were after. It could have been me.'

CHAPTER EIGHT

HE'S *RAPIDO* CLINT

'I'LL shoot two hundred!' announced the player who was shaking the two dice in his cupped right hand. 'Who wants it?'

It was a well known, if regrettable, fact that many people involved in the business of training racehorses also have a strong affinity for gambling. Nor do they restrict themselves to making wagers on the abilities of the animals in their care. A visit to the tack-room of practically every training stable thoughout the world on a Sunday afternoon would find some form of game of chance in progress. In England, it would probably be a card game such as pontoon, brag, nap, or prop-and-cop.

So the game of chance that was taking place in Charles Wagon's tack-room was unusual. However, only one of the participants was British.

Although Stanley 'Slick' Markey was one of the most dishonest jockeys ever to avoid being 'stood down' by the Stewards of the Jockey Club for his misdemeanours,[1] he had a curiously blind spot where other forms of gambling were concerned. A wiser man would have avoided becoming involved in a fast action game of chance for high stakes with which he had not previously come into contact. Yet, on the surface, the game of 'craps'[2] had seemed so simple when watching his American colleagues that he could not resist joining in.

1. See Part 2, 'Mr. Evans Does a Bit of Gas Work' in: GOOD EVANS by Edgar Wallace. J.T.E.

2. SCARNE ON DICE *by John Scarne* (with Clayton Rawson) Military Service Publishing Co., Washington D.C. 1952, is the definitive work on the game of 'craps'. J.T.E.

Basically, the game *was* simple. A player, known as the 'shooter' threw two dice. If the numbers on their upper surfaced totalled seven or eleven, a 'natural', it was a winning decision and called a 'pass'. Throwing the numbers two, three, or twelve, 'craps', was a losing decision and termed a 'missout'. Should the result be a four, five, six, eight, nine, or ten, that number became the 'shooter's' 'point'. He then continued to throw until repeating his point effected a winning decision. However, if he threw a seven before he made his 'point', he lost.

Before making his first throw, the 'shooter' placed whatever sum he wished on the playing surface, showing he wanted to wager that he would make a 'pass'. Any of the other players who were so inclined could cover the amount he had put down to back their belief that he would 'missout'. If a 'point' number appeared, the 'shooter' neither won nor lost. Instead, he continued to throw until he repeated his 'point' or a seven appeared.

There was, Markey had soon discovered, vastly more to craps than that. One could wager in a variety of ways among the other players and was not restricted to 'fading', covering the amount put down by the 'shooter'. Experimenting with the various forms of bets had proved costly. Nor had his attempts to recoup by doubling the amount previously wagered after each loss helped him out of his difficulties. Rather the opposite.

Apart from the 'shooter', all of the eight men gathered around the blanket covered table were clearly jockeys. Their small size, ages and the way they were dressed was evidence that they had risen over the rank of stable lad or apprentice. Just under six foot in height, the exception loomed above them. Attired after the fashion of a British farm labourer, he was burly and had a hard, vicious face. His harsh midwestern twang as he made his challenge while shaking the dice suggested that his appearance was deceptive. So did the big .45 Colt 1917 revolver thrust into his waist band.

'Not me,' declared Bucky Borofin, from Markey's side, in his lazy Southern drawl. 'You're way too hot for me, Kinch.'

'I don't fade-a nobody who makes six-a passes in a row,'

Angelo Pirelli went on, his Italian-American accent at odds with his blond hair. 'That's-a too lucky for me.'

Staring down at the pile in front of Stanton Kinch, Markey ran the tip of his tongue around his lips. There was greed and a calculating glint in his shifty eyes as he considered the statement made by the New York Italian jockey. Six times in a row, Kinch had thrown a 'natural'. He was allowed to continue 'shooting' until the dice produced either a 'point' or a 'missout'. To Markey's way of thinking, the odds were greatly against him 'shooting' a seventh 'natural' in succession.

'I – I'll fade you!' the English jockey announced, trying to keep his voice steady. 'If you'll take my marker.'

Markey was already adopting the other players' term for an 'i.o.u.'

'That'll be over fifteen hundred pounds – or whatever you call 'em – that you're in for, Slick,' warned Ivan Drobsky, whose reputation on American race courses was almost the equivalent of Markey's in England.

'I'm good for it!' Markey snapped.

'You'd better be, seeing as most of it's to me,' Kinch growled, continuing to shake the dice. 'Do you want it?'

'I said I'd fade you!' Markey spat back.

'Come seven!' Kinch chanted and his right hand shot forward.

Bouncing across the blanket, the two dice came to a halt in front of the English jockey. Almost sick with disappointment, he saw that one upper face showed three spots and the other four.

'And a "natural" it is, gents,' Drobsky announced. 'Hard luck, Slick. You're still shooter, Ki—!'

So engrossed had the players been in what was going on that none of them had noticed the door of the tack-room open. However, turning his gaze from Markey to Kinch, Drobsky became aware that a newcomer was present. What was more, studying the way he was clad, the New England jockey realized that he was a stranger. Noticing how Drobsky was behaving, the others turned their heads to follow his gaze.

'Who the he—?' Kinch began, taking in the comparatively

small size, youth and Western attire of the man who had entered, and letting his right hand move towards the butt of the black Colt.

'I'd forget *that*, was I you,' advised the young Texan who had been given a ride into Little Venner by Beryl Snowhill.

Gently as the words were spoken, they seemed to carry a greater menace than if they had been shouted violently. The Texan had advanced until he was about fifteen feet from the table before his presence was detected. Halting as soon as he was seen, he balanced on spread apart feet. His hat was dangling on his shoulders by its *barbiquejo* chin strap. While his left hand grasped and drew open the side of his jacket, the right was pointing towards it.

Not only had Kinch's words been brought to a halt, his hand's movement towards the revolver ended well clear of it. Suddenly, in some way he could not fathom out, he felt he was no longer looking at a *small* interloper. It seemed that the newcomer had grown, become very large and was charged with an aura of deadly menace.

'You'd best listen to him, Kinch,' Borofin drawled.

'Do you know him, Bucky?' Drobsky inquired.

'I'll say I do,' Borofin confessed, with an air of satisfied self importance. 'He's *Rapido* Clint.'

'*Rapido* Clint?' Kinch ejaculated, staring with even greater intensity at the newcomer. 'Is that right?'

'You-all try taking out that hog-leg, *hombre*,' the Texan suggested, still in the same quiet and yet somehow menace-filled tone. 'And I'll right soon give you the answer.'

'Go on, Kinch-boy,' grinned Borofin, having no liking for the burly man. 'I *could* be wrong, seeing's how I only had him pointed out to me the one time when I was riding in a meeting down to San Antone.'[3]

'Hey!' the bald Link Gruber put in, his Pacific North-West accent showing excitement. 'I've heard about you, Mr. Clint. You wiped out all the Mendez gang down in Texas, then cut the legs from under the O'Brien bunch when they wouldn't pay you for doing it.'

3. San Antone: colloquial name for San Antonio, seat of Bexar County, Texas. J.T.E.

'Now don't that just show you-all how things get all exaggerated,' the Texan drawled, without taking his eyes from Kinch's face. 'Shucks, I didn't but put blue windows in 'Lonzo Mendez, Mick O'Brien and maybe three each of their boys afore the rest was up and running.'

'Then, from what I heard,' the burly man growled, having his reputation for toughness to consider and feeling he should demonstrate it. 'That there "Cap" Fog of the Texas Rangers ran *you* clear down into Mexico.'

'That's what you-all heard, huh, *hombre*?'

Giving no prior warning of his intentions, either by a look or the tone of his voice, the Texan moved far faster than he was speaking. Gliding forward while he was talking, he lashed his right arm around and up almost simultaneously with the word, '*hombre*'. Clenching as it rose, the back of his fist crashed against the bottom of Kinch's jaw. Small the newcomer might be, but he was clearly very strong. Taken unawares, the force of the blow sent Kinch spinning away from the table to sprawl on his hands and knees. Spitting out obscenities, he rolled until he was sitting up. Then, glaring at his assailant – who was several feet away and well beyond reach – he grabbed at and began to tug the revolver from his waistband.

Once again, displaying the speed of movement which had earned him the nickname '*Rapido*', meaning exceptionally fast in the Spanish spoken by *Chicanos*,[4] the Texan darted forward. Even as the Colt was extracted, but before it could be brought into alignment, his right foot whipped upwards. The sharp toe of the Justin boot[5] took Kinch under the chin, snapping his head rearwards. Pitched over by the impact, losing his hold on the weapon, his shoulders met the floor with a solid thud. He was already unconscious and did not feel it.

'What the hell's going—?' bellowed a voice from the doorway. '*You!*'

4. *Chicano:* colloquial name for a Mexican born, or residing, in the United States. J.T.E.

5. Justin boots: originally made by Joseph Justin, the business being carried on to the present day by his family. The boots, designed with the specialized needs of cowhands in mind, achieved great popularity by virtue of their excellent quality. J.T.E.

'Me,' confirmed the Texan, recognizing the tones even before he had turned to look at the speaker.

Having had no desire to go into the house and tell *Him* what had happened in the yard behind the Starter's Hack, or that the attempt to borrow the publican's car had been unsuccessful, Wagon had taken a roundabout route back. He had just finished unsaddling the hunter and was unaware that the woman calling herself Olga Garvin had arrived. Wishing to delay the interview with *Him* for as long as possible, the trainer had decided to accompany the two 'stablehands' – who had been equally desirous to stay away from the house and were in their quarters above the hunter's loose-box – to see what kind of gambling was taking place in the tack-room.

'What the something or other, something, something[6] are *you* doing here?' Wagon snarled, glaring at the speaker and taking a couple of steps forward.

Much to the surprise of the jockeys and, in particular – knowing him as they did – the 'stablehands', in spite of his obvious rage at the sight of the small visitor, Wagon came to a halt instead of attacking. What was more, he seemed very ill-at-ease for all his foul mouthed question.

There was good cause for Wagon's reaction. The recollection of what had happened after he burst out of the back door at the Starter's Hack was still fresh in his memory. Nor would he ever forget it. Roaring his challenge as the interloper had turned to face him, he had lunged to make his attack.

And, somehow, the proposed victim had stopped being small!

In fact, the strangely dressed young man had appeared to swell like a balloon being blown up until he was larger than Wagon.

Even as the trainer was trying to decide what to make of the phenomenon, his right wrist had been caught by what

6. The author realizes that, in our present 'permissive society', he could include Wagon's exact words, but he sees no valid reason why he should need to. However, if so inclined the reader is at liberty to substitute them. J.T.E.

felt like the grip of a steel clamp. He had seen the stranger pivoting around without releasing his trapped limb. An instant later, some irresistible force had caused his feet to leave the ground. He had found that the world was turning topsy-turvy. Despite his instincts as a rider he had alighted on his back hard enough to jar the wind and wits from him. When he had recovered, the stranger was no longer in sight. The only consolation, apart from relief that the attack had not been continued, was he had been able to give the publican at least a passable excuse for his condition without revealing the truth.

Although puzzled by their employer's behaviour, Ollie and Mush, the 'stablehands', were aware of what was usually expected of them when they came into contact with trespassers. Lumbering by Wagon, they converged on the small intruder. If he was afraid, or realized their intentions, he gave no indication of it. Nor, despite Borofin for one – knowing what was portended – expecting him to do so, did he adopt the posture he had assumed when confronting Kinch. Instead, he stood apparently relaxed and without even as much as clenching his fists.

Neither of the 'stablehands' was particularly intelligent. Their duties as Wagon's 'minders' called for brawn rather than brain. For all that, they were not so stupid as to be unaware – as their employer and Kinch had become – of the change that seemed to come over their intended victim as they drew near. To find that he gave the impression of an inexplicable increase in size was such a shock that it impaired their usual smooth co-ordination and caused a certain hesitancy in their actions which allowed Ollie to draw slightly ahead of Mush.

Rapido Clint took instant and effective advantage of the pair's confusion!

Once again, the Texan demonstrated the devastating skill with which he could kick. However, his latest target was *not* the chin. Snapping forward, his left foot struck Ollie with considerable violence. Letting out a strangled screech of agony, the 'stablehand's' far from pleasant features turned an ashy shade of greenish-grey. Clutching at the stricken area, the most vulnerable and susceptible portion of the male anatomy for such an attack, he folded at the waist and collapsed almost fainting.

Startled by the unanticipated swing of events, it became Mush's turn to discover how dangerous the man called *Rapido* Clint could be. Even as his sluggish brain was giving a warning that the affair was not going as it should have, he saw the *big* stranger's right arm swinging with extraordinary alacrity in his direction. Yet the blow was not being struck in a manner to which he was accustomed. Instead of being clenched, the hand was open. Held horizontally, its fingers were extended together and the thumb curled across the palm.

Making a sound as if yelling, '*Kiai!*' for some reason, the Texan slashed with the edge of his hand into the front of Mush's throat. To the 'stablehand', it felt as if he had been struck with a blunt axe. Gasping and barely able to speak, he staggered backwards but did not go down.

Seeing his men's discomfiture and hoping to take advantage of the Texan's preoccupation with them, Wagon rushed forward. To the spectators, it seemed that his charge knocked the – to them, at any rate – small newcomer over.

For a brief instant, Wagon subscribed to the watchers' summation. He saw *Rapido* Clint falling backwards as if forced to do so by the weight of his attack. Except that, he suddenly realized, it was happening before his effort could have produced such an effect. Then he felt his reaching hands knocked away from their intended targets. An instant later, his jacket's lapels were grasped and, as he tried unavailingly to restrain his onwards impetus, a foot was rammed into his midriff. While his jacket was hauled downwards, the foot shoved in the opposite direction. Then followed an unnerving sensation similar to being thrown over the head of a horse. Performing a half somersault, his body came down spine first upon the unyielding wooden planks of the floor.

Having thrown his assailant by as neat a wrestling move as any of the onlookers had ever witnessed, *Rapido* Clint uncoiled his body in such a manner that he bounded to his feet.

And into what appeared to be trouble!

Half strangled by the after-effects of the blow to his throat, Mush was far from incapacitated. Wheezing what would have been vilifications if his vocal cords had been functioning correctly, he lunged forward and hurled a punch as the Texan returned to an upright position. Badly aimed, duc to its deliverer's condition, the fist caught Clint on his left shoulder instead of somewhere more harmful. It still arrived with sufficient power to send him reeling. He went over in a rolling plunge, but was sufficiently in possession of his faculties to snatch up Kinch's revolver in passing.

What was more, as Mush advanced with the intention of continuing the assault, the Texan ended his flight in a kneeling posture. Facing the burly 'stablehand', he thrust out the big revolver with a steadiness of hand that warned he had not been seriously, or even more than moderately, hurt by the blow.

'That's close enough, *hombre*!' Clint declared and, despite the Colt Model of 1917 revolver being equipped with a double action mechanism allowing pressure on the trigger to perform the whole firing cycle, he drew back the hammer with his thumb.

Hearing the menacing click and realizing what it meant, Mush came to a halt. He was looking into the .45 calibre muzzle (although it seemed vastly larger than that to his eyes) which was pointing unwaveringly at the centre of his face.

'You-all stay back,' the Texan went on, his voice almost caressing in its easy drawl and yet charged with a terrible threat and fatal certainty. 'All right now. Somebody'd best take me to meet the head he-hooper of this spread. I didn't trail all the way from Texas to fool around with – nor *kill* should I have to – any of his hired help, but to get taken on myself. And, from what I've seen so far, he *needs* some real capable help like *me*.'

CHAPTER NINE

THIS IS PURELY A SOCIAL VISIT

HAVING driven from Camden Town to the West End of London, Mr. J. G. Reeder parked the Frazer-Nash Fast Tourer in Leicester Square. Accompanied by Colonel Brian Besgrove-Woodstole, D.S.O., M.C. and Bar, he crossed New Coventry Street which at that hour on the still pleasant Sunday afternoon was almost deserted and turned into Leicester Place. They were, the detective had informed his guest during the journey, going to try to find William Maxwell Churgwin. Although not engaged in British crime prevention, the Colonel knew him to be one of the city's major criminals and the leader of a large gang.

A small, ferret-faced and snappily dressed man was locking the door of a building as Mr. Reeder and Besgrove-Woodstole turned the corner. They were both wearing boots with rubber soles and heels, so he was unaware of their presence until he swung around. Instantly, alarm showed on his features and he spun on his heel with his left hand reaching for the bell-button on the frame of the door.

Slipping through Mr. Reeder's fingers until he grasped it by the ferrule, the umbrella flashed forward and the crook of its handle hooked into the neck of the man's jacket. With a heave that seemed out of keeping when applied by such an apparently fragile person, the detective plucked his captive out of reach of the bell-button and slammed him back against the wall.

'Why it's Mr. Tupper!' Mr. Reeder declared, with an air of amazement, sliding the umbrella back into a conventional position.

'You haven't got nothing on me!' the small man whined,

in the somewhat nasal tones of one born within the sound of Bow Bells, thrusting away the key with which he had locked the door.

'Not a single, solitary thing in the – um – world,' the detective agreed, his manner very gentle, therefore – as his little captive was all too aware – full of promised malevolence. 'In fact, you are so – um – virtuous that you would have no objections if your good – um – lady wife learned where you have been spending your evenings recently.'

The effect of the words was both obvious and surprising to Besgrove-Woodstole. All of the little man's aura of self righteous truculence evaporated and he crouched back as if he had been struck.

' 'Ere now, Mr. Reeder—!' Tupper croaked.

'Who – or should it be "whom"? – is in the Pinhole Club?' the detective inquired. 'Would Mr. – um – Churgwin, for example, be amongst those present, I wonder?'

'Y – Yes,' Tupper confirmed and a sense of grievance, caused by his having been refused admission despite claiming membership, made him continue, 'And he's got a lot of real toffs up there. So if you're thinking of pulling a raid—'

'Perish the thought,' Mr. Reeder said reassuringly and held out his left hand palm upwards. 'This is purely a social visit. May I ask you for the – um – loan of your key?'

'*My* key?' Tupper yelped.

'As – and I confess this with – um – shame – neither the Colonel nor I are members, we can hardly gain admittance without it,' Mr. Reeder explained. 'Of course, if questioned, I will be – um – discreet as to how I obtained the means of ingress. On the other hand, I am an inveterate gossip and, should I not get in, I may find myself in the Elephant And Castle district later—'

' 'Ere!' Tupper gasped, taking out and handing over the key. 'Give me time to scarper and, don't forget, I ain't seen you.'

'Trust me,' Mr. Reeder called at the man's rapidly departing back.

'What was all that about?' Besgrove-Woodstole asked, as his companion made no attempt to use the key.

'Tupper is married to a very large and – um – aggressive

lady who would take the most violent exception if she discovered how he had been spending his leisure hours,' the detective replied and almost whispered in shocked tones. 'He is – um – unfaithful.'

Allowing a good three minutes to go by, Mr. Reeder inserted the key and opened the unmarked door from which Tupper had emerged. Frowning in puzzlement, the Colonel followed his host along a passage and up a flight of none too clean stairs. Much to Mr. Reeder's relief, the small booth at the top was unoccupied. Usually a man would have been in attendance. His absence simplified matters in the detective's opinion, as it allowed them to reach their destination unannounced. Opening his jacket, an action duplicated by his companion, Mr. Reeder led the way to a set of double doors beyond the booth. One side yielded when he turned the handle. Going through on his host's heels, Besgrove-Woodstole found that they had entered the main room of a luxuriously appointed night club which was offering its patrons an unusual form of entertainment.

Clad in the latest and most daring style of bathing suits, but which had been torn to the point of immodesty, two very dishevelled, clearly exhausted, but otherwise attractive and shapely young women were rolling over and over fighting with each other in the centre of what would normally have been the dance floor. Although their hands were covered in thin black leather gloves to prevent scratching, each bore marks gained in what must have been a lengthy struggle. They were being encouraged in their flagging efforts by some fifty or so spectators of both sexes. At least a dozen were people who Besgrove-Woodstole recognized as wealthy members of Society, although they belonged to a class with which he was disinclined to mingle.

From all appearances, Mr. Reeder and the Colonel had arrived at a critical moment. One of the contestants was straddling the other's supine body and, digging both hands into her hair, was banging her head on the padded mat which covered the floor. The other occupants of the room, even the man who should have been on duty in the booth, were so absorbed that none of them noticed the new arrivals. However, as the woman on the bottom went limp, a big, burly man wearing an immaculately tailored Saville Row suit happened to glance in their direction. Instantly, he came to his feet. Snapping an order which caused two of the women seated at his table to rise and pull the victress from her flaccid victim, he strode forward with a proprietorial air.

'Hello, Mr. Reeder,' the man greeted, waving a hand towards the dance floor. 'Just a little sporting contest and no real harm done. The girls had a bit of a disagreement and asked if they could settle it—'

'So it would – um – appear,' the detective answered, sweeping the room with his gaze and noticing that its occupants were considerably disconcerted at the sight of him. A fattish, porcine-featured young man sharing a table with a beautiful and expensively raimented lady started to rise hurriedly. 'Please don't let me drive you away, Mr. – um – Frithington-Evans, isn't it? Like yourself and – um – Lady Herban, the Colonel and I are here merely as – er – guests. This *isn't* a – raid, I believe is the – um – term.'

Looking as if he wished the floor would open up and swallow him, the man – a very rich racehorse owner of questionable morals[1] – sank back on to his chair. Although his companion was a married woman whose husband was out of the country, but would be unlikely to approve of her escort or her attendance at such an erotic form of entertainment, she seemed much less abashed by the presence of the famous detective.

While making his comment, Mr. Reeder had little interest in either Lady Mary Herban or Frithington-Evans. He had noticed in his examination of the room that, mingling with the members of Society who were present, and almost as well dressed, were the sub-leaders of every section from Churgwin's organization. Without exception, they were sitting in somewhat constrained attitudes and attracted the majority of the detective's attention. There was something about them suggesting that – although worried by his arrival –

1. Further details regarding Mr. Frithington-Evans and his connection with Lady Herban are divulged in Part IV 'The Freak Dinner' and Part XII, 'The Journalist' of MORE EDUCATED EVANS by Edgar Wallace. J.T.E.

none had guilty knowledge of the attack upon him and his companion.

Subjecting the occupants to a similar scrutiny, Besgrove-Woodstole duplicated his host's summations. Then, turning his gaze to Churgwin, the Colonel found something familiar in the gang leader's bearing. A moment's thought supplied the answer. A skilled hunter of big game, Churgwin's posture reminded him of a dangerous animal such as the Cape buffalo, *Syncerus Caffer Caffer*. Having become aware of a potentially threatening enemy near by, such a beast was wary yet knew it was so well protected that it had little to fear. If Churgwin had ordered the abortive assassination, he was such an accomplished actor that he was concealing any sign of perturbation over discovering it had failed.

'How did *you* get in, Mr. Reeder?' Churgwin demanded, throwing a look which boded little good for the discomfitured man who should have been in the booth preventing unauthorized entry.

'I have been in possession of a – um – membership key for some time,' the detective replied, with such disarming innocent frankness he might have been telling the truth. 'Collecting such things is a harmless – um – hobby of mine. This is the first time Colonel Besgrove-Woodstole and – But how – um – remiss of me. Do you know the – um – Colonel?'

'We haven't met,' Churgwin replied and there was nothing about his tone or expression, even to Mr. Reeder's exceptionally capable gaze, to imply the officers name held any special meaning for him. 'But—!'

'Perhaps we are delaying the next – um – bout?' the detective interrupted apologetically, knowing that the spectacle they had witnessed was a frequent feature of the Pinhole Club's entertainment. 'I must confess I'm not an – um – *aficionado* – if that is the appropriate foreign expression. Not that I would protest anybody else's right to participate or – um – spectate. But if we could have the privacy of your—' He held up his umbrella filled left hand in a gesture of gentle prohibition before the gang leader could speak. 'I am, of course, in – um – error. Like the Colonel and myself, you are but a member. But perhaps—?'

'Come with me,' Churgwin said, accepting that there

would be no point in continuing his pretence that he was not the owner.

'Would you care to have Mr. – um – Gulliver accompany you?' Mr. Reeder inquired, nodding to where the gang leader's solicitor was sitting and watching them.

'Do I need him?'

'That is merely a matter for your – um – conscience. Not that, I hasten to assure you, I – um – *know* of anything which might be troubling it.'

'Then we'll leave him where he is,' Churgwin decided. 'If you'll come with me—?'

'The – um – pleasure is all mine,' Mr. Reeder answered and swung his gaze around the room once more. Raising his left hand in salutation, he gave vent to his most extreme form of frivolity. 'Toodle-oo!'

'All right, Mr. Reeder,' Churgwin said, after he had escorted his unwelcome visitors into the Club's office. 'What's the game? Why've you come here?'

'Merely to settle my – um – insatiable curiosity,' the detective replied. 'Have you seen Bert the – um – Jump-Up recently?'

'Not in months,' Churgwin declared. 'After he turned down the—'

'Brighton job?' Mr. Reeder suggested. 'No – um – matter. May I have the use of the telephonic apparatus, please?'

'Of course,' Churgwin assented. 'Shall I wait outside?'

'It's of no – um – importance, everything will be on – er – record,' Mr. Reeder replied and the gang leader looked startled by the oblique reference to a piece of unauthorized equipment attached to the telephone, but which he had assumed to be a secret. Taking the earphone from the mouthpiece's pole-like stand, the detective dialled the number at his home which could be found in the appropriate London directory. By doing so, he knew his housekeeper would be very circumspect with anything of importance she might have to impart. 'Mrs. Grible? Is there – um – anything to report?'

'Nothing, sir,' the housekeeper replied. 'I called the Press Club and had a word with Mr. W. He said he'd see if any of the crime reporters had heard anything.'

Experience had taught Mr. Reeder's organization that newspaper reporters who specialized in criminal activities occasionally obtained information which would not have been given to the authorities. Sometimes the chairman of the Press Club (the gentleman to whom Mrs. Grible had spoken) would exert influence to produce information that otherwise might have been regarded as confidential

'Most – um – satisfactory,' Mr. Reeder praised. 'We will be continuing our investigations. I'm sorry about missing your – um – excellent lunch.'

'Yes, sir,' the housekeeper answered. 'Be careful, sir.'

'Rest assured that I have every – um – intention of doing so,' Mr. Reeder promised and hung up. Beaming benevolently at the gang leader, he went on, 'Thank you, Mr. – um – Churgwin. I don't think I need trouble you any – um – further. Where can I get in touch with you in the unlikely – um – event that I should wish to do so during the next few days?'

'On Lord Berringham's yacht,' Churgwin replied just a shade too quickly in Besgrove-Woodstole's opinion. 'He's asked me and some of my bo – our friends to go on a cruise in the Mediterranean. We'll be leaving early tomorrow morning.'

'Which of your – um – associates are included in the party?' the detective demanded and the words were a demand in spite of the mild way they had been uttered.

'Sid Hall, Chubby Vickery, Lumpy Tooth,' Churgwin obliged and continued until he had named each of his subordinate leaders.

'A – um – notable selection,' Mr. Reeder said, almost pensively. 'And you will be away how – um – long?'

'A fortnight, at least,' Churgwin answered.

'Enjoy yourselves,' Mr. Reeder enjoined, rising. 'Well, we must be on our – um – way. Good day to you, Mr. – um – Churgwin.'

'Good afternoon,' the gang leader replied, looking at the top of his desk. 'Be very careful, Mr. Reeder.'

'I *always* am,' the detective declared and, much to his guest's surprise, turned to leave without questioning what had clearly been a warning. As he and the Colonel were going down the stairs, he remarked, 'Whatever his multifarious illegal activities might be, Mr. – um – Churgwin was not responsible for the attempt. But, although I might be doing him an – um – injustice, I suspect that he is aware that measures are being contemplated for my – um – removal.'

'You're satisfied now that it is you they're after?'

'At the risk of appearing – um – immodest, Colonel, and with due respect to your position of importance, I – um – am.'

'But you don't think Churgwin's involved?'

'Not in my opinion, for what little *that* is – um – worth,' Mr. Reeder stated, with feeble certainty.

'Yet he knew it was going to happen,' Besgrove-Woodstole pointed out.

'No, Colonel,' the detective corrected. 'He knows something is – um – contemplated, but not that it has already taken place. If he had been aware of *that*, the cruise upon which he and his – um – confederates are to embark, in the interests of creating what I believe is termed an – um – alibi, would have already commenced.'

'If he knows it's being planned, he might know who's behind it.'

'Possibly.'

'Then why not go back and ask him?'

'Because, if I did, he would – um – lie,' Mr. Reeder answered in hushed tones as if ashamed to be levelling such a dire accusation. 'And I have no wish to be responsible for him having such a thing on his – um – conscience.'

Knowing his companion very well, Besgrove-Woodstole did not press the matter. He was confident that Mr. Reeder would have asked the requisite questions if there had been any chance of obtaining the answer.

On returning to the Frazer-Nash, the Colonel noticed that the detective was looking at its bonnet. Thinking nothing of it, he reached for the handle of the passenger's door.

'Wait!' Mr. Reeder hissed urgently. 'Stand back, Colonel!'

Frowning, Besgrove-Woodstole obeyed. He watched as, acting with great care, his companion unfastened and raised the hood. Glancing inside, the detective stiffened slightly.

'Just as I – um – suspected when I saw the cotton I had

tied around the clips of the bonnet was broken,' Mr. Reeder remarked. 'Most – um – enterprising on somebody's part.'

Stepping around the end of the car as gently as if treading on eggshells, the Colonel let out a low whistle. Whoever had opened the bonnet had done *much* more than merely break the strands of cotton. A bundle of six sticks of dynamite rested on the engine. Running from the detonator implanted in them, a piece of electric cable was attached to the vehicle's ignition wires.

'Good god!' Besgrove-Woodstole gasped, realizing what the sight implied. 'That was close!'

'Most – um – disconcerting,' Mr. Reeder admitted, with masterly, if gentle, understatement. Leaning forward, he peered at the device for some seconds before starting to render it harmless. 'I don't – um – think there would be time for anything more elaborate, Colonel,' he said at the completion of the task, lifting out the bundle and holding it in his companion's direction. 'But I feel it would be – um – advisable to make sure.'

'Do you think this was Churgwin's work?' Besgrove-Woodstole inquired, taking the dynamite and watching the detective carrying out a *very* thorough examination of the tourer.

'I – um – doubt it,' Mr. Reeder replied, bending to peer underneath the chassis. 'The Pinhole Club is a most – um – lucrative establishment. He is too intelligent to – what, in my opinion is vulgarly referred to as – urinate on his own – um – doorstep in such a fashion.'

'Then somebody must have followed us here!' Besgrove-Woodstole barked.

'We weren't – um – *followed*, Colonel,' Mr. Reeder contradicted apologetically. 'In the – um – prevailing conditions, I felt it incumbent upon me to watch out for such an – um – eventuality.'

'Then if we weren't followed—?'

'Our arrival was – um – anticipated.'

'You mean that somebody guessed we'd come here?'

'That is my – um – belief,' Mr. Reeder stated.

'But who—?' Besgrove-Woodstole began.

'That, Colonel, is what I wish I – um – knew,' Mr. Reeder

replied, in a tone which sent a shiver through the normally steel-nerved officer. 'The only person I can envisage as being possessed of such – um – brilliant planning ability is – er – dead.' He paused for a moment, looking at the bundle of dynamite in Besgrove-Woodstole's hand and then continued in an even more frightening manner. 'At least, I – um – sincerely hope he is.'

CHAPTER TEN

I'M GOING TO SEARCH YOU

Cyril Gambel, the elder of the two men who had met Beryl Snowhill's passenger on her arrival at Charles Wagon's house, had committed most of the major crimes in his life and considered himself to be very tough. For all that, he received a shock which brought him to a halt as he entered the tack-room. On fetching him, Bucky Borofin had mentioned there had been trouble; but had not gone into details of its full magnitude.

All of the other jockeys were gathered around the table, but the craps game was postponed. To one side of them, Kinch was groaning his way back to consciousness. Still looking dazed and breathing hard, the trainer was sitting on the floor against the wall. The 'stablehand', Mush, stood near his employer, but Ollie had not recovered from the effects of the kick and crouched in a huddled heap on the floor.

'You can put down that revolver,' Gambel told the author of these various misfortunes who was seated on the edge of the table, idly shaking the dice in his left hand.

'Are you the head he-hooper?' asked *Rapido* Clint, without offering to comply.

'Am I the *what*?' Gambel snapped, in his well bred English accent.

'The big augur,' the Texan explained, not much more succinctly, then translated, 'The top boss of the whole outfit.'

'I am as far as you're concerned,' Gambel stated stiffly.

'That far's not near enough by a good country mile,' Clint declared. 'I don't talk to no straw boss. Either I get to see the *hombre* who gives *you* orders, or I just plain get.'

'And what if I say you can't do either?' Gambel challenged, having his position of authority to consider and conscious that several of his subordinates were listening.

'*I'd* say those yahoos are a right smart answer to fool notions like *that*,' Clint answered, indicating his victims with a gesture from the big Colt Model 1917 revolver. 'Which same, I didn't have this old hog-leg when I handed *them* their needings.'

'Very well,' Gambel said quietly, staring at the revolver which had halted its movements to point with disconcerting steadiness at his stomach and remembering the orders he had been given. 'I'll take you to *Him*, but not with that gun in your hand.'

'Shucks, I don't conclude I'll need it no more,' the Texan drawled, operating the stud on the right side of the frame with his thumb and swinging out the cylinder. Having shaken the cartridges from the chamber, he tossed the unloaded weapon on to the body of its barely conscious owner. 'Let's go.'

'You'd better get on your feet and to the house, Wagon!' Gambel snarled. 'But I should keep out of *His* way for a while. *He's* not going to be pleased when *He* hears what's happened.'

With that, *His* second-in-command turned and Clint accompanied him from the tack-room. Such was Gambel's eagerness to carry out *His* instructions that he failed to notice the Texan was allowing him to take the lead and was, in fact, positioned so as to be able to step behind him if the need should arise. On reaching the house, Gambel entered first. Still drawing no conclusions from the way Clint was lagging, he led the way towards the open door of a room to the left side of the entrance hall.

'In there!' Gambel ordered, without looking back.

'Why sure,' Clint drawled and acted with the kind of speed that had helped him to cope with his larger assailants in the tack-room.

Giving Gambel not the slightest prior indication of his intentions, the Texan stepped closer. The criminal's first intimation that something was wrong came when he felt his right wrist seized and twisted behind his back. An instant later, a hand grasped the scruff of his neck with savage power. Before he could think of offering resistance, or yelling a warning, he found himself being propelled with considerable vigour through the door. Released, he staggered across the room and sprawled in front of the table at the centre. As he landed, the Luger automatic pistol slipped from his waistband and clattered to the floor.

'Looks like I've done you-all a mistrust, *hombre*,' Clint drawled, walking with a cat-like stealth across the threshold of what was usually Wagon's study in which such important personages as owners could be entertained. 'Only I've heard tell of how sometimes folk lie in wait behind doors. So I concluded I'd rather it was you-all'n not me's got whomped on the head should it be going to happen.'

Although Clint was addressing the man he had shoved, his gaze passed around the other occupants of the room. To the right of the table, Gambel's brother, Maurice, had let out a startled exclamation and was staring downwards. Such was his surprise at the unexpected turn of events, that the heavy calibre Webley revolver in his right hand was dangling with its muzzle pointing at the floor.

With a mocking smile playing on her pallidly beautiful face, Olga Garvin was also standing and studying Cyril Gambel. Raising her eyes, she subjected Clint to a brief but calculating scrutiny before turning to look at the man who was sitting by her side.

The latter was the main source of the Texan's attention. Clad in a multi-hued dressing gown with wider than usual sleeves, there was still a suggestion of what had been a magnificent physique about the man despite his shoulders being rounded and bent. He was undoubtedly very old. Lined and wrinkled like the texture of ancient parchment, his face had little expression except for his eyes. Deep set, they were light blue and had such a piercing, unwinking stare that they might have been devoid of lids. His mane of hair, neatly trimmed moustache and beard were pure white. Sitting erect in the high back carving chair, only his bony hands – moving as restlessly as two disturbed spiders – gave evidence that he was still alive.

'Well, you *brought* him to us all right, Cyril,' the woman

commented, directing another mocking glance to where – muttering obscenities – the organization's second-in-command was picking up the Luger and starting to rise. 'Wouldn't you say so, father?'

'He's here, I'll grant,' the old man conceded, speaking with a strangely thin and tense voice that had an anything but merry-sounding chuckle in it and which grew more strident as he continued, 'His hands *are* empty, but is he armed?'

'I haven't searched him,' Cyril admitted sullenly, looking across the table at the old man.

'Then I would strongly advise that you do it,' was the high pitched response to the confession. 'And immediately!'

'All right, you!' Cyril snarled at the Texan, after glancing at his brother. 'Hold out your arms. I'm going to search you!'

'Like hell you are,' Clint contradicted, his left hand rising to grasp the lapel and draw open the jacket while the right pointed across his chest. Once again, such was the strength of his personality, he produced the impression that he had grown larger and it gave the same aura of menace to his posture. '*Nobody* puts their hands through *Rapido* Clint!'

'We'll soon see about that!' Cyril spat out, taking a step forward and starting to raise the automatic pistol.

'The only way you can do it is *after* I'm dead, *hombre*,' Clint warned, showing neither alarm, nor concern even, over the sight of the brothers pointing their respective weapons in his direction. Something in his attitude brought Cyril to a halt. 'You've got to take the safety off on that Luger and, what I've seen of them, the Webley's mighty heavy on the trigger unless the hammer's back, which it isn't. You *might* get me, but I'll take at least one of you with me. Only I don't reckon's how your boss there behind the table'd want me killing.'

'And why wouldn't I?' demanded the old man, cocking his head on one side in a gesture as ludicrous as a vulture trying to ape the mannerisms of a perky house sparrow.

'Because you're real curious about me, sir,' Clint explained, adopting a more respectful attitude than he had shown to Gambel. 'And, like you-all know, but those two butt-dragging yahoos haven't figured, once I'm dead, you'll never get to know where I learned how to find you.'

'What do *you* have to say to that, Cyril?' Olga asked, derisively.

'Don't you-all go riding him so he does something *loco*, which means stupid, ma'am,' Clint advised, his voice losing the respect and hardening. 'Like I said, your daddy doesn't want *any of us* dead.'

'And what if I don't care?' the old man inquired.

'Say the word, sir, happen I'm wrong,' Clint suggested, the respect returning to his quiet drawl. 'Only it'd be a mortal shame for you-all to lose two good men.'

A flush of annoyance, caused by the way the Texan had addressed her, had come to Olga's cheeks. For all that, she could not resist a glance at the Gambel brothers. Much to her surprise, knowing their capabilities and considering that they held weapons while the young newcomer was still empty handed, she found they were displaying what she felt sure was perturbation.

Nor was the woman wrong regarding the two men's emotions.

Over the years, the Gambel brothers had met Parisian *apache*, Sicilian members of the *Mafia*, cold blooded German and Polish assassins and Russian anarchists who delighted in taking human life. Yet none of them had created such a state of chilling apprehension as the *big* Texan. *Rapido* Clint was something beyond either brother's comprehension. Every instinct they possessed warned that he was not bluffing and could do as he claimed.

'Good men are hard to come by,' the old man conceded, duplicating his daughter's summation and swinging his gaze to the brothers. 'I would advise you to put those guns away, gentlemen.'

'What about *him*?' Cyril demanded, glaring at the Texan.

'As far as I know, he isn't armed,' the old man replied. 'At least, I can't see *him* holding a weapon.'

Exchanging sulky glances, the brothers returned their weapons to their waist bands. After they had done so, Clint allowed his hands to fall to his sides.

'And now, my young friend,' the old man almost purred,

his right fist disappearing into the left sleeve of his dressing gown. 'Tell me about yourself.'

'Like I said, sir,' the Texan obliged, 'they call me *Rapido* Clint–'

'And what kind of crimes do you commit, *Mr. Rapido* Clint?' Olga put in, still smarting from her rebuff at the Texan's hands.

'Only one kind, ma'am,' Clint replied, showing no emotion over the question. 'I kill people – for money.'

'I hope that you're better at it than some of your other countrymen!' Olga barked.

'You kill people for money, do you?' the old man put in, before the Texan could answer.

'Yes, sir,' Clint confirmed in matter-of-fact tones.

'Including your employers?' the old man challenged.

'I gunned down Mick O'Brien because he sent some of his *pistoleros* to pay me off in lead instead of gold or paper money,' the Texan explained, still without emotion. 'And I've never heard tell of John Flack turning against any man *he* hired and who treated him square.'

'So you know *me*?' the old man ejaculated. 'But you can't! Poor old Mad John Flack is dead! That swine Reeder killed him!'

'Don't worry, father,' Olga said soothingly, laying a hand on the old man's shoulder as his voice grew shriller. 'We'll take our revenge.'

'When?' John Flack screeched, the right hand emerging to join the left in banging on the table. 'Those three fools failed in Brockley Road and that useless idiot did no better at Leicester Square.'

'Toomis is ready for him if he visits Birkstone, so is Gaston,' Olga pointed out, while the Gambel brothers showed a growing alarm. 'And you've had arrangements made at Gray's flat if he goes there. One of them is sure to get him.'

'Just as that damned "Actor" and his men, or Dumbrowski and his booby trap were sure to get him!' Flack snarled, then he made a visible effort and regained control of his emotions. His face became impassive and his voice, when he addressed the Texan, was as near normal as it ever sounded. 'Well, Mr. *Rapido* Clint, you who kill men for money. What do you think of Mr. J. G. Reeder?'

'I've heard tell about him, sir,' the Texan replied. 'And, sounds like what I heard could've been right. He must be slicker'n a well greased weasel happen he's stopped you-all having him gunned down.'

'But *you* could get him?' Olga suggested.

'I don't claim *that*, ma'am, seeing's how your daddy hasn't been able to get it done,' Clint replied, with the same sardonic air that Beryl Snowhill had found so aggravating and, if Olga's expression was any criterion, she too disliked it intensely. 'But, happen the price's right, I'd sure's sin's for sale in Cow-Town[1] give it a try.'

'You will, will you?' Flack cackled, not displeased by the capable young Texan's apparent respect and admiration for him. 'Very well, Mr. *Rapido* Clint, who kills men for money. If the need should arise, I'll pay you a thousand pounds, or its equivalent in U.S. dollars, to kill J. G. Reeder.'

'Any time you're ready, sir,' drawled the young man, exuding calm confidence. 'Just say the word, put up the money, and J. G. Reeder's dead.'

At that moment, a medium sized man carrying a sheet of paper came into the room. Although his attire was that of a farm labourer, his pallid, studious face and soft white hands were not in accord with the suggestion of bucolic employment.

'Bad luck, *Mr.* Clint!' Olga hissed, stalking towards the newcomer. 'This should tell us that he's already dead.'

1. Cow-Town: colloquial name for Fort Worth, Tarrant County, Texas.

CHAPTER ELEVEN

YOU DON'T LOOK SO TOUGH

CRUISING along Wardour Street from Oxford Street, Mr. J. G. Reeder passed several good parking places. Shortly before he reached the intersection of Old Compton Street, he seemed satisfied. He brought the Frazer-Nash Fast Tourer to a halt in front of a large dark green Albion two-ton van – its curved side windows a hangover from the horse-drawn van's era – owned, if the name painted boldly on its sides was any guide, by Sugden's Bakeries, Ltd., of Stepney. It appeared to have been left unattended by its driver. Taking his umbrella as he left the car, he waited for Colonel Brian Besgrove-Woodstole to join him. Strolling by the commercial vehicle without a second glance, the detective did not seem to be paying any great attention to his surroundings as he led the way to 'Luigi's', a small Italian restaurant at the other side of the street.

After having made sure that there were no further booby traps in the Tourer, Mr. Reeder had taken his guest to the Strand Palace Hotel. In addition to having a meal in the dining room, he had spent several minutes on the telephone. However, on his return, he had appeared to have no other interest in the world except poultry. Almost an hour had passed before they returned to the vehicle, which had been left under the watchful eye of the hotel's *commissionaire*. Setting off, they had not traversed any great distance before reaching what was apparently their destination.

Much to the Colonel's surprise, Mr. Reeder made no attempt to unbutton his jacket. So he followed the detective into Luigi's, but took the precaution they had both exercised at the Pinhole Club by making sure he had easy access to the big Webley revolver tucked into his waistband.

As at their previous point of investigation, there were a number of customers in the restaurant's dining room. However, none of them were prominent members of Society. Most of the men wore the kind of loud clothing generally associated with bookmakers in the lower price range and certain other followers of the Sport of Kings. The women had on copies of the latest fashions popular among film stars, displaying ostentatious amounts of jewellery and either smoking cigarettes in long holders or chewing gum.

Gazing around, Besgrove-Woodstole found they were getting a reaction similar to that with which the members of Churgwin's gang had greeted their entrance at the Pinhole Club. Coldly hostile scowls, uneasy glances at their leader, but nothing that remotely suggested any of them were aware of the attempt to murder the gentle detective. The Colonel decided that he too could have left his jacket buttoned, but did not intend to remedy the omission until he was certain.

Apparently oblivious of the hostility being directed his way, Mr. Reeder made what seemed to be a hesitant passage across the room. However, Besgrove-Woodstole saw that not even the largest and most brutal-looking of the occupants made any attempt to impede him, nor did they appear to want to meet his mild-appearing scrutiny.

Only two of the men openly displayed interest in Mr. Reeder's progress. Seated opposite each other at what was obviously the place of honour against the wall facing the front door, they were considerably better – if no quieter – dressed than the rest. Before Mr. Reeder had taken two steps forward, there had been a brief interplay between them.

Giving what had clearly been an order, the shorter and older of the men had caused the pair of beautiful young women sharing the table to rise hurriedly and walk away. Then he had made a *sotto voce* comment, obviously, identifying the detective. The taller man's head had snapped around. His broken nosed and thick-eared face was that of a boxer, but showed an intelligence which implied he was mentally superior to the average pug. He had stared for a moment, then whipped his gaze back to his table-mate and asked, no more loudly, what Besgrove-Woodstole had guessed to be, '*That's* Reeder?' On receiving a nod of confirmation, he had grinned. Hooking his thumbs into the armholes of a waistcoat capable of making anyone with delicate sartorial taste reach for a pair of dark glasses, he tilted his chair on its back legs. Then, having thrown a grin to the three burly men at the nearest table, he returned his scrutiny to the approaching detective.

If Mr. Reeder was aware of the attention being directed at him, he gave not the slightest indication of it. He might have been strolling through a gathering of his staunchest admirers rather than among some of the roughest and most savage racecourse thugs in England. As he walked, the umbrella slipped through his hand until he once again held it near the ferrule.

'Good afternoon, Mr. – um – Birkstone,' the detective greeted, coming to a halt close to the younger man's side of the table but addressing the elder of the two. 'I trust you and your – um – family are enjoying the best of – er – health?'

'So *you're* the great J. G. Reeder, are you?' the younger man put in speaking with a Nottingham accent, before his companion could reply. He still sat with his chair inclined to the rear. 'You don't look so tough to m—!'

The speech ended abruptly!

Even as Lou Birkstone was about to snarl a warning at his guest, whose name – believe it or not – was Robin Hood,[1] Mr. Reeder hooked the handle around the spacer rods of the chair's legs and heaved with such power that he plucked it from beneath its occupant. Letting out a startled howl, the Nottingham man collapsed with a bone-jarring thud to sit with his back against the wall.

Having no illusions regarding the danger, Besgrove-Woodstole sent his right hand to the butt of the Webley. However, he doubted whether he could free it from the grip of his waistband quickly enough to be of use.

1. Neither the author, nor the world's foremost fictionist genealogist, Philip José Farmer – author of such biographical works as TARZAN ALIVE and DOC SAVAGE, HIS APOCALYPTIC LIFE – on being consulted, have been able to trace any connection between this Robin Hood and the lineage of an earlier, more famous bearer of the name. J.T.E.

Chairs scraped back as, with startled and profane comments, the other occupants of the room began to rise. Hands went into pockets, with fingers slipping through the holes of brass knuckledusters, or grasping the cut-throat razors and coshes with which they maintained their leader's domination of race courses throughout Southern England.

Not one of the men completed the withdrawal of a weapon.

Reversing his umbrella with the deft skill of a drum major twirling a baton, Mr. Reeder grasped the handle and his right arm extended with considerable rapidity.

'Sit down, gentlemen, *please*,' the detective requested politely and almost humbly. 'I don't think that Mr. – um – Hood would wish you to help him to – er – rise.'

Seeing what was being done and listening to the comment, the Colonel decided that he was hearing another example of Mr. Reeder's masterly understatement.

Winded and in some pain from his unexpected precipitation to the floor, Hood still had sufficient control of his wits to be able to think. Which was fortunate for him. The steel ferrule of the umbrella had halted almost touching his right eyeball. It could not match the point of a needle, but – as it had not been blunted by being brought into contact with the ground as an aid to walking – was nevertheless extremely sharp. He observed that it had not stopped so fortuitously because that was as far as Mr. Reeder could reach. The detective's right elbow was still flexed and, if straightened, would make the deadly spike advance to a dangerous degree. Nor, with his head pressed against the wall, could Hood attempt to draw clear of it.

Having come to London to discuss a merger of interests with Birkstone, the Nottingham criminal had not previously seen the great Mr. J. G. Reeder. Knowing the awe with which the Londoners regarded the detective, he had been amazed to find it was given to such an ancient and puny looking specimen of manhood. So, as he had believed his host's stories of Mr. Reeder's malignancy were greatly exaggerated, he had decided to exhibit his superiority. Now Hood was rapidly revising his opinion. What was more, for all the apologetic timbre of his assailant's voice, he had an unpleasant feeling that he would lose his right eye if anybody tried to render him assistance.

'There's something else for *you* to consider, Mr. – um – Birkstone,' Mr. Reeder went on, still in the same tones, keeping the umbrella rock steady. 'Outside, concealed in the – um – motor vehicle purporting to belong to Sugden's Bakeries of Stepney, are several large and powerful members of the – er – Flying Squad. At the first hint of any – um – altercation, they will come in and I'm afraid that Mr. – um – Luigi's premises may suffer more damage than the breakage of Mr. – um – Hood's chair.'

'Sit down, all of yer!' Birkstone snarled, his voice harsh and Cockney. Most of the men obeyed instantly, but he had to turn and glare at the trio standing by the nearest table. 'That goes for you Nottingham blokes, too.'

'That's – um – better,' Mr. Reeder sighed, after the three men had complied, lowering the umbrella and peering almost benevolently at the man its point had been menacing. 'Have you a car, Mr. – um – Hood?'

'Yes,' the Nottingham gang leader admitted, with none of his earlier truculence.

'Then I would suggest that you and your – um – Merry Men climb into it and return to the – er – Greenwood, I believe it is called,' the detective said. 'Nottingham is a very pleasant – um – city and will doubtless be improved by your early return.'

'I'm here for—!' Hood began.

'I *know* what you are – um – here for,' Mr. Reeder interrupted, seeming repentant for such a breach of good manners. 'And, if you are still here by – um – six o'clock this evening, it will be my unpleasant duty to inform the authorities in – um – Birmingham—'

'How the he—!' Hood yelped and Birkstone showed a similar perturbation.

'Shush!' Mr. Reeder gasped, looking shocked. 'Language, *please*, there are ladies present. When did you say you are – um – leaving?'

'Before six,' Birkstone answered, with such definite authority that Hood stared at him for a moment, then gave a surly nod and started to rise.

'A most – um – judicious decision,' Mr. Reeder praised.

'Only how you've got the right to—!' Birkstone began.

'If you have a – um – complaint as to my behaviour,' Mr. Reeder put in mildly, 'I'm sure your good friend, Mr. – um – Benner would be only too pleased to take it up.'

'Here now!' Birkstone snarled. 'All them tales about me and my boys helping get him into Parliament were lies!'

'The most vile – um – calumnies, I'm sure,' Mr. Reeder stated, with such an aura of acceptance that he might have believed he was speaking the truth. 'I have no – um – desire to criticize *anybody's* political beliefs. Nor would I wish to do so. However, I do feel that Mr. Benner is – um – injudicious in his views on some matters.'

'Like making life easier in the nicks?' Birkstone suggested.

'While gentlemen of your – um – persuasion might welcome such – er – reforms, there are others – such as your – um – victims who would not agree,' Mr. Reeder pointed out mildly, knowing that only a clear conscience with regard to the shooting would have provoked the response. 'My main – um – objection to Mr. Benner is how he and his contemporaries would have us spend nothing on maintaining the strength of the nation's – um – Armed Forces. I consider this is a most – um – ill-advised economy and hope we don't have cause to regret it in the near future.'

A few years later, learning how his only son had been killed while serving with the ill-equipped British Expeditionary Force in France as it was driven back by the superior might of a nation which had not committed the folly of restricting its military strength, Birkstone was to remember the words and curse the day that his gang had helped exert pressure, causing the Right Hon. Horatio Benner to be returned as Member of Parliament for his Constituency.

'What do you want here, anyway?' Birkstone challenged, tiring of the subject. 'I don't care what pack of lies your "noses" have told you, Robin's only down here for a visit—'

'A *brief* visit,' Mr. Reeder elaborated. 'And as to my – um – "noses" – which I believe to be the derogatory name for an informer—'

'All right!' Birkstone snapped. 'What can we do for you?'

'Nothing more than offer to pay poor Mr. – um – Luigi for the damaged chair,' Mr. Reeder answered, knowing that the restaurant was owned by the gang leader and 'Luigi' was a mythical personage. 'Are you to be reached in – um – London for the next few days, or are you too going on a – um – cruise—?'

'A *cruise*!' Birkstone yelped. 'Did that something or oth—?'

'Language!' Mr. Reeder cautioned mildly. 'You are doing Mr. Churgwin an – um – injustice. Like yourself, whatever his other – um – faults, he has never been a – um – "nose" I believe is the term.'

'I'm going up to Birmingham for a few days,' Birkstone stated, grudgingly conceding that the detective had spoken the truth regarding his hated rival.

'Not for the purpose which brought Mr. Hood and his – um – Merry Men to see you?' Mr. Reeder inquired. 'As Chief Inspector Billers of the – um – Birmingham Constabulary said when I was speaking with him on the telephonic apparatus last – um – Tuesday—'

'Tuesday?' Birkstone croaked, for it had only been on Monday that he had contacted Hood to confirm his willingness to form a confederation and take over control of criminal activities in the neighbourhood of Birmingham.

'He said, rather forcibly and with the use of what I regard as being most undesirable – um – profanity, that he would not permit any extended – um – residence on either of your parts in his manor,' Mr. Reeder continued, ignoring the interruption. 'I merely mention this to save you the – um – expense of going. Having done so, I'll bid you all good afternoon.'

Nodding his head and beaming about benevolently, although nobody returned his salutation, the detective turned. With Besgrove-Woodstole at his side, he walked over to the door. There was a silence that could almost be felt as they reached it. On leaving, Mr. Reeder asked his companion to remain in the doorway until called.

Crossing to the Tourer, the detective opened the door and slipped behind the steering wheel. Wondering why he had been left, the Colonel saw his host suddenly drop to the empty passenger seat. An instant later, a hole appeared in the wind-shield and starred the glass. There was the distant crack of a rifle from the direction of Shaftesbury Avenue. Instantly, the rear doors of the 'Bakeries' van were thrown open and plainclothes men of the Flying Squad, led by Chief Inspector Gaylor, leapt out.

'Down there!' Besgrove-Woodstole bellowed, pointing to where the shot had been fired and hurrying to the car. Although he felt sure that his companion had taken the evasive action in time, it was still a relief to see the other sitting up unharmed. 'How did you know?'

'It was a result of my perverted – um – reasoning,' Mr. Reeder replied, climbing from the car and watching the detectives running along the street. 'As there had not been a further – um – attempt to tamper with the vehicle, I envisaged an assault from a longer distance. Regrettably, I appear to have – um – under-estimated how far.[2] The officers I caused to be positioned around what I incorrectly considered would be the chosen premises in Old Compton Street have waited in – um – vain. I also fear that Mr. Gaylor and his – associates will find the bird has – um – flown when they reach the spot from which the shot was fired.'

'It *is* you they're after,' Besgrove-Woodstole declared with firm finality.

'If I had believed – um – otherwise, Colonel,' Mr. Reeder replied. 'I would have asked you to remain in the restaurant, instead of merely out of the line of fire.'

'How did you know the sniper would wait until you got into the car?'

'Again, Colonel, suffering as I do from this – um – perverted sense of reasoning, I deduced that the assailant would wish to make sure of me. He would not, unless forced, shoot at a moving – um – target; which a gentleman of your military experience is doubtless aware is always more difficult to hit than one which is stationary. So I – um – concluded the attempt would be made once I was seated in the vehicle, but

2. Although there is no confirmation in the records examined by the author, he believes the shot was fired from a second floor window over the GEORGE AND DRAGON on Shaftesbury Avenue. J.T.E.

before I set it into motion, rather than while I was – um – walking towards it.'

'You were right, too,' Besgrove-Woodstole praised. 'Who's after you, Mr. Reeder?'

'That, unfortunately, I am unable to – um – decide,' Mr. Reeder confessed. 'As I said before, only one person springs to mind as intelligent enough—'

'Old Mad John Flack is dead,' Besgrove-Woodstole pointed out.

'All the – um – evidence leads one to that conclusion,' Mr. Reeder agreed. 'But I can only repeat what I said earlier. I hope the reports of his – um – demise were, in fact, correct. If not, I fear my – um – troubles are far from over.'

At that moment, in a telephone box on Shaftesbury Avenue, a respectably attired gentleman was making a telephone call which the detective would have found most interesting.

'Toomis missed, but I think he's got clear. Reeder's still outside Luigi's. Tell Gaston to get ready, let's see what he can do.'

CHAPTER TWELVE

ADIEU MON CHER OLGA

'PARKER!' Mr. J. G. Reeder called, bringing the Frazer-Nash Fast Tourer to a stop and looking across the street at No. 104, Grosvenor Square.

As the gentle detective had anticipated, although a spent cartridge case had been found, Chief Inspector Gaylor's men had failed to catch the sniper. While awaiting their report, Mr. Reeder and Colonel Brian Besgrove-Woodstole had removed the car's ruined windshield. Then he, his guest and Gaylor had returned to Luigi's. It was deserted of all but the staff and Lou Birkstone. Greeting them with an impassioned denial of responsibility for the shooting, the gang leader had been relieved when Mr. Reeder had stated a belief in his innocence, and had then requested the loan of a telephone. While this was being granted, Birkstone had insisted that he could not even hazard a guess as to who was behind the various attempts to kill the detective. Knowing that he would learn nothing and being in possession of one piece of information from Mrs. Grible, Mr. Reeder had told Gaylor that he was not anticipating any further trouble and they had gone their separate ways.

Going from Wardour Street to Piccadilly Circus by way of Shaftesbury Avenue, Mr. Reeder turned the Tourer along Regent Street. With the windshield removed, he and his companion had not troubled to replace the top and the vehicle was open. In spite of the detective's comment to Gaylor, Besgrove-Woodstole kept a careful watch through the rear view mirror. A Daimler had been behind them and he studied its occupants, but had seen nothing suspicious. Following the Daimler was one of the large red vans which the Post Office employed for carrying bulk collections of mail bags rather than making local parcel deliveries. The Colonel had regarded it with disfavour as it had effectively concealed whatever kind of traffic was behind it.

Although the Daimler had continued along Regent Street, the mail van had turned to follow the Frazer-Nash down Conduit Street on to New Bond Street. It was still about seventy-five yards behind as they used Brook Street as a means of reaching Grosvenor Square. All the time, Besgrove-Woodstole had been muttering his annoyance. He had tried to will the big vehicle to go some other way as it could offer excellent cover for any evilly disposed person who might be on their track. Just as he was on the point of commenting to his companion on the possibility of the van being used for such a purpose, Mr. Reeder applied the brakes and stopped the car.

Neatly dressed in a black bowler and jacket, with well creased pinstriped trousers, the fact that the man addressed by Mr. Reeder had come from up the area steps, and not from the front door of the house, suggested that he was not a guest of the owners. Turning his head on hearing his name called, he walked across the street. Of medium height, slender, he had the calmly deferential – yet far from servile – air of a top quality gentleman's personal gentleman such as was frequently employed in the area.

'Good afternoon, Mr. Reeder, sir,' the man exclaimed, starting to raise his hat. Its movement halted and, for a moment, his air of imperturbability faded as he noticed the absence of the windshield. 'If I may—?'

'Get on!' Mr. Reeder snapped, and there was no trace of the usual hesitancy in his voice, rather the words burst from him like the cracking of a bull whip.

Without waiting to question the order, or to have it enlarged upon, Parker sprang on to the Tourer's running board. Pausing only for long enough to ensure that his impromptu passenger was holding on tightly, the detective released the clutch and jabbed down the accelerator.

Having watched Parker's approach to the exclusion of everything else, the Colonel was puzzled by his host's behaviour. Feeling the Frazer-Nash lunging forward, he glanced into the rear view mirror and decided that he had been correct in harbouring suspicions about the post office van; but its purpose was far more sinister than he had envisaged. It was now rushing forward and building up considerable speed. More important, it showed no sign of turning aside to go around them.

Glancing behind him, Parker also took in the sight. Then he was compelled to devote all his attention and energies to clinging on and retaining his position.

Nearer came the large red van, an onrushing juggernaut capable of smashing into the back of the car with a force which would seriously injure, even if it failed to kill, the three occupants. What was more, there was evidence that the driver intended to cause a collision. The fact that the front bumper was strengthened by a welded steel bar gave confirmation to the supposition.

Spluttering furious curses, Besgrove-Woodstole tried to claw free the Webley revolver. Already the van was so close that, looking back, he could see the man behind the steering wheel clearly. Although the garments were such as might be worn by an authorized driver, the swarthy face was Gallic in its lines and set with savage determination. If further proof of his intent was needed, the stout webbing cross-straps attached to the seat and encircling his chest were definitely *not* standard Post Office equipment on its vehicles. They would, however, allow him to crash into the Tourer without too great a danger to himself.

All that the Colonel saw – and more!

In spite of the quick get-away, the car's rear end was only scant inches from the reinforced steel bumper of the van!

The contact between them was not made!

No other vehicle available in England could touch the Frazer-Nash Fast Tourer for its powers of acceleration. Which was very fortunate for Mr. Reeder and his two passengers. Under the impulsion of the well-tuned, supercharged engine – which was even more puissant than the power unit usually installed – the car began to draw away. Once that happened, the distance between it and its pursuer rapidly widened.

Seeing that his purpose had failed, the driver swung his

van with the intention of fleeing along Upper Grosvenor Street. However, he was travelling too fast for such a hurried change of direction. Even so, his skill at handling a heavy vehicle might have brought him through if the right front tyre had not burst. Feeling the van begin to skid, he did all he could to reduce speed and control the sidewards drift. He was only partly successful. While he was going more slowly, he could not halt before the vehicle struck a lamp-post. The impact slammed him forward, but the cross-straps restrained his impetus. Jerked back against the hard seat, he was momentarily stunned.

Keeping the van under observation, which he had been doing ever since he had noticed the reinforced bumper as it followed them along Regent Street – Mr. Reeder saw it was starting to turn away. Instantly, but remembering to warn Parker, he applied himself to stopping the swiftly travelling Tourer. With the valet clinging to the frame of the windshield in an anything but secure manner, he could not make an emergency halt. Instead, he had to reduce speed considerably before bringing a cessation to the vehicle's motion.

Showing the same surprising grasp of the situation that he had displayed since the beginning, considering the nature of his employment, Parker leapt from the running board almost before it was safe for him to do so. Alighting safely, he swung around to stare at the now halted van.

Fit and active as Besgrove-Woodstole was, he could not keep pace with his host in quitting the vehicle. Moving with a rapidity that would have done credit to a much younger man, the detective had already opened the door, swung from his place and, drawing the Colt Government automatic, had started to sprint in the direction of Upper Grosvenor Street with Parker hot on his heels before the Colonel had even reached the pavement.

Obscenities in French bubbled from the driver of the Post Office van as he recovered his wits. Flying down, his hands tried to operate the quick-release mechanism of the cross-straps. Hitherto faultless, it did not work. Hearing the patter of rapidly approaching feet and seeing people emerging from the surrounding buildings, he became aware that the door at his side was blocked by the lamp-post. A glance in the left side, rear view mirror warned him that two men were running up and were already very close.

Like most European criminals who operated in England, Gaston Porthos was all too aware of Mr. Reeder's reputation. Nor had the detective's escape from what was usually a successful method of assassination made him believe that the reputation was other than well-deserved. Although the second man did not appear to be armed, he realized that in his present position Mr. Reeder had no need of assistance.

Ever since taking up his chosen speciality in the field of crime, Porthos had known that one day he might be faced with some such predicament. Being cognizant with what his fate would be at the hands of the law, which took grave exception to professional killers no matter how novel the methods employed, he had taken certain precautions. Even if the British Government did not allow his extradition to pay the penalty for his work in France, he was wanted for a murder he had committed in Brighton. Either the guillotine of his native land, or an English hangman's noose awaited him if, as seemed likely, he should be captured. He had a Browning automatic in a shoulder holster, but the straps prevented him from reaching it. Nor would it avail him anything in his restricted position when opposed by a man of Mr. Reeder's ability. Accepting the inevitable, he took what looked like a chocolate from his uniform top pocket and, removing the tissue paper wrapping, popped it into his mouth.

'*Adieu, mon cher* Olga!' Porthos sighed and bit through the chocolate covering.

'Oh *bother*!' Mr. Reeder ejaculated, in what for him amounted to a burst of profanity, for he was near enough to see the Frenchman's action.

Even as the detective lunged forward, he saw Porthos stiffen convulsively and then go limp. For all his suspicions, he held the Colt ready to be used. As he was reaching out for the door's handle, he heard Besgrove-Woodstole calling from the other side of the vehicle.

'Be careful. He'll have to come out your way. This door's jammed.'

'I'm afraid he won't come, or – um – go, anywhere under

his own volition,' Mr. Reeder replied, knowing sufficient of the symptoms of cyanide poisoning to identify the results of an exceptionally potent dose. Holstering the Colt and buttoning his jacket, he went on, 'In fact, Colonel, I am reasonably sanguine that he will not leave before he is removed for a post mortem examination by the – um – Home Office pathologist.'

Already a small crowd was gathering. Some of them were known to Besgrove-Woodstole and the majority were able to identify Mr. Reeder from the photographs of him that had on occasion appeared in newspapers. So they were willing to obey when requested to keep at a distance, even before a constable, blowing his whistle to summon assistance, ran up.

'A nasty accident, Mr. Reeder,' the policeman stated.

'Nasty – um – yes,' the detective answered. 'But not an – um – accident as you mean the term. I would suggest you touch nothing until those detestable fellows from Scotland Yard arrive.'

'Whatever you say, sir,' the constable assented and peered at the van. 'Is that bloke dead?'

'Remarkably – um – so,' Mr. Reeder confirmed. 'Would you be so good as to obtain the use of a telephone and report what has happened?'

CHAPTER THIRTEEN

NEITHER WAS THE BLACK DEATH

FIFTEEN minutes later, having been summoned by radio while on his way back to Scotland Yard, Chief Inspector Frank Gaylor arrived at the corner of Upper Grosvenor Street and greeted Mr. J. G. Reeder sardonically.

'If *this* keeps up, we'll have to put on a special squad to follow you around.'

'Quite,' the detective conceded mildly. 'Would you inform the Brighton Police that they need waste no further – um – effort in searching for Gaston Porthos?'

'I wondered if that's who it might be,' Gaylor admitted. 'But I'd no idea he was back in this country.'

'Neither had I,' Mr. Reeder confessed. 'Otherwise, I might have anticipated such an – um – attempt. In fact, when I saw the cross-straps without being able to make out his face, I imagined it to be a mere crime of – um – imitation.'

'I can excuse my "noses" for not having heard he was coming over,' Gaylor stated, frowning. 'But that your lot hadn't heard beats me. And I got the feeling that Lou Birkstone knew something.'

'So did I and Mr. – um – Churgwin, too,' Mr. Reeder replied. 'But neither was inclined to divulge their knowledge even to avoid the possibility of arousing my – um – animosity by remaining silent. Not, I would hasten to add, that my – um – wrath is such a terrible thing—'

'Neither was the Black Death,' Gaylor sniffed, suffering from no delusions regarding the true nature of the gentle detective. 'What do you make of it?'

'There are times when I wish I wasn't cursed with my

horribly perverse – um – mind,' Mr. Reeder sighed. 'But this evil form of reasoning with which I hope you are nev—'

'My wife's waiting dinner for me,' Gaylor protested, rolling his eyes heavenwards.

'To my way of – um – thinking,' Mr. Reeder continued. 'Such a plethora of experts in the matter of – um – assassination could only have been assembled secretly by one man.'

'Go on!' Gaylor snorted, but his voice lacked conviction. 'Old Mad John Flack's dead.'

'So we have all – um – assumed,' Mr. Reeder admitted. 'But if he is, somebody at least as intelligent is not only adopting his – um – methods, but also appears to be able to exert an equal moral ascendancy over even major figures of the – um – underworld.'

'Whoo!' Gaylor breathed. 'If that old *gentleman* wasn't killed when the cliff caved in, we're in for a lively time.'

'I consider that, in my – um – simple way, I'm already having one,' Mr. Reeder remarked, but in spite of his abhorrence for profanity (the man from Scotland Yard had not said '*gentleman*') he agreed with the summation. 'The only – um – consolation we might draw is that there is no major gold bullion shipment in the near future upon which he could engage his attention.'

'And, with the lessons we learned from the "Terror Keep" job,' Gaylor growled, 'he won't find it so easy to take another.'

'That too has struck me,' Mr. Reeder said pensively. 'However, while he has concentrated the majority of his – um – organizing ability upon bullion robberies in the past, he has also dabbled in various other forms of criminal activity. Ah well, there is nothing to be learned here. I'm sure you wish to go home and trust you will give your lady wife my – um – apologies for delaying you.'

'Why don't you and the Colonel come and do it yourself?' Gaylor suggested.

'We have other – um – calls to make, I fear,' Mr. Reeder replied and looked at his guest who had stood listening to the conversation. 'Unless you have other – um – plans, Colonel?'

'I'll stick with you,' Colonel Brian Besgrove-Woodstole decided.

'Well, I'll be going then,' Gaylor stated. 'And, without offence, I hope I don't see you again today.'

'Equally without – um – offence, I concur,' Mr. Reeder answered.

'Excuse me, sir,' Parker put in, having remained unobtrusively in the background. 'Could I trouble you for a ride to the Captain's flat?'

'Certainly,' Mr. Reeder agreed, deducing that there was more to the valet's request than a mere desire to avoid having to make his own way to Park Place Villas, Paddington, where his employer was now in residence. 'Unless you have any – um – objections, Colonel?'

'None at all,' Besgrove-Woodstole declared.

'I hope you haven't been trying to contact me, sir,' Parker said, as he sat between the detective and the Colonel in the Frazer-Nash Fast Tourer. 'But, as Captain and Mrs. Gray aren't in residence, I took the afternoon off to visit a young lady of my acquaintance.'

'Lady Mary Herban's cook?' Mr. Reeder asked with a smile.

'Maid, sir,' Parker corrected. 'The reason I called Mrs. Grible was that, while it may not come within our province, there's a possibility that a racing coup is being planned.'

'By Mr. Frithington-Evans?'

'So it would seem, sir. Apparently he and Mr. Siniter had a quarrel in the Cheese Club last night. It ended with each engaging to wager a large sum, which will be donated to a designated charity by whomever wins, that the horse he is entering in the Gore-Hampton Selling Plate at Kempton will pass over the line first.'

'If that's all there is to it, I doubt whether it will come into the – um – purview of the Public Prosecutor's Office,' Mr. Reeder pointed out, although he knew Saul Siniter[1] to be a racehorse owner no more honest than Frithington-Evans and was aware that the Cheese Club in Camden Town was

1. Some details of Saul Siniter's career are given in Chapter Two, 'Mr. Evans Does a Bit of Gas Work', GOOD EVANS by Edgar Wallace. J.T.E.

devoted almost exclusively to bookmaking and kindred interests.[2] 'Do you know anything about the – um – race, Colonel?'

'I can't say I do,' Besgrove-Woodstole replied. 'There's only been one of our family with any money. He was a bookmaker and he never gave me anything except the advice not to bet on horses.'

'I'm afraid my own education in the Sport of – um – Kings is equally lacking,' Mr. Reeder confessed sadly. 'Perhaps you can enlighten us, Parker?'

'The race is only a minor one on the card at Kempton that day, sir,' the valet obliged, having acquired an interest in such matters because his employer had been actively engaged in horse racing during the 'Big Printer' case.[3] 'It never has a large field and normally there would be little interest or betting on it.'

'The ideal kind of – um – event if one, or two, owners were wishing to indulge in what I believe is called – er – skullduggery,' the detective guessed.

'That's what I thought, sir,' Parker replied.

'Then it might pay us to – um – look into the matter with greater interest,' Mr. Reeder decided.

'I hoped you would consider it so, sir,' Parker exclaimed. 'In fact, I took the liberty of asking Millie – Lady Herban's maid – to keep me informed on the pretence that I too wished to participate in the coup. She agreed.'

'Good man,' Mr. Reeder praised, for the valet was a most valuble source of information regarding the activities of a strata of Society beyond the access of the normal type of police 'nose'.

'You appear to have had an accident, sir,' Parker remarked, indicating the shattered windshield.

'It was no – um – accident,' Mr. Reeder corrected. 'Unless, of course, one assumes it was accidentally broken by a dum-dum bullet fired from a high powered rifle.'

Watching, while the detective gave an explanation of all that had happened since they had been strolling in the

2. Information regarding the Cheese Club can be found in Part VII, 'The Dreamer' of: EDUCATED EVANS by Edgar Wallace. J.T.E.

3. Told in: ROOM 13 by Edgar Wallace. J.T.E.

garden of Daffodil House, Besgrove-Woodstole noticed what was for Parker a *very* strong reaction. The valet's eyebrows moved a fraction of an inch and, sitting with his arms decorously folded, he drummed the fingers of his right hand no less than *three* times on his left bicep.

'We'll come up to the flat so I can call the Captain and – um – inform him,' Mr. Reeder finished, also having observed how the valet responded to the news and feeling even more certain that neither he nor his employer had envisaged the possibility of attempted assassinations.

'Very well, sir,' Parker agreed, without hesitation.

Silence fell after the valet's acceptance. The Tourer had turned from Edgware Road on to Maida Avenue. None of the trio in it anticipated further trouble. They had taken especial care to ensure that they were not followed, but all felt that their vigilance was worth while. All of the apartments in Park Place Villas had balconies from which – if Mr. Reeder's connection with Captain John Gray had become known – an evilly disposed person might have arranged to launch an attack. However, nothing happened and the detective brought his vehicle to a halt outside Number Thirty's front door.

Entering the building, Mr. Reeder and his companions went to the lift to ride up to the second floor. With Parker in the lead, they walked to the apartment taken by Captain Gray after his marriage. On arriving, although he took out a key, the valet did not offer to use it. Instead, he glanced at the top of the door and stiffened slightly.

'We appear to either have had, or have, visitors, sir,' Parker anounced, with no more emotion than if he had been commenting upon the weather. 'I applied the thread on leaving, as always, but it is broken.'

Not until Besgrove-Woodstole had stared hard for a few seconds was he able to locate a piece of black thread dangling from the upper edge of the door. He realized it was a similar precaution to that which his host had taken with the Frazer-Nash's bonnet. Then he noticed that Mr. Reeder was once again taking out the Colt Government Model automatic pistol.

'It might be – um – advisable to stand to one side of the

door, Colonel,' the detective said, almost casually, extending the umbrella in the valet's direction. 'Take this and give me the key, Parker.'

'Very well, sir,' the valet replied and made the exchange.

Waiting until his companions were standing against the wall at the hinged side of the door, Mr. Reeder reached around and placed the key in the keyhole. Turning it, he transferred his left hand to the knob and twisted. Then he began to push open the door. As it moved, there was a crack such as a mousetrap would make on being sprung. The sound was followed by two noises, a 'boing' and a 'pop' which all of them recognized from past experience with such things.

'Get down!' Mr. Reeder snapped, jerking the door closed rapidly and flinging himself to the floor.

Displaying an equal alacrity, Besgrove-Woodstole and Parker duplicated the gentle detective's actions. Even as they landed, there was an explosion in the apartment and the door was blown outwards.

'I never anticipated *that*!' Mr. Reeder ejaculated bitterly, rising and looking at the ceiling. 'Is anybody upstairs?'

'Not in the flat immediately above, sir,' Parker answered, sounding relieved. 'I suppose they used a mousetrap, with something to trigger it and a string fastened from its back-breaker bar to the pin of a Mills bomb?'

'That would be my – um – assumption, too,' Mr. Reeder admitted, reverting to his hesitant form of speech.

'How did they get in to fix it?' Besgrove-Woodstole demanded, having heard of booby traps being produced by such a comparatively simple method.

'At the moment, Colonel, I'm more worried by the – um – fact that they came here,' Mr. Reeder declared. 'It seems that our – um – secret must have been found out, Parker.'

'Yes, sir,' the valet answered, sounding worried, for he knew what could be at stake if – as seemed likely – the detective's fears were justified. 'I'm afraid it does.'

CHAPTER FOURTEEN

ALL OF WHICH MEANS YOU'VE FAILED

'You seem to find that paper interesting, Mr. *Rapido* Clint,' Mad John Flack remarked, staring from his place behind the study table to where the small Texan was standing by the window holding a week old copy of the *Sporting Chronicle*. 'I saw you looking at it before dinner. Are you *so* interested in British horse racing?'

Listening to the words, Clint decided they were further proof of something he had discovered earlier. The old man might on occasions behave in a manner which suggested how he had gained the nickname 'Mad', but he was also remarkably shrewd and discerning. Although he had not insisted that the Texan be searched, he had asked a number of pertinent questions which indicated that he had no intention of taking the other at face value.

After showing Flack the manner in which he was armed, Clint had explained how he had located Charles Wagon's training establishment. However he had refused to divulge the sources of his information and his refusal had been handled so tactfully that he had won the old man's approval. Hearing that a few dishonest jockeys and a number of professional killers were being sent to England, he had decided there was big money involved and had followed in search of employment. He had travelled over on a ship which was commissioned to collect a cargo of alcoholic beverages which were prohibited in the United States under the terms of the 'Volstead Act'.[1] Another of the passengers, although

1. 'Volstead Act': the Eighteenth (Prohibition) Amendment to the Constitution of the United States, defining intoxicating liquors as those containing more than one half of one percent alcohol and forbidding

Clint had ensured that they never met on the voyage, had been Link Gruber.

On arriving in the United Kingdom, Clint had trailed the jockey until losing him at Swindon. Having visted two other areas in Wiltshire where racehorses were trained, the Texan had reached Little Venner and learned the most likely place for Gruber to be hiding. His first attempt to verify this had been thwarted when he was seen by the trainer. Doubting whether he would be allowed to explain and despite being armed he had withdrawn and returned undetected feeling sure that he had reached his destination.

At the end of the explanation, Flack had demonstrated not only his shrewdness but his discernment. That he should have heard of Hogan Turtle, the man Clint had claimed could verify his *bona fides*, was not surprising. The Turtle family had long been very prominent in the criminal activities of the Lone Star State.[2] However, as Flack had shrewdly pointed out, in spite of employing the jargon of cowhands and gangsters, the newcomer's accent was that of a well educated Southron. Admitting that he was the black sheep of a wealthy Texas family, Clint had refused to supply further details. Once again, Flack had accepted his reticence.

Much to the unspoken disapproval of Wagon and the Gambel brothers, Flack had invited the Texan to stay in the house. Having managed to hire a car, the Right Hon. Horatio Benner, M.P. had arrived. Learning that Clint's luggage was at the room he had taken at the Starter's Hack, the old man had instructed that he accompanied Olga 'Garvin' Flack and Benner into Little Venner so he could collect it. The M.P. in particular had been displeased by the arrangement, but he had kept his thoughts to himself.

Olga had not intended visiting the village, much less in the company of the Texan or Benner, but she had been prevailed upon to do so by her father. As he had pointed out,

---

manufacture, transportation, or sale of such liquors for beverage purposes. Introduced by Representative Andrew J. Volstead of Minnesota, the Act was ratified in 1919 and repealed in 1933. J.T.E.

2. Details of the Turtle family's prominence among the outlaw element of Texas is given in: OLE DEVIL AND THE CAPLOCKS and SET TEXAS BACK ON HER FEET, also, by implication, in THE QUEST FOR BOWIE'S BLADE by J. T. Edson. J.T.E.

the girl who had given her a ride from Swindon might have recognized the M.P. In which case, his presence in the district was certain to arouse interest and it was undesirable he should give the impression that he was there secretly. So Olga had telephoned Beryl Snowhill. Apologizing for her unsociable behaviour in the car, she had asked the girl to let her make amends by meeting for a drink at the Royal Colours Hotel. Although Beryl had not been too eager, she had yielded to Olga's insistence and it was arranged they would get together at nine o'clock.

Between Clint's arrival and dinner time, the pallid faced 'country dweller' had delivered two more messages. Remembering a certain fitment he had noticed on the roof of the house, the Texan could guess how they had arrived. On each occasion, Flack had flown into a rage over learning there had been yet another failure to kill J. G. Reeder and Olga had succeeded in calming him down. Clint had been impressed by noticing how the Gambel brothers, Benner and Wagon had shown alarm during Flack's tantrums. Their behaviour had struck him as convincing proof, although he had not needed any, that their leader was an exceptionally malignant and dangerous person.

Waiting for Wagon's servants to announce that dinner was ready, Clint had picked up the copy of the *Sporting Chronicle.* It was opened at a page devoted to horse racing. The first thing to catch his eye was what he took to be a photograph of Bucky Borofin riding a horse which was being led by a large, triumphant looking woman. Reading the heading over the picture, he had found that he was in error regarding the identity of the jockey.

'LEM DOOBY BRINGS HOME FAVOURITE AT NEWMARKET'

The resemblance to Borofin was remarkable. What was more, the jockey behind Dooby might have been Ivan Drobsky. However, according to the small print beneath the picture, his name was Jim Gold.

An intelligent young man, Clint had realized that the resemblances were more than a mere chance coincidence. Noticing that Flack was watching him, he had seen a way to satisfy his curiosity and also strengthen his position. He had already treated the old master criminal with a respect that hinted at hero-worship and it had clearly been found most acceptable. However, as yet he had not been told what the other was organizing. He had wondered if a comment about the resemblances might produce an enlightening disclosure.

The group had been called for dinner before Clint could put his idea into operation. While the food had been good and he had learned something about the character of Mr. J. G. Reeder, the conversation had done nothing to inform him of what was being organized. He was too wise to ask until after he had prepared the ground and gained the old man's confidence.

After the meal, Olga, Benner and Maurice Gambel had gone upstairs and Wagon left to make an inspection of the stables. Telling Clint to accompany them, Flack had taken Cyril Gambel into the study. However, he and his second-in-command had started a softly spoken conversation at the table. Their attitudes had warned the Texan that he was not expected to join them. So he had resumed his examination of the Sporting Chronicle. Olga had just returned, dressed for the visit to Little Venner and carrying a handbag which was slightly larger than the current fashion, when her father had addressed Clint.

'I'd say that depends on who-all's doing the riding, sir,' the Texan replied, replacing the paper on the small table. 'Now if it's a couple—'

At that moment, there was an interruption. In spite of the curtains being drawn, it was possible to see the lights and hear a powerful car coming along the drive towards the front of the house.

'Who's this?' Gambel asked.

'I would advise you to go and see,' Flack answered.

'And *I'd* advise you to fasten your coat, or leave the Luger behind,' Olga went on. 'It may be one of the neighbours, or somebody who isn't connected with us.'

Complying with an angry gesture, Gambel stalked across the room and disappeared from sight. The other occupants listened to him crossing the hall and opening the front door. By then, the car had stopped. They heard his startled exclamation, followed by the sound of voices pitched too low for what was said to be audible, after which several pairs of feet approached the study.

On his return, Gambel proved to be accompanied by three men. One was tall, well built, blond haired, good looking and attired in the style of an English country gentleman. In his right hand, dangling with its muzzle directed at the floor, was a Colt 1917 .45 revolver. Flanking him, the others were shorter and more thickset. Obviously of Italian extraction, they had on long ulsters and each had their right hand thrust into the pocket. The blond's gaze swept the room, halting for a moment on *Rapido* Clint before dismissing him as one of the imported jockeys and of neither danger nor any importance.

'Go and stand over there with the punk, Gambel,' Joseph 'Joe the Actor' Steffens ordered. 'And keep your hands where I can see them all the time.'

'Well, gentlemen,' Flack greeted without cordiality, after his second-in-command had obeyed and the trio were standing in a loose arrowhead formation at the other side of the table. His restless hands moved until the right was touching the wide left sleeve of his dressing gown. 'Have you come to tell me why you *didn't* kill J. G. Reeder?'

'We missed him all right, but it wasn't *our* fault,' Steffens replied, showing annoyance rather than remorse over having failed to justify his employer's confidence. '*Your* man said he'd be alone and inside the house. Instead, he was walking in the garden with another feller. Then that damned driver *you* got for us shows up wearing what anybody with half an eye could see was a false beard, which's what gave the whole snap away. And, to cap it all, he lammed like a bat out of hell instead of stopping—'

'All of which means you've failed!' Flack interrupted, voice rising slightly.

'We may have done,' Steffens answered. 'But it wasn't *our* fault.'

'When do you intend to try again?' Olga inquired, holding her bag in both hands.

'*Again!*' Steffens snorted. 'Listen, girlie, you only get one stab at the kewpie doll in this game, particularly *that* kewpie doll. Do you think a feller as smart as Reeder would fall for it twice?'

'Then try another way!' Flack commanded.

'We only work *one* way,' Steffens stated. 'Which being so, we'll take our money and go work for somebody else.'

'*Money?*' Flack repeated. 'What *money*?'

'The balance of our pay,' Steffens elaborated and his tones grew harder as Gambel made as if to move forward. 'Stay put, limey. This's between your boss and us.'

'I promised to complete the payment *after* that swine Reeder was dead,' Flack pointed out. 'And, from what I've been told, he's still alive. Very much alive, in fact.'

'That's still none of our fault,' Steffens insisted, with an air of grim finality. 'So you can start shelling out.'

'Shelling out!' the old man spat furiously, his voice raising and his beard seeming to quiver and bristle in rage. '*Shelling out*, you say. And for what, might I ask? That swine Reeder is still alive. Why should I pay you?'

'Because I'm telling you to,' Steffens answered, starting to raise the Colt. 'So get doing it, you crazy old son-of-a—'

Giving his challenger no time to complete the demand, Flack produced a short, spear-pointed[3] knife from the sheath strapped to his left forearm. Before the Colt could be elevated into alignment, his right hand whipped up and down in a lightning swift motion.

There was a brief flicker of light on shining steel. Then the old man's weapon, speeding through the air with unerring accuracy, buried itself to the guard of the concave ivory hilt in the centre of Steffens' throat. An expression of horror mingled with agony came to his face. Releasing his hold on the Colt's butt so it fell unfired to the floor, he reeled backwards with both hands rising towards his neck.

Startled exclamations burst from the two Italians as their leader made a pirouette between them. When he collapsed, blood spurted from the severed jugular vein in the wake of the knife he had inadvertently wrenched out of his flesh. For all their surprise, the pair reacted with considerable rapidity.

3. Spear point: one where the double edges of the blade come together in symmetrical convex arcs. J.T.E.

Each began to jerk out the revolver he was grasping in his ulster's pocket.

Taken unprepared, although he should not have been as he was aware of the knife in his superior's sleeve and how quickly it could be brought into action, Gambel grabbed for and started to unbutton his jacket. It was obvious that he would not be able to arm himself quickly enough to intervene.

Showing an amazing agility for one so aged, Flack tipped over his chair and went from it in a backwards roll that many a far younger man would have been hard put to duplicate. Even as he landed, he was looking and holding his right hand towards his daughter.

Displaying no horror at what she had seen, Olga jerked open the bag. Her right hand disappeared into it, closing around the pearl grips of a wicked looking, old fashioned, black powder firing, but none the less deadly little Remington Double Derringer. Fetching out the .41 calibre superposed twin barrelled pistol, she tossed it – with a similar precision to that with which the knife had been aimed – in the direction of her father's extended palm.

For all the speed with which Olga was moving, her efforts – like those of Gambel – would have been too slow.

Old Mad John Flack might have died at that moment, but for the expertise of the man called *Rapido* Clint.

Setting his weight firmly on the balls of his feet, which were spread apart to the width of his shoulders, the Texan bent his legs slightly and inclined his torso forward. His left hand rose and pulled open the side of his jacket to leave unimpeded access for its mate. Flashing across at least as quickly as Flack had moved, the right hand closed around the ivory stocked butt of a big black Colt Government Model pistol held in the retention springs of an open fronted shoulder holster. Pivoting downwards, he liberated the weapon. Moving with the kind of devastating speed which had earned him his nickname, he turned it outwards until his right elbow was about eight inches ahead of his right hip.

Not until the muzzle was pointing away from him did Clint's forefinger enter the triggerguard, or his thumb thrust down the manual safety catch. For all that – although a bare

.6 of a second had elapsed since his hands' first motions – when the big automatic thundered, its .45 calibre bullet passed into the centre of Generoso Rizzito's forehead and shattered its way hideously out at the back of the skull.

Impelled by the pistol's recoil, the cocking slide jerked rearwards to eject the spent cartridge case and cock the hammer. Going forward, it fed the top round from the magazine into the barrel's chamber.

Swinging the Colt, knowing he had nothing further to fear from the first Italian, Clint saw Giovanni Aiello's revolver was clear of his pocket. However, the professional killer was suffering from indecision. He was not given an opportunity to make up his mind which enemy, the Texan or Flack – who was sitting up holding the Remington – presented the greater danger.

Aimed as its predecessor had been, by instinctive alignment and without the use of the sights, Clint's second bullet hit Aiello high in the left shoulder. Although he reeled, he did not release the revolver. Having had experience with the kind of man he was up against, the Texan did not hesitate. Changing the angle of the Colt's barrel slightly, he squeezed the trigger. Again there was the thunderous detonation from the heavy calibre weapon. Then a fourth shot left it. Struck twice in the left breast, either of which would have produced a fatal injury, Aiello was pitched backwards. The bullet Flack sent into him was unnecessary and he joined his dead companions on the floor.

'I'm right sorry I had to do that in front of you, ma'am,' Clint remarked in a matter-of-fact tone, glancing at the singularly unconcerned Olga and returning his gaze to her father. 'But it's like I told Bucky Borofin. It looks like your daddy needs some real *capable* help around him.'

CHAPTER FIFTEEN

YOU DON'T KNOW WHICH ARE THE SUCKER BETS

'HELLO there, Mr. Smith,' greeted the proprietor of the Starter's Hack public house, showing relief at the sight of his small guest entering the lounge. 'I thought you'd got lost until I heard you upstairs.'

'Shucks, no,' answered *Rapido* Clint, noticing that his arrival seemed to be disturbing Slick Markey, the only other occupant of the room. 'I've found me some work, so I just drifted in to collect my gear.'

'You took the room for a week,' Haggerty protested.

'Why sure,' Clint drawled. 'And, seeing's how I won't be able to stay on, you-all keep what I paid you. It's all my misfortune and none of your own, which's opposite to what the song says.'[1]

'That's good of you, sir,' Haggerty stated, although he had never heard the song to which the Texan had referred. 'Will you take something with me?'

'I was hoping you and Mr. Markey'd take something with me,' Clint suggested. 'I'll have me a whisky. Can't get used to drinking warm beer, unless there isn't any other kind to be had.'

'I'll have the same,' Markey grunted, deciding that the newcomer had not been sent after him and always willing to accept a free drink.

'And me, if that's all right with you, sir,' the publican

1. Chorus of an old trail driving song:
'Whoopee ti yi ho, get along little dogies,
It's all your misfortune and none of my own,
Whoopee ti yi ho, get along little dogies,
You know that Wyoming will be your new home.'

went on, accepting the pound note which the Texan had taken from one pocket of his Levi's pants. 'Then I'll have to go and see what the lads in the taproom want.'

Watching Haggerty depart after having drunk his health, Clint thought that he was not sorry for an excuse to leave.

'How'd you-all make out in the crap game?' the Texan asked, swinging his gaze to the sullen-faced jockey.

'Bad!' Markey almost spat the word out.

'It's a whole heap harder than it looks,' Clint remarked, tossing off his drink. 'Especially when you don't know which are the sucker bets.'

'Sucker bets?' Markey repeated, in tones redolent of suspicion. 'What're they?'

'Things like offering even money that the shooter won't throw a six or eight in his next two rolls,' the Texan explained. 'There're a whole slew of them. They sound all right, but they sure's hell aren't.'

'Tell me the rest of 'em!' Markey requested.

'Shucks, I don't know them all,' Clint answered, but gave several examples.

'I took some of 'em and won a couple,' the jockey stated at the end of the recital.

'Only you lost a whole heap more than you won,' the Texan guessed. 'Hell, they're not certain winners for the feller's makes them. But they're a whole lot better than even money bets, you'll never win one for one.'

'You're right about me losing a lot more than I won,' Markey admitted.

'There's other ways which don't give you-all even that much of a chance, though,' Clint warned, reaching into his leather jacket's right side pocket and extracting a pair of dice.

'How do you mean?' Markey demanded, drawing an inference from the Texan's manner.

'Take a look,' Clint countered, dropping the dice on the bar counter.

'There doesn't look like there's anything wrong with them,' the jockey growled, picking up the cubes and studying them without comprehension.

'You-all try shooting an even number with them,' Clint

challenged. 'Then you'll right soon find out what's wrong with them.'

'Are they loaded?' Markey hissed angrily, after making about a dozen throws all of which produced odd numbers, having heard that it was possible to affix weights in dice and ensure they fell in a favourable manner.

'They're a heap more certain than any old "loads" would make them,' Clint replied. 'Back to home, we call them "dispatchers", because they'll surely dispatch you-all to the cleaners faster'n a jack-rabbit with its butt on fire getting chased by a coyote.'

'I still don't see—!' the jockey protested, scowling at the two dice on the counter.

'That's 'cause you can only see *three* sides of each dice.'

'Huh?'

'You-all put a mirror at the back of them galloping dominoes, or pick one up and turn it over. The count of the spots on the opposite sides *should* come to seven.'

'Hey!' Markey yelped, after he had carried out the experiment. 'There's only one spot on each side!'

'You'll find it's the same with the three and five sides,' the Texan drawled. 'And the other dice's got nothing but twos, fours and sixes.'

Although Markey was not conversant with the mathematics involved in working out the correct odds for the various bets in the game of 'craps', he was able to appreciate the meaning of the two dice being made in such an eccentric fashion. With such a combination of numbers on them, there was no way of adding their combined total to produce an even number.

'They don't make it for certain sure, mind,' Clint continued, as the jockey began to splutter indignantly. 'But they give the "shooter" one hell of a good chance of throwing a "natural" on his come out.'

'I can see *that*!' Markey snarled, thinking back to how Kinch had thrown no less than seven consecutive 'passes' at a considerable loss to himself and how the Texan had picked up the dice they were using. 'Are *these* the pair we were playing with?'

'I surely wouldn't take it kind was you-all to think I'd be

toting my own "dispatchers",' Clint warned, in the quietly menacing way which he could produce so effectively. 'And, was I you-all, I'd stay well clear of crap games until you know a whole heap more about how it's played – and how you can get flim-flammed.'

'Do you know?' Markey asked.

'Some,' Clint conceded. 'About fair games – and cheating.'

'Here,' Markey said, as the other set down his empty glass and made as if to turn away. 'Have a drink on me and tell me some more about it.'

Accepting the offer, Clint started to give Markey an insight into some of the many ways in which one could be cheated in a game of 'craps'. By the time he had finished, the jockey was red with anger and convinced that the heavy losses he had suffered in the past few days were not caused by bad luck.

Learning how Clint had travelled to Little Venner that evening, Markey declined a suggestion that he used the same means to go back. He also asked the Texan not to mention to Olga Flack that he was visiting the Starter's Hack. Acceding to the request, Clint collected his belongings from the room he had rented and, saying good night to the publican, took his departure. Markey remained at the bar, scowling angrily and muttering to himself. Then, reaching a decision, he called and asked Haggerty to join him.

CHAPTER SIXTEEN

THE LADY SAID LET GO!

BERYL SNOWHILL could not regard the meeting she had reluctantly agreed to at the Royal Colours Hotel as being a resounding, or even a moderate, success. In spite of the fact that the woman she knew as Olga Garvin was trying to behave in a more sociable manner than she had during the drive from Swindon, she could not hide the fact that she was preoccupied and had not really wished to visit Little Venner.

Although Olga had good cause for her perturbation, it did not stem out of revulsion over seeing three men killed. Throughout much of her life, she had been on the fringes of her father's violent and often bloody career. In fact, she had been a willing and active participant in it. So she had mingled with some of the world's most desperate and dangerous criminals. It had been because they were on terms of intimacy that Gaston Porthos had taken the chance of returning to England when her father had requested his services. She had heard of his suicide shortly after the shootings at Charles Wagon's house, but felt neither regret nor remorse over the news.

One of the reasons for Olga's emotional state was *Rapido* Clint. She had never met anybody who had disturbed her as much as he had during their short acquaintance, nor one who could display such terrifying speed when the need arose. Even as she had been throwing the Remington Double Derringer to her father and wondering if he would be in time, she had seen the Texan's right hand begin to move. Before the weapon had reached Flack, Clint had drawn the big Colt automatic pistol and killed the first of his two victims. There had been something almost inhumanly mechanical in the merciless precision with which he had terminated the second Italian's life.

Even more than Clint's deadly skill with firearms, Olga found herself put out by his attitude towards her. Unlike almost every other man with whom she had been brought into contact, he seemed completely impervious to her charms. His behaviour had been polite, but far from subservient or respectful. To make matters worse, the way in which he had won over her father's approval was saving him from the consequences that would otherwise have been the penalty following an expression of her disapproval.

Fortunately, the room in which the shooting had taken place was sound proof. So none of Wagon's small domestic staff, nor the occupants of the training stable, had been aware of the incident. The Right Hon. Horatio Benner, M.P., had only found out when he and the trainer were fetched by Cyril Gambel. Both had been frightened and alarmed by the unanticipated turn of events. In fact, the M.P. had stated his intention of leaving immediately. He had been anything but pleased when Flack had informed him, in no uncertain manner, that he must stay as had been arranged. Knowing better than to argue, he had been in such a pitiable state of nerves that he had sought solace in a type of cigarette – supplied by Olga – in which the tobacco had been substituted with flakes from the dried leaves of the *cannabis sativa* plant.

One of the effects produced by inhaling the *marihuana's* smoke was to give Benner a kind of bravado which he never knew at any other time, another being a belief that he was irresistible to women. His demeanour, on arriving at Little Venner, was indicative that the narcotic had produced this frame of mind.

Wearing a stylish dress, Beryl looked even more attractive than she had while delivering the parcel that afternoon. On being introduced, Benner's greeting had been fulsome and his clammy hand shake was more of a suggestive squeeze until she had withdrawn her hand from his grasp. She refused his offer of a cigarette, which he usually found induced a receptive frame of mind, pointing out that she did not smoke. Although she did not suspect the real reason, thinking it to be no more than jealousy over the attentions being paid to her, she noticed that Olga showed irritation when he tried to force her to take one on the grounds that it was time she started.

Much to Beryl's relief, none of her friends were at the Flying Colours Hotel that night. In fact, she and her companions had the lounge to themselves. For all that, she had been pleased when Olga – demanding rather than suggesting – elected to make use of a small alcove table instead of staying somewhere in more open view. Knowing Benner when he was under the influence of *marihuana* and wanting to avoid any chance of an unpleasant scene, Olga sat alongside the girl. The precaution did not entirely work. On the first occasion Benner's foot touched Beryl's, she thought it was an accident. After it had happened the fourth time, each having been accompanied by a lascivious leer or a sly innuendo, she had responded with a sharp kick to his shin. Anger had diffused his sullen face, but a coldly prohibitive glare from Olga – who had known what was happening – caused him to control his temper and lapse into scowling silence which did little to make the evening more enjoyable.

After only a short while, Beryl began to wonder why Olga had insisted upon the meeting. It had soon become clear that they had no common interests. Nor, with the exception of Wagon, had they any mutual acquaintances. Olga claimed that she and Benner were partners in the ownership of a horse and had come to spend a few days watching it being trained for an unspecified race. However, although Beryl had suspected Olga's motives, she did not appear to have any interest in obtaining information regarding the animals in training at General Snowhill's stable. All she had done was to give a broad hint by saying that she and the M.P. would not have time to become involved in the social life of the district.

All in all, Beryl was not sorry when ten o'clock came. Excusing herself on the grounds of having to rise early the following morning so as to watch some of the horses at work, she announced that she would have to be going home. In spite of Olga expressing reluctance to break up the party, the girl had sensed that she too was relieved for a chance to bring it to an end.

However, as the party were leaving the alcove, a waiter came over and told Olga that there was a telephone call for her.

'I'll see Beryl to her car while you take it,' Benner offered.

'There's no need!' the girl stated definitely and, hoping she sounded more sincere than she was feeling, turned to the woman. 'Thank you for a lovely evening, Olga.'

'Perhaps we'll have another chance to do it before I leave,' the woman replied, without enthusiasm or a great deal of conviction. 'I'll give you a call if I'm free. I won't keep you waiting long, Horatio.'

'All right,' the M.P. answered and swung on his heel to go into the gentlemen's toilet.

Turning, as Olga strolled across to the telephone, Beryl left the hotel by the side entrance which gave access to the car park. Walking towards the MG Super Sports tourer, she heard masculine footsteps approaching rapidly from her rear. Then, as she remembered that the toilets could be entered from the car park, a hand caught her right bicep and she felt herself being jerked around.

'What—?' the girl began, having guessed the identity of her assailant. Then, as the M.P. caught hold of her other arm and began to drag her towards him, she let out an angry hiss, 'Let go of me!'

'What's wrong, you rotten little Roedean snob?' Benner snarled, surprised by the strength with which his captive was struggling. 'Aren't I good en—?'

'*Hombre*, the lady said let go!' drawled a quiet voice which both of them recognized. 'So you just sort of take your cotton-picking hands off her.'

Spitting out a low curse, Benner swung his head around without complying. Both he and the girl stared to where, having placed his suitcase in the boot of Olga's car, the small Texan was approaching out of the darkness.

Normally, particularly as he had been told of what *Rapido* Clint had done to the two Italian gangsters, the M.P. would have showed discretion. However, the *marihuana* was working on him and giving him a false courage. Considering only that height and weight were in his favour, he decided to teach the interloper a lesson and prove to the girl he was a man with whom it did not pay to trifle.

'You mind your own something-or-other business!' Benner snarled, shoving Beryl away from him and striding to meet the Texan. His voice began to rise as he went on, 'No dirty little hireling killer's—!'

Which was as far as the M.P. was allowed to go with his indiscreet comment.

Rapido Clint gave another demonstration of how effectively he could fight without the need for weapons other than his hands. Knotting his right fist as he ducked under Benner's inept round arm swing at his head, he hurled it forward. The M.P. had never been kicked in the stomach by a horse, but the sensation he experienced was a close approximation of how it would feel. Driven backwards by the force of the blow, he was also folded over at the waist. Nausea threatened to engulf him as he collapsed, winded and helpless, at the girl's feet.

'*You*!' Beryl gasped, staring at her rescuer.

'*Me*, ma'am,' Clint agreed, glancing at his victim and deciding no further attentions were necessary. 'I reckon you-all can head for wherever you were going. He won't be bothering you any more.'

'Th – Thank you,' the girl replied, then dropped her gaze to the huddled and moaning figure of the M.P. 'But what about him?'

'Don't pay him no never-mind, ma'am,' the Texan drawled. 'I'll see that he gets back.'

'*Back*?' Beryl repeated, an interrogative note in her voice.

'I've got me a riding chore over to the place where he's staying,' Clint explained.

'A *riding* chore—?' Beryl said, sounding puzzled. Then realization came to her. 'Do you mean that *you* have gone to work for Charles Wagon?'

'Shucks,' Clint drawled, deciding that the girl's tone and attitude were anything but complimentary to his supposed employer. 'He's not such a bad *hombre* happen you-all get to know him.'

'Perhaps, but—,' Beryl began, then heard the side door of the hotel open.

Turning her head, the girl saw Olga was coming from the building. The woman stopped for a moment, staring from Beryl to the two men, then strode forward showing signs of anger. Much as Beryl wanted to leave the vicinity and avoid becoming any further involved in the unpleasant incident, she stood her ground. She intended to make sure that her rescuer's actions were not misunderstood by Olga nor misrepresented by Benner.

'What happened to him?' the woman demanded, halting and indicating the moaning M.P. with an almost contemptuous gesture.

'He got something in his stomach that disagreed with him,' Clint answered, before the girl could speak. 'Fellers often get took that way when they start in to pawing and mean-mouthing a lady against her wishes.'

Knowing Benner, Olga had suspected that he had followed the girl when she found he was missing at the conclusion of her telephone call. She had followed, hoping to arrive before he behaved in a stupid fashion. From what she could see and had been told, her fears were justified. However, the Texan must have intervened. While indifferent to how this had been done and considering the M.P. had in all probability deserved whatever punishment he had received, she wanted to prevent Beryl from complaining that he had tried to molest her when she reached her home.

'You must have misunderstood Horatio, dear,' Olga told Beryl, forcing herself to sound more pleasant than she was feeling. 'If he likes a person, he tends to be a little demonstrative. But he doesn't mean anything by it. It's just his sense of humour.'

'I *didn't* find it funny,' the girl stated.

'I'll bet he doesn't – now,' Clint commented dryly and opened the MG's door. 'Anyways, ma'am, we'll see him safe to home.'

'This young man hit him in self defence,' Beryl declared, looking straight at the woman.

'I'm sure he did, dear,' Olga replied. 'But *none* of us want to be involved in a scene, do we?'

'I don't,' Beryl admitted.

'Then I'd suggest that we forget it,' Olga proposed. 'And that we all go before somebody comes along to see us.'

'Very well,' Beryl acceded, boarding her car. She looked up at the woman for a moment and went on, her voice holding a note of warning, 'There won't be any repercussions for this young man, will there?'

'I'll see that there aren't,' Olga promised. 'Good night.'

Confident that she had achieved her purpose, Beryl started the MG and drove from the car park. Not until she had covered about half a mile did she remember the way in which Benner had referred to her rescuer. She wondered if the Texan had tried to impress his employer, or the M.P. and Olga, by pretending to be a gangster. Then she dismissed the notion. Nobody, she felt sure, would take seriously a claim made by such a small and insignificant looking person that he was a hired killer.

CHAPTER SEVENTEEN

CHOMPED, WHOMPED AND STOMPED

STANDING side by side in silence, Olga Flack and *Rapido* Clint watched Beryl Snowhill taking her departure. After she had gone beyond their range of vision, the woman let out an angry snort and turned towards the small Texan with the intention of giving instructions. However, without waiting to hear what she was going to say, he bent over the figure which was crouching huddled and moaning at their feet. Grasping the Right Hon. Horatio Benner by the back of his jacket's collar and the seat of his trousers, Clint displayed the strength of a Hercules in miniature by hauling him into an upright posture. Nor did the Texan allow his attentions to end there.

Before the M.P. could begin to comprehend what was happening, he found himself being hustled towards the black 1927 Daimler Royal Double-Six-50 car – the Gambel brothers had cured its engine's malfunction shortly after Olga's arrival from Swindon – in which his party had travelled from Charles Wagon's training stables. All the false courage induced by the *marihuana* had been driven from him by the Texan's blow, but he started to struggle weakly and babble a protest just as he reached the vehicle. Instantly, he was twirled around with an irresistible force and rammed backwards against its side. The powerful hands left their holds on his garments, but his assailant's right forearm was thrust savagely across the front of his throat, effectively silencing him.

'Keep your god-damned mouth shut!' Clint commanded, his softly spoken words charged with more menace than many a larger man could have attained with shouted threats.

'Just make one more sound, or cause me another lil mite of fuss, and I'll kick your teeth down your throat, then stomp your face flat for mumbling. Get the hell into that back seat. *Pronto!*'

On being released, although he had no knowledge of Spanish, the rapidity with which Benner responded suggested he was aware that the word '*pronto*' meant 'with all haste!' when employed in such a manner. Nor did he offer to point out that, on the way to Little Venner, he had automatically claimed the right to ride at the front alongside Olga. Instead, he turned as soon as he was released and jerked open the appropriate door. Practically diving in, he moved straight across and crouched in the furthest corner. Nor did he say a word when, throwing an anything but sympathetic look at him, the woman took her place behind the steering wheel.

'Looks like we're not any too soon in lighting a shuck[1], ma'am,' Clint remarked, as he sat on the Daimler's front passenger seat and closed the door, nodding to where the bulky shape of the village constable was approaching. 'And it's real lucky I was on hand to cut in when I did.'

'I hope for your sake that my father agrees with you,' Olga answered, setting the vehicle into motion. She realized that the Texan had acted in their best interests, but wanted to try and destroy his attitude of calm assurance.

'You *know* he will,' Clint corrected, with the kind of relaxed self assurance which – particularly as she knew he was right – irritated the woman. He indicated Benner with a contemptuous jerk of his right thumb. 'Fact being, lady, I'd say your daddy'll allow I didn't hit that muggle-smoking[2] son-of-a-bi – gun hard enough, what I found him doing.'

'He was only having a little harmless fun,' Olga protested, determined not to show her agreement with the Texan's

1. Lighting a shuck: cowhands' expression for leaving hurriedly. In the trail drive and round up night camps, 'shucks', dried corn cobs, were available to supply illumination for anybody who had to leave the firelight and walk in the darkness. As the 'shuck' burned quickly, a person using one had to move fast if he wanted to benefit from its light. J.T.E.

2. Muggle-smoker: an early colloquial name for a user of *marihuana*. J.T.E.

summation of how her father would react to the news, but her voice lacked conviction.

'That wasn't harmless, nor fun,' Clint contradicted firmly. 'And *you-all* know it. From what I saw of her and the way you-all've been telling it, that lil lady's for real high toned quality. Her kin-folks'd get's riled as a tail-stomped and stick-teased diamondback[3] was she to go home and tell them's how that *loco* yahoo'd started to lay hands on and mean-mouth her like he was doing.'

'You seem *very* concerned about *her*,' Olga sniffed, seeking for some other way to avoid conceding that the Texan was correct.

'Seeing's I've been took on's hired help, I'm concerned about *anything* that could spoil whatever it is your daddy's setting up,' Clint replied, increasing the woman's annoyance by displaying neither resentment nor any other visible emotion over what she had hoped would be a counter irritant. 'She did me a good turn this afternoon, for sure. Happen she hadn't helped me to get clear, there'd've been fuss with Wagon and his two yahoos—.'

'And *you* could have been hurt,' Olga interrupted, still seeking for a way to provoke her passenger.

'I *could* have,' Clint admitted calmly. ' 'Cepting that it didn't come off *that* ways when we got 'round to locking horns. And, happen I had been, it's likely your daddy'd be dead now. Gambel couldn't've taken out Joe the Actor's two *pistoleros* before they made wolf bait of him and your daddy both. Then, what I've heard tell about the way those Italian jaspers treated women-folk, you'd likely've got 'round to wishing they'd killed you straight off too.'

'I'm not exactly fragile,' Olga gritted, once again faced with the unpalatable knowledge that she was hearing the truth.

'Lady, I've never, not even for one itty-bitty minute, thought *you* were,' Clint answered and, as the woman moved restlessly on the seat in her annoyance, gave an inclination of his head in Benner's direction. 'Is *he* important to whatever deal your daddy's got in mind, ma'am?'

3. Diamondback: *Crotalus Adamanteus*, the diamondback rattlesnake. J.T.E.

'*Very*!' Olga said shortly, but with great emphasis, her manner implying that any further discussion of the subject was prohibited.

'Then I'd say he's luckier than he deserves to be,' the Texan declared. ' 'Cause, lady, your daddy's a man to stand aside from when he's riled.'

Olga did not reply, but there was a calculating glint in her eyes as she darted a glance at Clint and increased the Daimler's speed. However, during the return journey, her gaze repeatedly flickered to the small figure by her side. She hoped that he would attempt to continue the questioning and present her with another opportunity of snubbing him. Instead, he lounged back on the seat and whistled – although she did not identify it – the old cowhand tune '*The Streets of Laredo*'. Unused to such cavalier treatment on the part of her father's employees, she was in a far from amiable mood as she turned the vehicle along the drive leading to the house.

'*Hombre*!' Clint remarked, twisting around so that he could look at and address the M.P., as the vehicle was stopping in front of the building. 'Mr. Flack's not going to take kind to what I caught you trying to pull at the hotel. *I'm* not fixing to tell him. *You* can do what you want, mind. But, was I you-all, I'd head straight to my room, say nothing and hope the lady here does the same.'

Although Benner did not answer, the speed with which he quit the vehicle as soon as it stopped implied he was going to take the Texan's advice. He had disappeared into the house and was scuttling towards the stairs before either of his travelling companions had stepped from the car.

Throwing a cold glare at Clint as he went around and opened the Daimler's boot, Olga stalked after the M.P. without speaking. Unloading the suitcase which held his belongings the Texan strolled leisurely and quietly towards the open front door. As he drew near, he heard Maurice Gambel's voice and slowed down.

'You've *got* to speak to your father, Olga. We should be bringing the men down here and making sure they know what will be wanted from them. But he insists he won't let them leave London until Reeder's dead.'

'I'll do what I can,' the woman promised, but she did not sound hopeful. 'You know what he's like where Reeder is concerned.'

'I *do*!' Gambel spat out, holding his voice down in a way that showed he did not want his words to carry too far. He went on angrily, but in no louder tones, 'Damn it all! There's close to five hundred thousand pounds at stake, not counting what we'll make on this betting coup. And he's putting it all in jeopardy just to satisfy a grudge.'

'I said I'd do what I can!' Olga snapped and, throwing a glance pregnant with meaning towards the door, raised her voice. 'Do you need any help with your luggage, Mr. Clint?'

'No, ma'am,' the Texan replied, realizing that the question was intended to warn Gambel of his presence and to prevent him from hearing what was being said. He strolled into the house carrying the large suitcase with no sign of effort, continuing, 'I reckon I'll go straight up to my room unless your daddy wants me for anything.'

'He's already gone to bed,' Gambel announced, scowling at the Texan. 'And he left word that he isn't to be disturbed.'

'Then I reckon a man can't do better than follow his lead,' Clint drawled, having surmised that the other man would not have been speaking as he had if old Mad John Flack was in the study. 'Good night, you-all.'

As the Texan went up the stairs, he heard Olga following him. However, without needing to look back, his ears informed him that Gambel was not accompanying her. The sound of the front door being closed and locked suggested why this was.

On entering the small back bedroom which had been assigned to him, Clint glanced around. It was furnished with a single bed, a small dressing table, a washstand and one chair. There was nothing to suggest that anybody had been in while he was absent. Nor, despite there being no way he could have fastened the door from the outside, had he expected otherwise.

Closing and putting the catch on the door, Clint crossed to place his suitcase on the bed. Peeling off his leather jacket, he hung it over the back of the chair. Passing behind his waist belt, a strap on the back of the shoulder holster held it firmly in position. He opened the press-stud, drew the strap free and took off the rig. Liberating the Colt Government Model automatic pistol, he laid the holster on the seat of the chair. After he had unloaded the weapon, he opened his suitcase. Feeling among the clothing it held, he produced a box of .45 calibre cartridges, an empty magazine and a small bundle containing the means to clean the pistol.

Working with deft speed, Clint stripped, cleaned and re-assembled the Colt. Emptying the bullets from the magazine he had removed, he filled the spare and inserted it into the pistol's butt. Not until he had drawn back the cocking slide and recharged the chamber did he show any signs of relaxing.

A second delving into the suitcase brought into view a metal bootjack in the shape of a cricket.[4] Placing this on the floor, he inserted the back of his right boot into the U-shaped prongs of its 'head'. With his other foot on the 'cricket's' body, he applied leverage to remove the tightly fitting footwear and reversed the process. He did not remove any more of his clothing. Instead, he crossed the room and turned off the light. Returning, he lay on the bed and tucked the Colt under the pillow. With that precaution taken, he closed his eyes and went to sleep.

Although the knock on Clint's door was not loud, it proved sufficient to achieve its purpose. Swinging his legs from the bed, he rose with the Colt in his hand and was as alert as if he had been fully awake instead of fast asleep an instant before. Crossing the room without making a sound, he halted against the wall at the right side of the door.

'Who-all's there?' Clint inquired quietly, his right thumb resting on the Colt's manual safety catch.

'It's me, Mr. Clint,' Olga's voice replied, speaking no louder. 'Open the door, please. I want to speak with you.'

Noticing the way in which his visitor was addressing him, the Texan was puzzled. It was as if she did not wish to disturb the occupants of the other rooms. Yet nothing he had seen of her caused him to believe that she would show such consideration under ordinary circumstances.

4. Cricket: a leaping orthopterus insect, *Gryllus Domesticus*. Something like a grasshopper in appearance, having six legs and a pair of long antennae.

Switching on the light, Clint waited for a few seconds until his eyes had adjusted themselves to the increased illumination. Then, still standing against the wall, he reached down to draw back the catch and open the door. Looking around warily, he satisfied himself that his visitor was alone. However, the fact that she wore a silk negligee and carried a bottle of brandy did nothing to explain her presence.

'May I come in?' Olga inquired, smiling seductively.

'Does your daddy want me for something, ma'am?' Clint asked, although he felt certain that the answer would *not* be in the affirmative. He moved to block the doorway and tucked the Colt into his waist band.

'Of course not,' Olga replied, struggling to retain her friendly expression. 'I feel I've been treating you rather badly, particularly as you did save our lives this evening. So I thought we might drink to a more – favourable – association in the future.'

'I'd surely admire to, ma'am,' Clint drawled, without offering to step aside. 'Only this's neither the time, nor the place.'

'How do you mean?' Olga asked, her face and voice losing every suggestion of seductive promise.

'Your daddy wouldn't take kind to it,' Clint explained in his unemotional drawl. 'And any man who comes close to you-all without his "go to it" 's going to get chomped, whomped and stomped so fast and hard he'll think the hogs've jumped him. Which I'm not figuring to let *that* happen to *me*.'

'I didn't think *you* were afraid of *anybody!*' Olga spat out.

'Happen a man's fast with a gun as I am, ma'am, he's not got a whole heap of need to be,' Clint replied, still as calmly as if discussing the weather or some other commonplace matter. 'But there's a mighty big difference 'tween not being scared and acting *loco* to try and prove it. I'm not scared of a diamondback rattler, nor even an old Texas flat-head grizzly,[5] but I wouldn't go patting neither the one of them barehanded to show I'm not. Which being the way the trail's headed, I'll say thank you 'most to death for your kind offer.

5. Texas flat-head grizzly: *Ursus Texensis Texensis*, the sub-species of flat-headed grizzly bear with a range from the Davis Mountains, Texas, to southwestern Colorado.

But it'll have to wait until *after* I've heard your daddy say it's all right before I'll take you up on it.'

'Do you know what you are?' Olga hissed, her face ugly with disappointment.

'Yes, ma'am,' Clint assured her, his tone sardonic. 'I'm just a half-smart lil ole Texas boy who hasn't been around much. But I've got just enough savvy *not* to get suckered into something that'd put me in *real* bad with the feller's hands out the money comes pay day. So I'll be saying good night again.'

With that, the Texan closed the door and secured it with its catch.

Realizing that her motives had been understood by her intended victim, Olga stood for a moment in the semi darkness. Then, with a hiss that sounded almost bestial in its fury, she swung on her heel. As she did, she discovered that her failure to entrap Clint had not gone unobserved. A door further along the passage was open and a figure stood in it.

Filled with anxiety over how Flack might regard his behaviour at the hotel, Benner had been unable to sleep. However, smoking a couple of *marihuana* cigarettes had improved his spirits. He had been on the point of going to bed when, hearing voices outside his room, he had decided to eavesdrop.

'Hard luck, Olga,' the M.P. jeered, as the woman stalked towards him. 'You did—.'

The rest of Benner's comment went unsaid. Spitting out an obscenity, Olga hurled the bottle of brandy at him. Although it missed, it struck the wall and burst close enough to spray him with fragments of glass and liquor. Giving a startled yelp, he retreated hurriedly and slammed the door.

Having noticed Benner spying on them, Clint had not returned to his bed after bringing the conversation to its abrupt termination. Instead, giving the woman time to turn away, he clicked off the light and opened his door a few inches. He hoped he might learn something, but was also ready to protect Olga if the M.P. had been smoking *marihuana* and had regained the kind of spurious courage which caused him to molest the girl in Little Venner. From what the Texan saw, backed by his summation of Olga's true nature, he decided no rescue would be required. So, still smiling sardonically, he closed and fastened the door. Strolling to the bed, he lay down and was soon once more sleeping peacefully.

There was nothing gentle or furtive about the next knocking to disturb Clint's slumbers. Sitting up, with the Colt in his right hand, he found that it was daylight. Going across the room, he unfastened and opened the door.

'Come downstairs straight away,' ordered Cyril Gambel.

'You asking, or telling me?' Clint challenged, moving until the other man could see the pistol he was holding.

'Mr. Flack wants to see you,' Gambel elaborated, scowling.

'Why'n't you say so straight off?' Clint asked. 'All right. I'll come down just as soon's I've pulled my boots on.'

In spite of his promise, the Texan delayed for long enough to don the shoulder holster as well as his footwear. Having affixed the securing strap and slipped the Colt into the arms of the retention spring, he went to the ground floor. Guided by voices, he entered the study. Flack was seated at the table and attired as on the previous day. Olga, Gambel, Wagon and Kinch were present. While the woman and her father's second-in-command were still clad in their night-wear and showed signs of having recently been called from their respective beds, the other two men – whose faces expressed considerable alarm – were dressed.

'Good morning, Mr. Clint,' Flack greeted, in a completely neutral tone. 'I trust you slept well?'

'Well enough, sir,' the Texan replied, wondering if there was a hidden meaning to the old man's words. 'Only I don't reckon you've sent for me just to ask *that*.'

'I didn't,' Flack conceded. 'While you were in Little Venner last night, did you by any chance see one of our men?'

'Why sure,' Clint drawled, showing none of the tension he could feel rising. 'I met Slick Markey down to the saloon I'd taken a room at.'

'Then why didn't you say something about it when you got back?' Gambel demanded.

'I'm pretty smart, *hombre*, but I haven't gotten around to

reading minds yet,' the Texan answered. 'Nobody's got around to telling me what kind of deal's going down hereabouts yet. I conclude it's something to do with rigging a horse race and can figure's how you'd not want the American hard-boots to be seen out and about, them being look-alikes for some English jock's and all. But there wasn't any call that I could see for Markey having to stay out of sight. Has he run out on you, sir?'

'Did you think he was going to?' Gambel barked.

'Did you?' Flack repeated, when Clint made no response to his second-in-command.

'If I had, sir, I'd've fetched him back,' the Texan stated. 'We got to talking about shooting craps. Seems like he'd been a heavy loser and was asking about ways he could get cheated. So I told him a few—.'

'Huh!' Gambel snorted, while Kinch looked even more worried and uneasy. '*That* wasn't a very clever thing to—.'

'*Hombre*!' Clint interrupted coldly and firmly. 'Way I see it, a man who doesn't have enough savvy to unfasten his coat and leave his gun clear before he brings in Joe the Actor's bunch hasn't any call to go judging how smart other folks might be.' His gaze returned to the old man and he went on in a respectfully polite manner, 'I'd say that Markey didn't come back last night, sir.'

'He didn't,' Flack admitted, after flickering a glance filled with suspicious calculation at his second-in-command. 'He wasn't in his room this morning and his bed hasn't been slept in.'

'Is his gear still there?' Clint inquired.

'Yes,' Flack replied.

'Then he could've got so drunk after I left him that he wasn't able to make it back here,' the Texan suggested.

'*We* had thought of *that*,' Olga put in.

'Only he wasn't hitting the Taos Lightning bad enough for it to seem likely when I pulled out,' Clint continued, as if the woman had not spoken. 'If he had been, I'd've stayed around and made sure he didn't talk out of turn.'

At that moment, showing signs of having dressed quickly, Maurice Gambel strode in and said, 'Come on, Wagon. We'll go and look for him.'

'Do you reckon he's gotten riled over the money he's lost and pulled up stakes, sir?' Clint asked, as the two men were leaving.

'It's possible,' Flack answered and stared for a moment at the now visibly frightened Kinch. Then he swung his coldly reptilian eyes back to the Texan. 'Have you any more suitable, or less unusual, clothing than you are wearing?'

'Got me some city-bought duds in my grip, sir,' Clint replied. 'I didn't pick them up over here, but they're not too different from what I've seen being worn.'

'Then I'd advise you to change into them,' Flack stated. 'You are going to London with my daughter as soon as we find out what has happened to Markey.'

'*Bueno!*' the Texan enthused. 'Once I get there, I'll be able to have a crack at earning my pay by killing J. G. Reeder.'

CHAPTER EIGHTEEN

HAVEN'T *YOU* HEARD ABOUT IT?

'WE'VE been keeping Bert the Jump-Up's home under observation as you asked, sir,' Detective Sergeant Challoner reported by telephone from Camden Town, shortly before five o'clock on Monday afternoon. 'His widow hasn't come back from his mother's and nobody else has been near.'

'I feared that might be the – um – case,' Mr. J. G. Reeder admitted. 'You may as well bring the surveillance to an end, sergeant. Thank you for your co-operation.'

Never had the gentle detective spent such a worrying and unproductive period as he had gone through since the first attempt to kill him the previous afternoon.

Investigating the incident at Captain Gray's flat, Mr. Reeder had speculated upon what had happened but was unable to locate any evidence to confirm his suppositions. He felt sure that two men were involved. One had opened the door, allowing the other to enter. Then, while the booby trap was being set, he had gained access to the unoccupied apartment upstairs and lowered a rope ladder up which his accomplice had climbed at the completion of the work. However, in spite of extensive inquiries by the police, nobody could be found who had seen the intruders.

Usually, Mr. Reeder would only have needed to ask questions in the right places to be told who was responsible. The underworld was a hotbed of gossip and secrets could rarely be kept. On this occasion, no information had been forthcoming. In fact, he had found there was a marked reluctance to communicate in any way with him. Men who had good cause to be grateful to him and had shown their gratitude by 'nosing' had been unavailable when he tried to get in touch with them. Some, alerted by the mysterious yet highly efficient means with which news passes between criminals, had gone so far as to leave London rather than be placed in the invidious position of having to refuse a person to whom they were in debt.

Being wise in such matters, Mr. Reeder had not tried to press the issue with those informants who had remained in town but were uncommunicative. They were too valuable to the functioning of his organization for him to do anything that would destroy his rapport with them. Nor was there need. Their silence had suggested the solution.

By the time Mr. Reeder had parted company with Colonel Brian Besgrove-Woodstole, although he had no direct proof, he was convinced that he was in contention with old Mad John Flack. No other person was capable of inducing such a condition of terror at all levels of the underworld. He had always been notorious for his completely ruthless nature and the diabolical ingenuity he had shown in dealing with anybody who aroused his wrath. Using his knowledge of chemistry, he could kill in unexpected and terrible ways. The fact that he had escaped what should have been certain death during the collapse of the passages underneath 'Terror Keep' would have increased the already close to supernatural dread with which he was regarded.

Added to the effect upon the underworld in general and Mr. Reeder's erstwhile loyal informants in particular, there had been an ever growing number of suggestions that Flack was still alive and seeking vengeance. The reports which had reached the detective during Sunday evening, and since his arrival at the Public Prosecutor's Office on Monday morning, had served to strengthen his assumption.

Mr. Reeder's reasoning was as follows.

No trace had been found of Joseph 'Jo the Actor' Steffens and his men. However, their unannounced arrival in England was significant. They were well known in their specialized field. Only a person of great importance and well connected in international criminal circles could have secured their services. While men like Steffens did not openly advertise their movements, some hint of their coming would almost certainly leak out. When that happened, a 'nose' was sure to have informed against any normal employer. They would be disinclined to do so if they learned that Mad John Flack, with his terrible reputation, had brought the American trio across the Atlantic Ocean.

While Mr. Reeder and Besgrove-Woodstole had been having a belated dinner at Daffodil House, on Sunday night, a report had arrived from an expert of Scotland Yard's Explosives Department. The manner in which the sticks of dynamite found in the Frazer-Nash Fast Tourer had been fastened together, the type of detonator, the way it had been crimped to the firing wires and how they were coupled to the engine's electrical system were peculiar to a professional assassin, Igor Dumbrowski. As he was known to be active in political as well as criminal circles, the Colonel had contacted Military Intelligence's Duty Officer at the War Office. According to the files, Dumbrowski was currently employed by one of the anarchist factions in France. Just after noon on Monday, Mr. Reeder was informed that he had disappeared from his usual haunts and his present whereabouts were not known.

The spent cartridge case found by the detectives after the shooting in Wardour Street and the damage done to the Tourer's windshield had been informative. The weapon employed was of the high velocity .257 Roberts calibre and the tip of the bullet had been carved with an 'X' to create a dumdum effect on impact. Gregory Toomis, a soldier-of-fortune in the Far East invariably used a Winchester Model 54 rifle of that calibre and dumdum[1] bullets when carrying out sniping assignments. Although no legal charges had ever been made against him, British Military Intelligence took considerable interest in his activities. On being radioed for information, all Besgrove-Woodstole's men in the Far East could say was that Toomis could not be found but he was believed to be engaged in his usual line of work elsewhere. However, the records at the War Office had disclosed that he had once been a close associate of 'Colonel Hothling' who, before his arrest in the 'Terror Keep' case, was Flack's second-in-command.

1. Dumdum bullet: one with a soft nose which expands on impact, inflicting a large, jagged wound. Said to have originated at the Dumdum Arsenal near Calcutta, India.

Appreciating the danger of coming back to England so soon after the murder he had committed in Brighton, Gaston Porthos would have needed some greater inducement than money to tempt him from the comparative safety of his homeland. He was suspected of having worked for Flack in the past and to have been enamoured of the old man's daughter. Knowing something of her capability where handling members of his sex was concerned, Mr. Reeder felt sure that she might have exerted considerable influence in persuading Porthos to cross the Channel.

Despite the lack of proof, the matter of the entry into Captain Gray's flat and the settling of the booby trap had been informative. In Mr. Reeder's estimation, there were not more than six men in the world capable of unfastening the type of lock fitted on the door without leaving traces of the tampering. The only one he knew to be in England was incarcerated in Dartmoor Prison and could be discounted. Consulting with Mr. Golden, who had access to a greater store of information than he had available in London, Mr. Reeder had decided upon the probable identity of the culprits. Although there were such things as crimes of imitation, generally criminals developed and stuck to a *modus operandi* which had proved successful. So the detective believed the incident was the work of two Swiss brothers, one an expert at opening locks and the other equally adept in the use of explosives. They were not professional assassins, but had used similar methods to kill a fence who had cheated and threatened to betray them. Less than an hour ago, a message from the police in Zurich had notified Mr. Reeder that the Tell brothers were last seen boarding an airliner destined for Sweden. As yet, there was no further news of their movements.

One of Flack's greatest attributes had always been his ability to obtain the services of top criminal specialists from all over the world and at very short notice. Another was the way he could bring them into England in spite of the watch kept by the police and other interested authorities for such undesirable visitors.

Satisfied that he was up against the malignant old master criminal, Mr. Reeder had nevertheless refused an offer of a police escort. In addition to preferring to rely upon his own precautions, he had no desire to place the officers' lives in jeopardy. He had been successful in reaching the Public Prosecutor's Office without incident and spent the day there carrying out routine tasks, fending off various journalists who wished to obtain further details about the attempts upon his life, or studying the reports which had arrived. Although he had felt sure it would be pointless, he had arranged for a watch to be kept on Carrington Mews. The task had fallen upon the local detectives with the results he had anticipated.

'By the way, sir,' Sergeant Challoner said, before Mr. Reeder could hang up the telephone receiver. 'What do you make of that business at the Cheese?'

'Do you mean the wager between Messrs. Frithington-Evans and – um – Siniter?' the detective asked, knowing of the 'Miller's' interest in horse racing.

'There *must* be more than just *that* behind it,' the sergeant protested. 'Why should either of them go to so much trouble if it was nothing more than a spur of the moment side bet?'

'I'm afraid I don't understand,' Mr. Reeder began.

'Why did they have to bring the others in?'

'Others. What others might these be?'

'Shenley, Burroughs, Graveny and Broughton.'

'I'm afraid I'm still no – um – wiser, sergeant,' Mr. Reeder confessed, although he knew something of the men in question.

'Haven't *you* heard about it?' the Miller asked, so surprised that the straw he was holding slipped from between his fingers and fell unheeded to his desk.

'I've heard of the wager between the two – um – gentlemen, but that is the extent of my knowledge,' Mr. Reeder explained. While his reputation for being exceptionally well informed was justified and advantageous in some respects, it also caused many people to believe he must be aware of everything that happened. 'Perhaps you would enlighten me.'

'Frithington-Evans and Siniter started it,' the Miller obliged. 'Then the other four – there are only six entries in the race – got involved and every one of them is hot.'

'By "hot", you imply that none of them are overburdened

by – um – scruples?' Mr. Reeder put in mildly, remembering that all four owned racehorses as well as having somewhat dubious business interests.

'I'd be surprised if *any* of them had even *heard* of scruples,' the Miller stated. 'Anyway, it finished with each of them putting down a monkey[2] as an unofficial purse, winner takes all. Then Messinger—'

'Would that be the Honourable Claud Messinger?'

'Yes, sir. All six were his guests for lunch. He suggested that, to make sure everything was fair and above board, each of them would put up a completely honest and straight jockey and stay away from the course on the day of the race.'

'A not unwise precaution under the – um – circumstances,' Mr. Reeder conceded. 'However, like yourself, I am surprised that the – um – Honourable Claud – if I may be so familiar – suggested it. Far be it for me to dispense gossip, but it is rumoured that he too not infrequently displays a lamentable lack of scruples.'

'I've never known him to show *any* scruples,' the Miller sniffed, being one with Mr. Reeder in suffering no delusions over the character of the Hon. Claud Messinger. 'But, if there's a fiddle going on, how will it be worked? I've been studying the form of the horses and there's nothing much between them, particularly when they'll have jockeys up like Lem Dooby and the others who've been picked. Not one of them would think of throwing a race and they always ride to win.'

'You say that there is no appreciable difference in how the six – um – horses have performed in the past?'

'Not enough to be able to say one's the clear favourite and there's nothing to suggest any of them has been held back for something special. They're just average horses. The kind that get run for the stakes in the minor races on a meeting's card.'

'Hum!' said Mr. Reeder pensively, although a lesser man facing such a serious personal threat might have told the sergeant he had more important matters demanding his attention. 'In which case, apart from the unsavoury characters of the men concerned, this might be no more than a chance

2. Monkey: betting term for five hundred pounds.

argument ending in a – um – sporting wager. I'm afraid that no possibility suggests itself to me as yet. However, I will give the matter my consideration – such as it is – and inform you if I learn anything informative.'

'I'd be grateful if you would, sir,' the Miller declared, in the tones of one who did not doubt there would be a successful outcome. 'And, if I learn anything else, I'll let you know.'

'Thank you,' Mr. Reeder responded and replaced the receiver.

For all his awareness that his life was in grave peril, the gentle detective did not put aside the matter raised by the Miller. Instead, leaning back on his chair, he sat thinking about it with as much serious attention as he had devoted to his private affairs. After considering other possibilities, he began to form a theory which he found so fantastic that his first inclination was to discard it. In fact, if he had not accepted the likelihood of Flack being alive, he would have done so. Although there was no record of the old man ever having been involved in a race course swindle, he was always versatile when it came to organizing various types of crime. The scheme envisaged by the detective was so unlikely that it could have sprung from Flack's warped, devious, yet brilliant mentality. However, on the face of it, the idea was so improbable that Mr. Reeder decided to look more carefully into it before mentioning it to the Miller.

Glancing at the clock on the wall, Mr. Reeder found the time to be almost six. As he had done on several occasions during the day, he rose and went to look cautiously out of the window. Despite his belief that he was being watched, he failed to locate the observers. Satisfied that *he* had been seen by *them*, he went into another room from which this would not be possible. Having done, so, he carried out similar preparations to those by which he had ensured his safe arrival that morning. With these completed he made his departure.

CHAPTER NINETEEN

WE'LL USE HIM TO TRAP REEDER

MR. J. G. REEDER's method of leaving the Public Prosecutor's Office proved to be as effective as the means he had employed to arrive unnoticed. In fact, if Mad John Flack's well concealed watchers had not received several glimpses of him throughout the day, they would have been unaware that he had somehow passed them and was on the premises. During the later afternoon, they had witnessed the exodus of the Director of Public Prosecutions, the Assistant Director and various lesser members of the department. One of the last persons to leave was a tall, lithe, good looking young man. Dressed in the fashion expected of an up-and-coming barrister when attending the Law Courts, he strode forth jauntily at quarter past six. However, there was no sign of the distinctively archaic attired Mr. Reeder emerging.

'But the old so-and-so *had* got out!' complained the tall, powerful and well dressed Toby Asquith, as he stood before Olga Flack and Maurice Gambel in the former's room at the Great Western Hotel. 'I sent in one of my men pretending he was delivering a message at half past six and the cleaners said everybody but them had gone home. So I left the men to keep watch and drove out to Brockley Road. And there he was, as large as life, in his front garden. I was thinking of taking a shot at him as I went by, but I saw that ugly old something-or-other Ma Grible was at an upstairs window with what looked like a rifle.'

When Gambel and Charles Wagon had been unable to learn more than that Slick Markey was not at the training stable, much to their and Olga's annoyance, *Rapido* Clint had earned increasing approbation from her father by finding out what had happened to him. Visiting the Starter's Hack, the Texan was told that Markey had tried to borrow the owner's car and had drank heavily when he was refused. He had become so intoxicated that he had fallen asleep while sitting in the outside toilet and was not found until Monday morning. The last the publican had seen of him, he was boarding a bus bound for Swindon with the intention of catching a train to London.

Having alerted Asquith, who was in charge of his organization in London, Flack had sent Olga, Gambel and Clint – the latter now wearing less noticeable clothing – after the jockey. Going to Swindon in the Daimler, they had ascertained that Markey had carried out his intention and duplicated his mode of travel. On reaching London, they had taken three adjoining rooms at the Great Western Hotel. However, when Asquith had arrived to report just after half past eight, Olga had not invited the Texan to join them. In her opinion, he had already attained too much of her father's favour. So, antagonized by the way he had treated her, she was determined to prevent him from strengthening his position. It was a desire with which Gambel was in complete agreement.

'My men have got Slick Markey,' Asquith went on hurriedly, noticing the anger that had come to Olga's face and how Gambel was not hiding satisfaction at what he had just been saying. 'Two of them waited until the chorus girl he goes around with had left for the theatre and fetched him out of her flat.'

Asquith's elegant raiment and cultured manner of speech had resulted in the hotel reception clerk regarding him as a socially acceptable visitor when he arrived and asked to see 'Miss Garvin'. However, he was known to the police as an intelligent but ruthless criminal who preferred to resort to violence rather than more subtle methods. Tough and courageous as he undoubtedly was, he had felt increasingly uneasy while he was making his report. Well paid as his position in Flack's organization might be, it was anything but a sinecure. The old man was notorious for being intolerant of errors, bungling, or failure.

Thinking of his employer's intolerance, Asquith wished

that Gambel was not present when he was telling Olga of his activities. There was considerable rivalry between himself and the brothers, both of whom would be delighted to be given a chance to show him in a bad light. He had tried to console himself with the thought that the various abortive attempts to kill J. G. Reeder had been the faults of the men making them. When he had been told what was expected of him, he had protested at having to have so many prospective assassins ready to take action on the same day. Pointing out how the detective had escaped death on other occasions, Flack had insisted that the plan was adopted. Claiming that Mr. Reeder would guess who had been responsible if he survived the murder bids, Flack had also ordered that the imported killers were removed from England with all dispatch.

Except in two cases, Asquith had carried out the latter instruction. Gregory Toomis, Igor Dumbrowski and the Tell brothers had been safely sent off to their respective destinations. Gaston Porthos' death had removed the need for any effort on his behalf. Unfortunately, Joseph 'Joe the Actor' Steffens and his confederates had refused to cooperate. After killing Bert the Jump-Up and abandoning the Clyno, both supplied by Asquith, they had disdained the arrangements made for their departure. Instead, they had taken the more powerful get-away vehicle and paid the visit which had placed Flack's life in danger. Although Asquith had not been present when the change in plans took place, he knew the Gambels would try to see he received part of the blame for the deviation. Nor would his standing be improved by his failure to achieve anything against the detective that day. So he was pleased that he had been able to finish up with some positive tidings.

'Is he alive?' Olga demanded, her attitude suggesting that her mood was changing for the better after what she had just heard.

'Yes,' Asquith replied, guessing the woman was hoping for such an answer. 'The boys coshed him to get him out of the flat, but he's recovered and isn't badly hurt.'

'Good!' Olga stated, a calculating gleam coming into her eyes. 'We'll use him to trap Reeder.'

'How?' Gambel wanted to know.

'Is Stivvins Wharf still empty?' Olga inquired, ignoring the question.

'Yes,' Asquith confirmed. '"Honest John" Staines tried to work the fiddle[1] with it on that chap Tibbetts who's been making such a name in the City, but it didn't come off.[2] Since then, they've even got rid of the caretaker.'

'Perfect!' Olga ejaculated, turning over in her mind all she knew of Stivvins Wharf and its surroundings. 'This is what we'll do.'

'It stands a good chance of working, Miss Flack,' Asquith enthused, at the end of the explanation. 'We won't have any trouble making Slick do his part and Reeder's never hesitated to act on his own. Even if he doesn't, there's no way he can bring the police without us seeing them in time to get away. You couldn't have picked a better place for us to get him.'

'How about Clint?' Gambel put in, glancing at the left wall of the room.

'How about him?' Olga countered.

'We're not taking him with us, are we?' Gambel elaborated.

'Certainly *not*!' Olga declared firmly, sharing her companion's disinclination to have the Texan accompany them in case her scheme should fail. She also wanted to see how he would react when he was informed that J. G. Reeder had been killed without his help, depriving him of the opportunity to earn his fee. 'I'll tell him that father has called to say you and I have to go out, but he must stay here in case there are any messages.'

'He won't argue if he thinks that's what your father wants

1. Work the fiddle: originally a confidence trick where one of the team would leave an object such as a violin temporarily on some pretence with a shopkeeper. After he had gone, a confederate arrived. Examining the object, the confederate claimed it was valuable and expressed a desire to buy it regardless of what it cost. He would then depart, promising to return later and conclude the purchase. When the 'owner' came back, the shopkeeper would buy the object with the idea of turning a quick profit and waited in vain for the 'purchaser' to put in an appearance. J.T.E.

2. Details of how the 'fiddle' went wrong are given in Chapter Three, 'Bones and the Wharfingers', BONES IN LONDON by Edgar Wallace. J.T.E.

him to do,' Gambel concluded. 'Even if he gets suspicious later, he won't know where we've gone and he doesn't know London well enough to be able to find us.'

'He may want to know how he can get in touch with us if he needs to,' Olga warned and looked at Asquith. 'We'll give him the telephone number of your club and say they'll know how to reach us. That ought to satisfy him.'

'Who is this chap and why do you need to satisfy him?' Asquith asked.

'So you see, he's not a man you can impose your will on,' Olga finished, after delivering a brief and accurate description of the Texan's ability in defending himself. 'And we don't want a disturbance here. We'll do as I said and that way there won't be any.'

In spite of the woman's and Gambel's delight over their belief that at last they were going to get the better of *Rapido* Clint, he was not unaware of their intentions. The rooms of the Great Western Hotel at that period were not completely soundproof. While he was unable to make out the words, he had heard Olga and the two men talking next door. Drawing the correct conclusion as to why he had not been invited to join them, he had converted the tumbler from his washstand into a simple but effective listening device. With its bottom to his ear and the top pressed against the dividing wall, he was able to hear all that was said.

There was a wry grin on the Texan's face as he lowered the tumbler at the end of the conversation. He could think of no way in which he could dispute the alleged orders from Flack without admitting he had been eavesdropping. Such a confession might lead to the disturbance Olga was anxious to avoid and which would not serve his purpose either. Yet he had no desire to miss taking part in such a potentially interesting expedition. It was obvious that Olga and Gambel had no intention of allowing him to accompany them. Although he knew where their destination was to be, Gambel had been correct when stating that he was completely unfamiliar with the topography of London. He might be unable to locate Stivvins Wharf by his own endeavours, or could reach it too late to participate in the proposed trapping of J. G. Reeder.

CHAPTER TWENTY

YOUR NAME IS ALVIN DUSTINE FOG

'Do you want to know who's trying to get you killed?' asked a male voice, in a Liverpool accent, having contacted Mr. J. G. Reeder via his publicly listed telephone in the study of Daffodil House.

In the course of his career, the gentle detective had received sufficient similar messages to be able to draw conclusions from the tone and responses of the person who was addressing him. More in hope than expectancy, he gave two presses on the bell button beside the telephone. It was a signal for his housekeeper to try to have the source of the call traced.

'I – um – *know* who it is,' Mr. Reeder replied and heard a faint sound like whispering in the background which suggested that there was more than one person listening to him. 'It is, of course, that criminal lunatic, old Crazy John Flack, who, if there was any – um – justice, would have been hanged years ago.'

'Do you know what he's planning next for you?' the speaker inquired.

'I would prefer to know with whom I am in – um – conversation,' Mr. Reeder countered, deciding that the ancient villain was not one of his audience. Flack would never have remained silent on hearing the way in which he had been mentioned. 'Who is this, please?'

'That doesn't matter,' the caller protested.

'Oh but it does,' Mr. Reeder replied, wanting to maintain the conversation for as long as possible. 'I am not in the habit of speaking with strang—'

'*Listen!*' hissed the speaker, having received *sotto voce* prompting from another of the listeners. 'I'm only going to say this once. If you want to know, come out to Stivvins' Wharf—'

'Would that be in the direction of – um – Henley?'

'No. It's in the opposite direction, off the main Woolwich Road. Come there by eleven tonight and I'll tell you everything.'

'Everything?' Mr. Reeder repeated, still playing for time in which the call could be traced. 'Good heavens. Not even the – um – Encyclopedia Britannica claims to do that. What a veritable cornucopia of inform—'

'Come alone!' the speaker almost shouted, once again receiving instructions from the background. 'If you bring the police, or anybody else, it's all off.'

'How do I know this isn't an – um – ill-conceived practical joke?' Mr. Reeder demanded, although he thought no such thing. 'After all, John – um – Flack is dead.'

'You know better than that,' the caller replied, in accordance with the orders he was being given. 'And you'll find out whether I'm joking or not if you don't come.'

'Wait a moment, *please*!' the detective requested, putting a note of urgency into his voice which he hoped would produce compliance and keep the conversation going for at least a little while longer. Locating the source of the call was a lengthy process and he doubted whether it had been achieved yet. Remembering the theory he had formed with regard to the problem presented to him by 'the Miller', he went on, 'I will come only if you can supply information about the – um – horse racing coup which the venerable Mr. Flack is engineering.'

'How the— did you know ab—?' the man at the other end of the wires commenced in profanely startled tones, then he or one of the other listeners hung up his receiver with considerable violence.

'So Mr. – um – Flack *is* involved,' Mr. Reeder mused, as he replaced his instrument in a more gentle fashion. 'I wonder where he might be?'

'They didn't have time to make the trace, sir,' Mrs. Grible reported, entering the study soon afterwards. She looked at the Colt Government Model automatic pistol her employer was slipping into his trousers' waist band holster. 'Are you going out?'

'Yes,' Mr. Reeder admitted and gave a full account of the conversation.

'It's a trap!' the housekeeper stated.

'The – um – contingency has not escaped me,' Mr. Reeder replied mildly. 'Could you see if we have a map of the appropriate area, please?'

Examining the large scale ordinance survey map produced by Mrs. Grible, the detective could see why Stivvins' Wharf had been selected as the rendezvous. The area was devoted to industrial interests, with few people residing in it. Situated some distance from the main Woolwich road, the Wharf was hidden from view of that thoroughfare by two blocks of factory buildings which were unlikely to be occupied at night. Access to it was only possible along a straight and narrow street, or from the river. To make matters worse, or better depending upon one's point of view, the Thames flowed in a straight line at that point and it would be impossible for a boat of any kind to approach the waterfront unnoticed.

'You're still going, aren't you, sir?' the housekeeper said, more as a statement than a question, knowing that he could never resist a challenge.

'I am,' Mr. Reeder confirmed.

'Then I wish that Mr. Grant and Captain Gray were back,' Mrs. Grible declared.

'Don't you think I'm – um – old enough to go out alone at night?' Mr. Reeder asked chidingly, but with a smile that robbed the words of any sting and made him seem far younger than he looked.

'It's not that, sir,' Mrs. Grible protested. 'They'd be able to help. You can't have the police anywhere near enough for them to be able to reach you quickly when the trap's sprung—' She paused as an idea occurred to her, then continued, 'Not unless you could have them put in an old barge, or something else that doesn't look like a patrol boat.'

'Regrettably, there isn't sufficient time to make such elaborate preparations,' Mr. Reeder pointed out. 'That is why they stipulated I must arrive by eleven o'clock. However, I intend to take some – um – precautions.'

Telling the housekeeper what he would require and what he wanted her to do, the detective went upstairs. In his bedroom, he changed into a dark blue shirt. Opening his chest of drawers, he removed a case containing a well-stocked theatrical make-up kit. Having selected a small round box, he put it in his jacket pocket and replaced the case.

On returning to the ground floor, Mr. Reeder walked into the dining room. It was in darkness. Without switching on the light, he crossed to the bay window and made a careful examination of Brockley Road. He saw nothing to suggest that any of his enemies were lurking along that respectable thoroughfare. Nor was he expecting to be in any danger until *after* he had reached Stivvins' Wharf. His well-founded reputation for springing traps of his own upon intended trappers would make people who had called him act with caution. Having taken the trouble to select an area which offered them excellent opportunities for detecting and avoiding any precautions he might implement, they would be content to let him arrive rather than try to attack him *en route*.

Ending his scrutiny, Mr. Reeder went into the entrance hall. He collected his hat from the rack and accepted the umbrella Mrs. Grible had prepared for him. It looked much the same as the others in the stand and the only difference would not be noticeable in the darkness. Inserted under the furled canopy, its end and the ring of its friction primer[1] emerging, was a tubular magnesium flare. It was capable of producing an almost instantaneous brilliant glare which would not only illuminate his immediate vicinity, but be visible for a great distance in spite of the surrounding buildings. Probably the police officers, who the housekeeper was going to ensure were as close as possible, could not arrive quickly enough to bottle up every avenue of escape. Instead, he was hoping that the glow would frighten his assailants away and, even if he did not manage to have anybody

1. Friction primer: a device whereby a rasp-like metal bar is drawn across a highly combustible compound to create a flame which in turn ignites another substance. J.T.E.

captured, might allow him to identify them for arrest at a later date.

For all the detective's estimation of his enemies' probable intentions, he was very alert as he drove the Frazer-Nash Fast Tourer with its top up – the windshield had been replaced during the morning – through the streets towards Woolwich Road. He was too appreciative of Flack's intelligence to have overlooked the possibility that his own reasoning on the subject had been anticipated and measures taken to make the most of it. With time of the essence, however, he realized that he could not take as circuitous a route as he would have wished. In spite of that, the journey was uneventful.

As usual, Mrs. Grible proved to have carried out her duties in a satisfactory manner. Mr. Reeder found the party of policemen he had instructed her to summon waiting on the side street which he had decided was sufficiently far from his destination to prevent his enemies learning of their presence. Leaving the Tourer in the officers' care, he took out the round box from his make-up kit. Opening it, he covered his face with the black powder it contained. With that precaution taken, he resumed his journey on foot.

The night was dark and there was no moon. Even on Woolwich Road, due to the stone throwing proclivities of the local urchins, the street lighting varied between fragmentary and non-existent. Unfortunately for Mr. Reeder, one of the surviving lamps illuminated the entrance but did not shine along the narrow access road. However, the fact that it was lined on both sides by the high perimeter walls – their tops encrusted with jagged chunks of broken glass to discourage intruders – of two factories was advantageous to him. While he could not enter the road unseen, by looking along each wall in turn. he was able to ascertain that nobody was lying in wait for him outside the Wharf.

Grasping the umbrella firmly in his left fist, Mr. Reeder unbuttoned his jacket. Wanting to be able to ignite the magnesium flare with the minimum of delay if it should be needed, a task which required both hands, he did not offer to draw the pistol. Scanning the terrain ahead constantly, making the most of his well-developed night vision, his ears sought to detect any warning sounds as he advanced warily along the potholed access road towards the dilapidated entrance gates. They were open and, exercising even greater care, he stepped through.

Stopping just inside the bounds of Stivvins' Wharf, the gentle detective gazed about him. Even without the disturbing belief that men were lurking somewhere on the premises with the intention of killing him, the scene struck him as being one of dreary desolation. It also offered too many places of concealment for his peace of mind.

To Mr. Reeder's right was what had once been a weighbridge and its office. As the latter's door was closed and the windows boarded over, he doubted whether any of his enemies would be inside. In fact, he surmised that – realizing how the river offered them a safer avenue of escape than the road – they would be closer to the waterfront. Some distance away, across a yard liberally bespattered with litter of various kinds, was a vast and decaying structure that had been a combined warehouse and precious metals' refinery. Beyond it, along the edge of the Thames, were a few battered derricks which *must* have seen better days and the remains of three smaller unidentifiable buildings.

Everything was deathly still as Mr. Reeder began to advance in the direction of the warehouse. Even as his eyes were sweeping along its wall, searching for the various access points, he heard a clock in the distance chiming eleven. Drawing closer, he could make out some of the objects of his examination. Although the doors appeared to have survived the onslaught of time and the local population, many of the windows had been denuded of their panes and frames.

Suddenly there was a brief suggestion of movement, which the detective sensed as much as saw or heard, behind the oblong outline of the glassless window he was approaching. Instantly, he froze in his tracks and his right forefinger sought for the primer ring of the magnesium flare.

'It's Corporal Hibbertson, Mr. Reeder,' announced a voice, which for all its quiet pitch, the detective recognized was that of Colonel Besgrove-Woodstole's batman. 'Don't shoot, or show a light, sir. They're down behind the buildings by the river. Four of them are on the bank, with what look like shotguns. There're another two on the motorboat they came across in.'

'Thank you, corporal,' Mr. Reeder replied in no louder tones. 'Is the – um – Colonel with you?'

'No, sir,' Hibbertson answered. 'There's only me and his cousin from America. He's down at the other end of the warehouse, keeping an eye on them.'

'Take this magnesium flare and be ready to set it off, please,' Mr. Reeder requested, realizing this was neither the time nor the place for him to satisfy his curiosity regarding the corporal's presence or about Besgrove-Woodstole's 'cousin from America'. He extracted the tube from the umbrella and, handing it over, drew his Colt. 'I'm going to spring the trap. Do you know *exactly* where the Colonel's – um – foreign relative is situated?'

'He's at the end window on the ground floor – sir,' Hibbertson explained, the slight pause before the honorific indicating a professional soldier's annoyance at a civilian thinking he might have omitted to obtain such basic but important information. 'Shall I come with you?'

'I think not,' Mr. Reeder decided, amused by the other's attitude. 'one target is – um – sufficient, corporal.'

'Whatever you say, sir,' Hibbertson assented. 'Good luck.'

Comforted by the knowledge that he had assistance so readily available, although puzzled by how it came to be there, Mr. Reeder stepped forward. Remembering how some of the waiting men were armed, he was too wise to let himself become distracted by pondering on his good fortune or allow it to make him grow careless. Instead, he paid an even greater attention to his surroundings. Feeling ahead of him with each foot in turn, so it would locate and avoid anything which might otherwise have been kicked and make a noise, he watched for the first hint to betray his assailants exact positions. He was confident that they would have great difficulty in seeing him. Having moved at an angle to the entrance gates, he was no longer 'sky-lined' against the illuminated entrance of the access road.

Contriving to move in silence, the detective went nearer and nearer to the bank of the river. By the time he was level with the next to the last window of the warehouse, he was growing concerned. He knew that he was already in range of the shotguns and he still had not succeeeded in pinpointing their users.

Doing so was growing increasingly urgent!

It was, in fact, literally a matter of life or death!

'Is that you, Mr. Reeder?'

The words originated from beyond the central of the three ruined buildings. In spite of the very frightened timbre the voice now held and the possibility of distortion caused by passing along the telephone wires, the detective could tell he was being addressed by the man whose call had brought him to Stivvins' Wharf. He also deduced that the man was not speaking voluntarily.

Coming to a halt at the first word, Mr. Reeder realized that his assailants were trying to locate him. So he glanced around quickly. By sheer bad fortune, the nearest window was one of those which had retained its fittings. He doubted whether he would be able to open it quietly enough to avoid detection. Nor was he greatly enamoured with the idea of plunging through the glass, particularly as he could not see what lay behind it. The nearest available shelter, the composition of which he was unable to ascertain, was a barely adequate mound of rubbish some feet to his left.

'It is,' the detective called back, having decided upon his strategy.

Even as Mr. Reeder spoke, the beam of a powerful electric torch stabbed with disconcerting – but, fortunately, not complete – accuracy through the darkness.

Having anticipated such an eventuality, although the light was being directed nearer to him than was desirable, Mr. Reeder was ready to counter it. As the beam moved towards him, his left thumb pressed the catch on the handle of his umbrella. Released from restraint, having been designed to act in such a manner, the canopy sprang open. Throwing it forward so it was illuminated, he propelled himself to the left with all the speed he could muster.

Three thunderous bellows told of gunpowder being detonated and the triple red glows of the muzzle-blasts erupted from between the buildings.

Spotlighted by the torch, the barrels having followed its

questing beam, the umbrella was flung backwards as the shotguns' charges tore into it. However, its owner had passed beyond the spread of the buckshot balls. Landing on the ground, he continued to roll until he was flattened behind the mound. Just as he was disappearing, the light picked him up again and he discovered that his chosen shelter was far less substantial than he had imagined. In his considered opinion, it would not even offer him protection from the flying lead if his assailants stayed where they were. If they advanced, his position would become untenable.

'You've missed the old—!' a furious voice bellowed from the shore, as Mr. Reeder was reaching his unpalatable conclusions. 'Aaagh!'

The words were terminated in a startled and pain-filled yelp as a heavy calibre handgun crashed from the last window of the warehouse. Either having been thrown or – more probably – knocked from the speaker's grasp, the torch was extinguished as it struck the ground and the scene was once more consumed by the darkness.

'He's got mates there!' yelled a second voice. 'Scarper!'

Realizing that a *very* rapid departure was called for, one of the men in the boat started its powerful engine and his companions on the bank turned to join him. Hearing and counting them jumping aboard, Mr. Reeder came to his feet and, when he was sure that none of them had stayed behind, walked forward. Before he reached the ruined buildings, the vessel was set into motion and went in a curve towards the other side of the river. As it departed, conscious that his rescuer had not offered to come and join him, he heard the man who had called earlier start shouting in alarm, but could not make out what was being said.

A shotgun thundered!

It was *not* aimed at the gentle detective!

The shouting ended in a scream and there was the splash of something fairly large falling into the water from the boat.

'Shall I set off the flare, Mr. Reeder?' Hibbertson called, taking the precaution of asking before doing something which might endanger the gentle detective.

'I'd sooner he didn't, happen that's all right with you-all,' called the man whose timely intervention had extracted Mr. Reeder from an exceptionally precarious situation. His accent was that of a well-educated Southron[2] and the tones were pitched so they would not carry far. Furthermore, despite the request, he did not offer to leave the blackness of the building. 'They're going like a bat out of the hot place and likely won't chance doing anything, but I'd sooner they didn't see lil ole me.'

'Very well,' the gentle detective assented, deducing that his rescuer was concerned with something more than merely avoiding being revealed as a target for the fleeing criminals' weapons. 'Thank you, corporal, but don't – um – ignite it.'

'*Bueno, gracias,*' the Southron drawled, but remained where he was. 'You're likely wondering who the Sam Hill I am?'

'On the – um – contrary,' Mr. Reeder replied, applying the manual safety catch and returning his pistol to its holster. 'Your name is Alvin Dustine Fog. It is said that, in addition to being the most competent – um – gun fighter of your generation, you are the youngest man ever to attain the rank of captain in the Texas Rangers and, because of this, you have acquired the sobriquet – um – "Cap".'

'I'd tell a man you know *all* about me,' the still concealed Southron chuckled.

'Not – um – all,' the detective corrected apologetically. 'I did not know you were in this country. Nor, I imagine, did Colonel Besgrove-Woodstole. Or he might have offered to – um – "trade", I believe is the term you American gentlemen employ, the information for something I know and in which he is very interested.'

'Whee-doggie!' 'Cap' Fog ejaculated, leaning against the window's ledge and studying Mr. Reeder, who had walked over while speaking, with interest. 'Is whatever old Mad John Flack's setting up likely to get the Colonel and his boys from British Military Intelligence on their trail?'

'Nothing so – um – dramatic, as far as I'm aware,' Mr. Reeder said mildly. 'He would have made the exchange to

2. Southron: a citizen of – particularly one who is still in sympathy with – the former Confederate States of America. J.T.E.

obtain the names of the – um – chickens we are entering for the National Poultry Show.'

'It looks like those jaspers will make it across before your police boats arrive,' the Southron remarked, leaning forward and looking to where, their crews having heard the shooting, a launch organized by Mrs. Grible was rushing from each direction. 'Have you-all anybody waiting over there to nail them?'

'Not sufficient to block every avenue of – um – escape,' Mr. Reeder admitted regretfully. 'It is probable that they will evade – um – apprehension.'

'I don't reckon they'll be fixing to have another stab at you-all tonight, anyways,' 'Cap' Fog guessed. 'But you're not out of the tall, dark and piney woods yet. There's somebody been set on your trail who's a whole heap meaner than any of those yahoos who've tried to make wolf bait[3] of you so far.'

'Who might – um – that be, pray?' Mr. Reeder inquired, displaying what might have been mistaken as alarm by anybody who did not know him, or who was a less shrewd judge of character than the shadowy figure in the warehouse.

'Just about the most deadly and dangerous *pistolero valiente*[4] ever to come out of Texas, same as his grandpappy afore him,'[5] 'Cap' Fog answered soberly. 'Fact being, I've heard tell he might be even better than me and I'm reckoned to be a regular snake at getting a hog-leg out and smoking. His name's *Rapido* Clint and, happen he comes gunning for you-all, you're likely to wind up dead.'

3. 'Make wolf bait': cowhand term meaning to kill. Derived from the practice of shooting an animal and, having poisoned the carcase, leaving it where it fell as a means of ridding a range of wolves. J.T.E.

4. *Pistolero valiente:* an exceptionally competent gun fighter, mostly one who sells his skill to the highest bidder. J.T.E.

5. Details of this earlier *Rapido* Clint are given in: BEGUINAGE by J. T. Edson.

CHAPTER TWENTY-ONE

CAUGHT 'TWEEN A ROCK AND A HARD PLACE

'So that sneaky old J. G. Reeder done licked you-all again, huh?' *Rapido* Clint greeted, before Olga Flack could speak, as he and Maurice Gambel entered her room at a quarter past seven on Tuesday morning.

The woman was so taken aback by the implication she read in the Texan's words that she refrained from launching her intended demand to be told why he had caused her to be woken up at such an ungodly hour. Almost the only consolation she had been able to draw from the previous night's events was that she had believed he was not aware they had taken place. Now it appeared she had not even that slight solace. What was more, she knew that she could no longer refuse to make use of his services. In spite of realizing that her father would not give his attention to their major project – the horse race coup was merely a moderately profitable intellectual exercise as far as he was concerned – as long as his hated enemy was alive, part of her still hoped that Clint would be as unsuccessful as all the other would-be assassins.

On reporting to Olga the previous night, Toby Asquith had assured her that he and his men had escaped from the abortive ambush at Stivvins' Wharf without being seen, or leaving anything which might identify them. Although Slick Markey had become panic stricken and was shot by one of Asquith's subordinates when he tried to leap from the motorboat, he had had nothing on his person that could lead the police to her. So she had considered that it was safe for her to remain in London.

It had been very late when Olga had returned to the Great Western Hotel with Gambel and she was in anything but an amiable mood. Nor was her temper improved when, just after seven o'clock, a maid had arrived saying that the 'American gentleman' next door had left instructions for their party to be called at that time. Before she could vent her pent up rage on the hotel's employee, she had been informed that Clint was already awake and wished to see her on a matter of the greatest urgency. Wondering if her father had been in touch with him during her absence, she had told the maid to let the Texan and Gambel know she would be available in a quarter of an hour. That had not given her time to dress, so she was clad in her dressing gown when they arrived.

'How did you know—?' Gambel began angrily, asking the question which was uppermost in Olga's mind.

'Well now,' Clint drawled. 'I figured it was that way from how Miss Flack banged the door and took to stomping around in here—'

'I meant how did you know we'd gone after Reeder?' Gambel corrected.

'Got all sneaky and listened through the wall with a glass,' the Texan explained cheerfully, unabashed at his admission of eavesdropping. 'Happen you know the trick?'

'I know it!' Gambel admitted. 'But you never said anything—'

'Wasn't no call for me to,' Clint answered, calmly crossing the room to sit with his left rump on the corner of the chest of drawers. 'I reckoned he'd be too slick for you-all. So I didn't bother calling you down when you sort of stretched the truth by saying's how your daddy'd passed the word for you to go out.' His gaze had swung to the woman as he was speaking. '*Now* maybe you'll let *me* take the cards and deal the hand.'

'Do you think you can do any better than us?' Olga was unable to prevent herself from demanding.

'Lady,' Clint replied drily. 'I for certain sure couldn't do any *worse*.'

'Why you—!' Gambel spat out, clenching his fists and taking a step forward.

'All right, *hombre*!' Clint drawled and, although his left hand rose to draw open the side of his jacket while the right pointed towards it, he remained seated. 'Happen you reckon I can't take Reeder, or *you* comes to that, come ahead and try to prove it. Only it's going to be settled now. Put up, or set back and let me talk to the boss lady. Name which it's to be.'

'Very well, Mr. Clint,' Olga gritted, when Gambel – having stopped at the Texan's first word – showed no sign of taking up the challenge. 'We'll let *you* kill J. G. Reeder.'

'Something just told me you-all might. First off, though I want you—'

'So you need *our* help?'

'Why sure, ma'am. Like this *hombre* told it last night, I'm off my home range and don't know sic 'em about the trails in this neck of the woods. So I need somebody on hand's does. Trouble being, I don't reckon you Limeys could get me what would be the most use.'

'And what might that be?' Olga inquired, being determined to supply every possible assistance so that the Texan could have no excuse if he was unable to carry out his promise.

'A good driver—' Clint commenced.

'*That's* easy enough to arrange!' Olga interrupted.

'Likely ma'am. Only, was this the good old U.S. of A., the folks's I'd be working for could likely fix me up with a hack and its driver.'

'A "hack"?'

'What you'd call a taxi cab over here,' Clint elaborated, his whole attitude implying that he felt he was requesting the unobtainable.

'We can get them for you,' Olga promised, knowing that Asquith had access to such a vehicle and, in fact, frequently acted as its driver.

'And I want to know what time those jaspers who were watching Reeder first saw him in his office,' Clint went on.

'Why?' Olga wanted to know, growing interested in spite of herself.

'Because that's where I'm fixing to take him,' Clint replied. 'Outside, on the street, as he's going in.'

'Huh!' Gambel snorted. 'Asquith's men were watching all day and they never saw him arrive, or leave.'

'Lordy lord! I swan if I hadn't clear forgotten *that*!' Clint ejaculated, directing a derisive glance at the other man and slapping his forehead in mock exasperation. He guessed from the glare Olga had thrown at Gambel, hoping he had overlooked the point, she would rather it was not called to his attention. 'Thing being, they didn't see him come or go. But they for sure saw him more than once while he was in there.'

'Several times,' Olga admitted. 'He kept peeping out of the window—'

'And making sure he'd be seen, so's folks'd know he was there.'

'What are you getting at?'

'How long will it take for you to raise this jasper with the hack, ma'am?' Clint asked. 'Because time's one thing we don't have a whole heap to spare.'

'Go and call Asquith, Maurice,' Olga ordered, impressed in spite of herself. 'When will you need it, Mr. Clint?'

'It'll have to be here soon enough to get me to Reeder's office just afore nine, I'd reckon,' the Texan replied. 'But I'd admire to hear what you think on that.'

'Can you explain, please?' Olga said and it was a request rather than her usual demand.

'I mind what your daddy said at dinner on Sunday,' Clint obliged, realizing he was being offered an olive branch. ''Bout how he'd got the Indian sign on every owlhoot and stool pigeon in this neck of the woods so bad that none of them would dare talk to Reeder.'

'He has, too,' Olga stated, recollecting how her father had made such a boast as a means of impressing the Texan.

'Well, ma'am. There's been so many tries and misses at getting Reeder that that there sign could start wearing off. Way it looks to me, your daddy and Reeder both are caught 'tween a rock and a hard place. Your daddy's got to nail Reeder's hide to the wall and *pronto*, or folks'll get to thinking his war medicine's gone bad.'

'Go on.'

'Trouble being for Reeder, he can't just sit back somewheres safe and wait it out,' Clint continued. 'He's built up a powerful reputation as one *hombre* who can't be scared. So he's got to go on the same way's he always has. That's why he let himself be seen once he'd made it to his office, knowing there was no way he could be reached in it. He figures that, when word gets out, folks'll conclude he's smarter than your daddy and isn't spooked one lil bit – And we *both* know he's right.'

'That's true,' Olga conceded.

'Way your daddy told it,' Clint went on. ''Cepting when he's hide-bound on some chore that keeps him away, he reaches his office just afore nine o'clock.'

'He's very regular in his habits,' Olga admitted. 'Father says he does it as a challenge to anybody who might want to try and kill him. Whitehall wouldn't be the easiest place to get at him.'

'That's what he's counting on,' Clint declared. 'Only, today I'm fixing to call his bluff.'

'How?' Gambel asked, showing considerable interest.

'By going over there and killing him,' Clint answered and his manner showed that he considered no further explanation was necessary, nor would any be given. 'While you're calling this Asquith jasper, tell him to keep all his watchers away today.'

'Why?' Olga inquired.

'Because we're up against one hell – if you'll excuse the word, ma'am – of a smart *hombre*,' Clint explained. 'I'll bet that, even if he didn't see them yesterday, he'll have figured out where they was hid and 'll have them staked out. Taking him's not going to be easy and I want all the edge I can get. When he hears they're not there, he'll conclude it's 'cause they're starting to reckon he's too smart for your daddy and he won't be so alert as if he's on the look-out for them.'

'Do it, Maurice,' Olga commanded. 'There is one thing, though, Mr. Clint. I'm willing to let you handle the affair as you wish, but I want to go with you.'

'Does Reeder know you?' Clint asked, showing no surprise at the request.

'Rather well,' Olga admitted with a frosty smile. 'But I can arrange it so he won't recognize me.'

'Happen you can do that, ma'am,' Clint drawled, 'I'd admire to have you along. And you'd best get us seats on the ten o'clock train to Swindon, *hombre*. We'll be back with you before it pulls out.'

'Pick me one with my back to the engine, Maurice,' Olga said, putting her seal of approval on the matter.

'What if something goes wrong?' Gambel grumbled.

'That's a chance I'm willing to take,' Olga answered, standing up. 'Now, as Mr. Clint pointed out, we don't have too much time to make all the arrangements. You both go and do whatever you have to. I'll be packed and you'll see to getting all the luggage on the train, Maurice.'

Watching the men leave, the woman unfastened the sash of her dressing gown. She was impressed by Clint's shrewd assessment of the situation and his preparations, such as learning when there would be a train suitable for their departure. However, she wished that she could have learned why he was so confident. If she knew that, she might still be able to arrange for J. G. Reeder's death without allowing him to carry it out.

Having packed her suitcases, with the exception of the items she retained in her somewhat large and bulky handbag, Olga dressed. She joined the men in the dining room and they had just finished eating breakfast when a porter came to announce that their taxi had arrived. Dressed in old clothes and a flat cap, with a realistic looking false walrus moustache to aid the disguise, Asquith was behind the wheel. His appearance was so close to that of the genuine driver only a close examination could have detected the deception.

Receiving his instructions as they set off, Asquith transported the couple from Praed Street, Paddington, towards Whitehall. As the Texan had laid great emphasis upon the importance of arriving no later than ten minutes to nine, he kept a careful check on the time and displayed a superb driving skill which would have made him the envy of many a professional musher.[1] In fact, if he had felt so inclined, he would have been just as competent as Bert the Jump-Up to handle the Clyno Royal sedan during the first abortive attempt to kill Mr. Reeder. Turning the vehicle on to Rich-

1. Musher: colloquial name for a taxi driver, English and American usage. J.T.E.

mond Terrace, he halted outside Number One. This was the building which housed the Public Prosecutor's Office.

During the journey, Olga had wiped off every trace of her faultless make-up and replaced it with a much less skilfully applied and matching selection from her handbag. Then she had donned a pair of most unbecoming hornrimmed spectacles and a rather shapeless hat which obscured all her hair. Slumping down on the seat in an anything but elegant posture, she effected such a change that she aroused Clint's unspoken admiration. Gone was her air of beauty and sophistication. She seemed to have become a plain, dowdy woman. As in Asquith's case, unless one knew her well and was allowed to look closely, she would go unrecognized.

'Whooee!' Clint ejaculated, gazing along Richmond Terrace in the direction of the Victoria Embankment. 'Was I part Comanch', I'd swear old *Kah-Dih*[2] was looking right favourable on us. Here he comes now.'

Staring over Asquith's shoulder, Olga failed to locate anything that could have accounted for the Texan's comment. There were several pedestrians approaching, but none of them was even remotely like the man for whom they had come looking.

'I don't see him!' the woman ejaculated.

'Yes you do, ma'am,' the Texan contradicted, opening the taxi's door. 'And so did Asquith's *hombres*. Only they're like you-all. They wasn't counting on him being all sneaking and showing up in disguise.'

With that, the Texan unfastened his jacket and stepped from the vehicle. Once on the pavement, without closing the door, he turned as if to address the driver. There was nothing in his attitude to suggest that he had any other purpose in mind.

Exercising all her strength of will, Olga forced herself to retain the unflattering posture as she repeated her scrutiny of the people who were coming towards them. One of the closest was a tall, heavy-set, ancient and venerable man in the garb of a Roman Catholic priest. A round topped black

2. *Kah-Dih:* the Great Spirit of the Comanche Indians. J.T.E.

hat was perched somewhat precariously on a veritable mane of white hair. Whiskers and bushy eyebrows almost obscured his features as he peered about him in what seemed to be a short-sighted fashion. Despite the day being pleasantly warm, he wore a crumpled old black cloak-coat from beneath which showed trousers badly in need of pressing. In his left hand, he grasped a new and tightly furled umbrella.

An umbrella!

The one thing which Mr. J. G. Reeder was almost never without!

What was more, the very newness of the umbrella gave a clue. Not only was such a neat item out of keeping with the rest of the 'priest's' rather slovenly attire, the detective had had an umbrella damaged beyond repair during the ambush at Stivvins' Wharf.

Even as the implications were starting to strike Olga, Clint straightened. In a deceptively casual seeming manner, he swung towards the 'priest'.

Halting in the same crouching stance he had adopted when dealing with the Italian gangsters on Sunday night, Clint began the smoothly flowing and lightning fast motions by which he could draw the Colt Government Model automatic pistol from its shoulder holster and fire in less than a second.

From the way in which the 'priest' responded, he knew what the sight portended. Halting, he started to throw the umbrella at the Texan with an under-arm swing that was vastly different from the bumbling way in which he had been moving up to that moment. However, such was the deadly speed employed by Clint that his pistol had come out and roared just after the umbrella left its owner's grasp. Twice more, in rapid succession, the big automatic vomited forth a bullet. Olga saw puffs of what appeared to be dust fly in a small triangle from the left breast of the cloak coat as the missiles struck home.

Reeling backwards, the stricken man's hands rose spasmodically. While the left clasped over the point of impact, the right went on to clutch at his beard. His hat and 'hair' slipped from his head. An instant later, as he was falling, an involuntary gesture tore away his face's adornment to reveal the agony distorted features and sandy side whiskers of J. G. Reeder.

CHAPTER TWENTY-TWO

THAT'S WHAT YOUR DADDY WANTED

LEAVING the jacket's lapel, as Mr. J. G. Reeder was crashing supine to the pavement, *Rapido* Clint's left hand stabbed out to catch the umbrella which was flying in his direction. At the same time, his right arm swung until the Colt Government Model automatic pistol was lined at Asquith. Shock and alarm came to the man's face. He wondered if the Texan had somehow learned of certain proposals which had been made to him. Even if he had contemplated treachery, finding himself staring into the muzzle of that deadly weapon would have caused him to discard the notion.

Having taken what he regarded as a sound precaution against being deserted, or worse, Clint did not waste a second. Still clutching the umbrella and his automatic, he flung himself through the open door of the taxi.

'You did it!' Olga enthused, as Asquith set the vehicle into motion, so beside herself with delight over the successful outcome that she beamed at the Texan.

'That's what your daddy wanted, ma'am,' Clint reminded her, laying his weapon on the seat between them so that he could close the door of the rapidly accelerating taxi.

So swiftly had the whole incident taken place that, building up its speed, the vehicle was departing along Richmond Terrace before any of the pedestrians could fully comprehend what had happened. It had turned left on the Victoria Embankment by the time the constable who was on duty outside Number Ten, Downing Street, attracted by the screams and shouts which rang out – he had thought that the shots were merely the result of a vehicle backfiring – dashed across Whitehall blowing on his whistle.

Displaying the same deft ability and knowledge of London's geography he had used while bringing his passengers from the Great Western Hotel, Asquith drove swiftly until making a left turn on to Northumberland Avenue. Going right at the Embankment brought them to Charing Cross. Reducing the pace as they entered Villiers Street, he joined the flow of traffic in the vicinity of the railway station. From there, in the company of numerous similar looking vehicles, he continued the journey at a pace which was unlikely to attract attention.

'Looks like I done you-all an injust' back there, *amigo*,' Clint remarked in a friendly tone, opening the taxi's communication panel as soon as the reduction in speed made conversation with its driver feasible. 'Only I've known it happen that a *pistolero* got left behind, accidentally on purpose, after he'd done his work.'

'There was a suggestion that I should,' Asquith admitted, glancing over his shoulder. 'I'm pleased I didn't consider it.'

'I *didn't* suggest it!' Olga Flack declared hastily, as the Texan looked at her.

'Never reckoned *you* did, ma'am,' Clint said soothingly and returned the pistol to his shoulder holster. Then he held out the umbrella, continuing, 'Here. I reckon your daddy'd admire to have this.'

Accepting the trophy, Olga gazed at it. There was a silver plate set in the handle and she read its inscription.

'Presented to J. G. Reeder by his colleagues at the Public Prosecutor's Office as a tribute to the part he played in disposing of Mad John Flack.'

'He will!' the woman confirmed vehemently. 'Thank you very much, Mr. Clint.'

'Back home to Texas they say you keep calling somebody "mister" you don't like them too well,' Clint drawled.

'We're a little more formal in England,' Olga answered with a smile, opening her handbag. 'I'd better make myself look more presentable before we get to the station.'

'Well,' Clint said, when the application of the make-up was complete. 'Now old Reeder's dead, you're daddy'll likely be willing to get those fellers together to make ready for whatever he's got in mind.'

'So you *did* hear Cyril Gambel on Sunday night,' Olga commented, but with none of the asperity that would have been evident before the successful conclusion of the Texan's assignment.

'Why sure,' Clint confessed, with a grin which made him appear very young and friendly. 'I guess I'm just a lil old sneaky at heart and he's got him a carrying voice even when he's trying to talk quiet.'

'The gentleman's right, Miss Flack,' Asquith put in, having been listening. 'I can gather them together and have them down to Little Venner just after dark tonight.'

'It's maybe none of my never-mind, but I'd leave it until at least tomorrow was I you-all,' Clint drawled. 'With somebody's important's Reeder being gunned down, the john-laws'll be jumping around like bullfrogs on a red hot stove-top. They're going to be watching every which way of leaving town *real* careful; checking who-all's on the trains and in cars and such. They'll not let that old horse-box of yours—'

'You know about *that*?' Olga interrupted.

'Guessed,' Clint corrected. 'Not that *that* needed much doing. Even after dark, maybe because it was after seeing what kind of a longhorn Wagon is, nobody's going to think much about seeing a horse box arrive at his place. Only the police on the road blocks aren't about to let it pass without wanting to look inside. That happens, them being such nosey cusses and all, they're going to start wanting to know how come some real big owlhoots are riding in it instead of horses.'

'You're right,' Olga conceded without hesitation. Not only had the Texan been correct in deducing how the various visitors were transported secretly to Charles Wagon's training stable, but he was just as right with his other summations. 'Tell them to stand by, Mr. Asquith. I'll make sure that father calls for them to come tomorrow.'

'I'd be obliged if you would, Miss Flack,' Asquith stated. 'We're all getting concerned by the waiting. Time's getting short and you don't lay on twelve bank hold ups simultaneously without plenty of preparation, particularly with so many different cities involved.'

'Whee-dogie!' Clint ejaculated. 'So *that's* what your daddy's big deal is!'

'That's what it is,' Olga agreed, closing the glass panel between them and Asquith.

'Your daddy's even slicker than I figured,' the Texan praised and, unknowingly duplicating the theory which Mr. Reeder had formed regarding the matter, continued, 'Taking all those banks's going to make what he gets for switching Bucky Borofin and the other hard-boots with the English jock's they feature look like chicken feed.'

'Arranging the coup amused father, but this is only a start,' Olga replied, accepting that after Clint's success there was no way she could prevent Flack from taking him into their organization. She also decided that, as he would be joining, he had qualities which could make him a useful ally if she could win him over. With the jealousies and ambitions of the other members posing a constant threat, she might have need of his services. 'Now Reeder's dead, there's nothing and nobody who can stop us building a criminal empire such as the world has never seen.'

'You and your daddy're the ones who can do it, Miss Flack,' the Texan declared and, in addition to dropping the patronizing 'ma'am' or 'lady' he had previously employed, there was a more respectful timbre to his tones. 'But it'll call for help that you can't get from us owlhoots.'

'Such as?' Olga challenged, noticing the change of attitude and pleased by it.

'Folks like shyster lawyers, judges who'll take orders on how to handle trials, or politicians to raise fuss and vote how you want, but who pass as honest God-fearing citizens,' Clint elaborated. 'Take that Benner *hombre*. What I've heard, your daddy helped get him elected to Parliament; but he didn't strike me as a jasper who'd stay loyal or trustworthy. So I reckon you've got him down at Little Venner to make him an accessory before, during and after those bank stick-ups. That way, he'll be in so deep he can't back out.'

'That's correct,' Olga confirmed, deciding that the Texan's shrewd assessment was further evidence of his intelligence and discernment. Combined with his deadly proficiency as a fighting man, provided she was able to keep him under control, it would make him a valuable weapon in her hands. 'He's an unpleasant, stupid, money-and power-hungry coward. So we need a really strong hold over him. And, as you said, once he's implicated and compromised, we'll have it.'

'Will that Markey *hombre* being killed do anything to spoil the horse racing deal your daddy's set up?' Clint asked.

'I doubt it,' Olga replied. 'As his death wasn't mentioned in the papers this morning, it's possible that his body hasn't been found.[1] If it has, there's nothing to connect him with Wagon, or us, and he'd already served his purpose by teaching the American jockeys the things they need to know about British racing.'

'That's right fortunate,' Clint drawled. 'I'd hate to think of your daddy's deal being spoiled by something's should never have happened.'

Although the comment might have caused a rift in the improved relationship between Olga and the Texan, it was prevented from happening by their realization that the vehicle was approaching Paddington Station. As it drew to a halt on the arriving taxis' rank, looking through the window, they found that Maurice Gambel was hovering in the background displaying a worried expression. The route selected by Asquith had been deliberately less than direct and the hands of the station's clock pointed to ten, so there was some cause for his concern. Relief flickered briefly on his face as he recognized Asquith, but faded when Clint emerged. Gambel threw an interrogative scowl at the taxi's driver, who met it with cool indifference.

'You-all got us the seats, *hombre*?' the Texan demanded over his shoulder as, deftly blocking off the advancing man, he helped Olga to alight.

'Yes,' Gambel answered sullenly, then his gaze went to the umbrella in the woman's hand. 'Is that—?'

'It is,' Olga confirmed, holding the umbrella out. 'Take it, you're more suitably dressed than either of us to be carrying it.'

'A porter's taken our luggage to the compartment I've

1. The body was not recovered by the River Police until late on Tuesday afternoon. J.T.E.

reserved,' Gambel said, obeying and drawing the correct conclusion from the way the woman was looking around.

'I just knew he was good for *something*,' Clint announced, oozing insolence. He took Olga's arm in the proprietary manner which might be expected of the man who had earned her father's approbation by killing J. G. Reeder. Then he made a gesture of annoyance and released her. 'Damned if I haven't forgotten to pay off thishere good driver.'

Turning, the Texan took some money from his trousers' pocket and handed it to Asquith. Accepting his payment the 'musher' threw a grin and a wink at his 'passenger'. Repeating the gestures, Clint took a handkerchief from his pocket. Shaking it a couple of times to open it out, he blew his nose and replaced it. Resuming his grip on Olga's arm, he gave a jerk of his head which was clearly a command rather than a request for Gambel to accompany them and led her towards the platform area. Scowling furiously, Gambel glanced at Asquith. Receiving no sympathy from that source, he stalked angrily after the couple.

Not until the trio were walking beside the train was Gambel allowed to take the lead and then it was only so he could guide them to their compartment. Once this had been indicated, Clint pushed by him. Entering the reserved first class compartment, the Texan placed Olga in the rearwards facing window seat and sat beside her. Scowling, but making no comment, Gambel set himself down facing them.

Nothing was said by any of the three during the few minutes before the train was set into motion. However, when it started and was passing beyond the end of the platform, Clint glanced to make sure nobody was going by in the corridor. Satisfied that they were unobserved, he came to his feet. Sensing danger from the cold glint in the Texan's eyes, Gambel also began to rise. As he was doing so, a set of hard knuckles lashed across his face in a powerful back hand blow and knocked him down again.

'That's for trying to have me left behind, or killed, back there after I'd made wolf bait out of Reeder,' Clint drawled, his soft voice chilling and his body exuding a sense of savage readiness. 'The last *hombre* who tried to double-cross me lived just long enough to figure how a thing like that might rile me. Only thing stopping me showing you-all is Miss Flack's daddy could need you.'

At about the same time that the Texan was delivering the warning, a medium sized slender man in the uniform of a railway porter entered a public telephone box and dialled a number. Standing with other similar officials at the arriving taxis' rank, he had not been a very diligent employee of the Great Western Railway as he had never offered to take any of the incoming passengers' luggage.

'It won't be today, sir,' the man said, when the connection was made, and his accent was more cultured than that of the average railway porter.

CHAPTER TWENTY-THREE

YOU'LL HAVE TO PASS *ME* FIRST

BERYL SNOWHILL was a young lady with an inquiring mind. When puzzled by, or interested in, something, she could never resist attempting to satisfy her curiosity. Finding herself both interested in and puzzled by the young Texan who had come into her life so dramatically upon two occasions, she had decided to put her mind at ease about him. So, although she had left her uncle's home with the intention of attending a cinema show in Swindon, she stopped her MG Super Sports Tourer outside the main entrance to Charles Wagon's training stables.

Since they had parted on Sunday night, the girl had found her thoughts continually turning to her rescuer. In fact, hoping to see him, she had spent a considerable amount of Monday morning and afternoon riding near the boundary of General Snowhill's and Wagon's Properties. Failing to do so, she had visited Little Venner with no greater success during the evening and wondered if he had been dismissed by the trainer at the Right Hon. Horatio Benner's instigation.

Seeing the *Daily Megaphone's* front page story at breakfast on Tuesday morning had caused Beryl to give the Texan further consideration. At first, she had read the story headed, '*J. G. REEDER MURDERED! Famous Detective Shot By American Gangster!*' with no more than casual interest. Then she had come to a paragraph which captured her full and undivided attention.

'The murderer, who is still at large, has been identified as James Bowie 'Rapido' *Clint. No photographs are available, but he is described as being about five foot six in height,*

powerfully built, with black, curly hair, tanned features and grey eyes, is aged twenty-five but looks younger, speaks with a pronounced Texas accent. When last seen, he was bare-headed, wearing a brown suit, white shirt and a plain dark tie. Although he has never been arrested, the United States of America's Federal Bureau of Investigation report that he is a notorious professional killer. They warn that he is always armed and an expert with firearms, but is also skilled at un-armed combat. He is very dangerous and should be approached with caution.'

Remembering how Benner had referred to her rescuer as a 'dirty little hireling killer', Beryl had also realized that – apart from the way in which James Bowie '*Rapido*' Clint was dressed – the description was identical with that of the young Texan.

Such was the girl's state of mental turmoil that she could not carry on reading. If she had, she would have learned the police had 'good reason to believe' Clint had already left London and was thought to be in the North of England. Also how Mr. Reeder's murder was causing considerable friction between Scotland Yard and the Public Prosecutor's Office. The former were stating that they could not be held responsible. In spite of several previous attempts to kill him, the detective had refused –with his superior's agreement and authority – to allow the police to take any precautions whatsoever for his protection.

Much as Beryl had tried to tell herself that there was nothing more than a hideous coincidence involved, she could not shake off a sense of perturbation. Nor could she decide upon what action to take. In addition to being disinclined to make a fool of herself, she had doubted whether the local constable could deal with her Texan if he should be Clint. Not, she had repeatedly told herself, that the polite young man she had met could possibly be a dangerous professional killer, despite the way he had knocked Benner down. One thing of which she had been certain, a visit by the police – even if, as she felt confident would happen, it established his innocence – would make Wagon discharge him.

The girl had still been undecided upon her line of action

when she set out for Swindon, yet she had known that she could not relax until the matter was settled one way or the other.

By the time Beryl had come into sight of Wagon's establishment, she had made a plan. She would call at the house on the pretence of asking if Olga 'Garvin' would like to accompany her to the cinema. Having done so, she could ask after the Texan's welfare in a way which would avoid arousing suspicion. If there should be any, she could make it appear that the visit was to ensure he had not been victimized in any way for his treatment of the M.P.

Forcing herself to ignore the nagging question of what she would do if her Texan and Clint should be the same person, the girl walked along the drive. She looked at the front of the house, but saw no sign of anybody having seen her. Hearing voices and activity behind the building, she acted on impulse. Instead of going to the door and knocking, she went around the end of the building. On reaching the stables' yard, she found Olga, the Texan, Wagon and two small men watching another who was equally diminutive and having difficulty persuading a recalcitrant racehorse to enter a loose box. Much to her relief, although her common sense warned that it proved nothing, she noticed the Texan was dressed as he had been on their first meeting.

Crossing the yard without attracting its occupants' attention, Beryl identified the three small men. Her sense of puzzlement was increased rather than diminished by seeing them. 'Hot' trainers usually tried to attract the patronage of a few honest owners to lend an air of respectability to their stables and, in spite of a growing dislike, she had been charitable enough to consider Olga in that light. However, as each was known to be completely straight in his dealings, she would never have expected to find any – much less *all* – of those three particular jockeys at Wagon's notoriously dishonest establishment.

'Hey now, Ivan-boy,' called one of the small onlookers as the horse backed away and, to the accompaniment of much profanity, dragged its handler after it. 'Why don't you-all leave that old cold-jawed hay-burner[1] out here and have Wagon build a stable 'round it?'

Shock brought Beryl to a halt, but it did not stem from the kind of language being employed by the man holding the horse. During the years she had spent around stables, she had grown inured to the use of profanity under such trying conditions. What had provoked the reaction was a realization that there was something strange about the way the two men were speaking.

Neither had an English accent!

That was not surprising in the case of the one Beryl had taken to be Lem Dooby. However, instead of his usual Australian dialect, his words had sounded much the same as the Texan's drawl. What was more, as an Englishman, Jim Gold's voice should have announced his Yorkshire origin; but the speaker was cursing in a hard American twang.

One thing became clear to the girl. She had beeen mistaken in her identification. Yet the resemblance was remarkable.

Suddenly, Beryl began to appreciate the precarious nature of her situation and was alarmed by the conclusions she was drawing. While she was aware that 'ringing the changes' with identical horses had been done on more than one occasion – in fact, Wagon was said to have practised such a subterfuge – she had never heard of anybody attempting a similar trick with jockeys. There was, however, something she could be sure of. If such a thing was being contemplated, the perpetrators would not want witnesses. What was more, considering the expense involved in organizing such an endeavour and the sum of money which must be at stake, they were likely to take severe measures to deal with a person who saw the substitute riders.

Even as Beryl was on the point of departing, hoping to do so without her presence being discovered, one of Wagon's burly 'stablehands' came from the tackroom. Giving a bellow of surprise, he lumbered towards her. Spinning on her heel, as the other occupants turned in her direction, she fled across the yard along the route by which she had arrived. She

1. Cold-jawed hay-burner: American racing term for an unruly horse.

heard Olga scream an order to catch her and the pounding of several pairs of feet, but did not try to look back.

Dashing around the corner of the house, the girl found herself confronted by a bulky, hard faced man dressed like a farm labourer. He grabbed for her and, unable to halt or swerve aside, she felt his hands close upon her shoulders. It was fortunate for her that she came from a sturdy and self reliant stock. Although frightened, she was not paralysed by fear. Out lashed her right leg, the toe of her sensible walking shoe making contact with her captor's shin. Giving vent to a savage imprecation, he thrust her away from him with such force that she staggered several feet and had no control over her movements. As she felt herself toppling backwards, two strong arms enfolded her from the rear. Rendered helpless to resist by the crushing pressure and lifted from the ground, she could not struggle. Face distorted with rage and drawing back his knotted fist, the man she had kicked began to advance.

'Back off Kinch!' roared the Texan's voice.

'Nobody kicks me,' the man snarled, glaring at the small figure which lunged between him and his intended victim. 'I'm going to bust her up good!'

'You'll have to pass *me* first,' *Rapido* Clint warned in his menacingly gentle fashion, adopting his posture of readiness.

Looking over her rescuer's shoulder, Beryl could see the change that came to her would-be assailant. Although he loomed above his challenger, he only took one more step forward. Coming to a halt, he kept his fist raised for several seconds and seemed to be trying to stare the other man down. Then his gaze dropped and the arm sank to his side. Muttering under his breath, he bent to rub his shin gingerly.

'Put her down, *hombre*,' the Texan ordered, glancing back.

'Yus, Mr. Clint,' rumbled the 'stablehand's' punch drunk tones in the girl's ear as he complied. 'Wot hevver you say.'

All the slight relief Beryl had felt was wiped away by hearing the name the man holding her had spoken. Her rescuer, the small and insignificant young man she had helped in the belief that he was in danger from Wagon's wrath, was, in reality, the professional killer who had murdered Mr.

J. G. Reeder. Even though he had prevented the man from attacking her and told the 'stablehand' to put her down, she doubted whether she could count upon his continued protection.

'Thank you, young man,' Beryl said, forcing herself to speak calmly under the scrutiny of the woman and men who surrounded her. 'I realize I shouldn't have come around to the yard without being invited, so I'll be going—.'

'You don't really think it's going to be *that* easy,' Olga purred. 'Do you?'

'I don't know what you mean,' Beryl countered, noticing that the man she had thought was Lem Dooby looked from her to Clint and back with a worried expression. 'You can't keep me here against my will.'

'Why not?' Olga challenged.

'My people know I've come,' Beryl bluffed desperately. 'If I don't go back soon, they'll come to fetch me.'

'How did she come here?' Olga demanded.

'In her jalopy,' answered Kinch, to whom the question had been directed. 'She left it on the road.'

'Fetch it in and hide it in the garage,' Olga commanded, studying the girl's appearance with a mocking gaze. 'If they come, they'll be told that you've taken me to visit a cinema in Swindon.' Her sneer increased as she saw the expression which came to the girl's face and her eyes flickered to the Texan. 'I seem to have struck a nerve, Mr. Clint.'

'It looks that way,' Clint admitted, also studying Beryl. 'Could be that's what she told her folks she was fixing to do.'

'So they won't be worried if you don't arrive home in a little while,' Olga went on, resuming her scrutiny of the girl. 'If they call, or come, earlier, they won't see you and that's what they'll be told. Or, later, we'll insist you've left after bringing me back. When they come looking, they'll find you – but you won't be able to tell them what you've seen here. You'll have been killed in a car crash.'

CHAPTER TWENTY-FOUR

YOU ARE 'CAP' FOG

'MY father wants to see you in the dining room, Mr. Clint,' Olga Flack announced, as the Texan answered her knock. 'He says you're to bring the girl down with you.'

Something in the woman's voice and attitude disturbed *Rapido* Clint. An attribute which he had always found to be of the greatest use in his exacting line of work was that he was extremely sensitive to atmosphere. However, in this case, he could detect no cause for the uneasy sensation which was assailing him.

Relations between Olga and Clint might have improved following his success at Richmond Terrace, but circumstances had prevented anything more intimate from developing. They had arrived at Charles Wagon's training stables without incident and old Mad John Flack was thrown into transports of delight on being presented with Mr. J. G. Reeder's umbrella as proof that his hated enemy was dead.

The blow had fallen early in the evening while they were listening to a British Broadcasting Corporation's news report. Not only was it announced that the identity of Mr. Reeder's murderer was known, but Clint's description had been given. Following his accusation of treachery directed at Maurice, there had been a heated altercation between the Texan and the Gambel brothers. It had required Flack's intervention to prevent an eruption of violence. He had persuaded Clint that the brothers were not responsible, doing it in such a way as to leave them in no doubt as to his high regard for their accuser.

If the Gambels' sullen acquiescence was any guide to their

emotions, they had not approved of their leader's feelings towards the Texan. However, there had been some slight consolation for them. Out of consideration for the news they had heard, Flack had regretfully agreed with Clint's statement that it would be unwise for him to stay in England. So the old man had promised to send him back to the United States as soon as a safe passage could be arranged. From that point, realizing he would be of no use to her, although still remaining friendly, Olga had lost her interest in Clint.

With the matter of the Texan's future settled, the party had turned their attention to business. Agreeing to the urgency of gathering the leaders of the bank hold up teams for consultation, Flack had pointed out that the police's attempts to capture Mr. Reeder's killer would place restrictions on their freedom to make the journey from London. It had been Clint who suggested the difficulties might not be of lengthy duration. He had said that there was frequently rivalry between the various law enforcement agencies in the United States and where two branches were involved, neither would be willing to accept the blame if something went wrong with an operation. From what Olga had told him on the train, a similar situation existed where Scotland Yard and the Public Prosecutor's Office were concerned. The news broadcast had mentioned how the police were complaining about Mr. Reeder's officially sanctioned refusal to co-operate by accepting their protection.

In Clint's opinion, if the police could be persuaded that he had already escaped from London, they would be unlikely to continue the time and man-power consuming task of maintaining road blocks around the city. Agreeing that this was possible, Flack had sent for the radio operator whose apparatus kept him in contact with Toby Asquith and had given the necessary instructions. From the reports received on Tuesday afternoon, the story of Clint's departure had been accepted and he was correct in his assumption. The police were no longer checking on traffic leaving the city. So the old man had arranged for the subordinate gang leaders to join him that night.

'You-all heard the lady, ma'am,' the Texan drawled, looking at the girl who had been in his custody since her capture. 'Let's go down and see what's doing.'

It said much for Beryl Snowhill's courage that she retained an appearance of composure as she preceded Clint from the room. There was a certain stiffness about her and her face had lost much of its colour, but she was holding her deep inner anxieties firmly in check.

Neither Beryl, Olga nor Clint spoke as they went downstairs. A glance at her wristwatch told the girl the time was half past ten. As yet, nobody would be worried by her absence. Nor, as she had forced herself to admit during her hours of captivity, were her family likely to be able to do anything on her behalf when they realized she was missing.

'Have those fellers from London arrived yet?' Clint inquired, as they reached the entrance hall.

'No,' Olga answered shortly.

Even as the woman spoke, the beam of a vehicle's headlights showed through the hall's windows as it turned into the drive. From the sound of its engine and heavy crunching of its wheels on the gravel, it was much larger than a car.

'This's it now, I reckon,' Clint drawled, still puzzled by the way Olga was behaving.

Without deigning to reply, the woman led the way to the dining room's main entrance. Once there, she allowed Clint and Beryl to go in front of her. Following, she slipped her right hand inside the front of her blouse. Entering with his left hand on the girl's arm, Clint stiffened slighty at the sight which met his eyes. Wagon was leaving by one of the room's other doors, presumably to greet the new arrivals in the stable yard, but the Texan paid no attention to him. Something of even greater importance and sinister portent held his interest.

Flack was sitting at the far side of the table, with his hands out of sight on his lap. Standing on either side of the old man, each with his jacket unbuttoned and a firearm prominent in his waist band, the Gambel brothers exuded malicious satisfaction. Face pale and haggard, the Right Hon. Horatio Benner crouched rather than sat on an armchair by the room's curtain-covered French windows. In front of the door opposite to the one through which the trainer was departing, Kinch lounged alongside what to Clint was the most significant sight of all.

Gagged tightly, Bucky Borofin was bound to the chair against which Kinch was leaning.

'You wanted me for something, sir?' the Texan asked, face expressionless and voice devoid of all emotion.

'I do, Mr. Clint. Indeed I do,' Flack replied, displaying just as little sign of what he might be feeling or thinking. He indicated a sheet of paper that lay before him with a wave of his right hand, then pointed at the captive. 'It seems we have a traitor in our midst. According to my informants in the United States, this is Special Agent Buckingham of the Federal Bureau of Investigation.'

'That takes some believing, sir,' Clint objected, releasing the girl and stepping forward. Before she could follow him, Olga had grasped her arm and restrained her. 'I've heard tell of him for a fair spell and he's always been a crooked jockey.'

'My sources are *always* accurate, Mr. Clint,' Flack declared, gesturing with his exposed right hand. 'You will kill him for me.'

'Why sure,' the Texan agreed, without hesitation. 'I'll take him along with me when I go to fix the girl's accident and leave him where he won't be found.'

'No, Mr. Clint,' the old man contradicted and pointed again at Borofin. 'You will kill him here and now!'

'That's out!' Clint stated flatly. 'I'm already so bad wanted I can't stay over here. Which being, I'm damned if I'm going back with this many witnesses able to say they've seen me kill a G-man.'

'You'll kill him,' Olga put in, pressing the muzzle of the Remington Double Derringer she had had concealed inside her blouse against Beryl's temple and drawing back the hammer with her thumb. 'Or I'll blow her brains out.'

'Not in front of witnesses,' Clint repeated, tense as a compressed coil spring beneath his apparently relaxed exterior.

'Is that the reason, Mr. Clint?' Flack challenged and his left hand rose into view grasping a long barrelled Mauser automatic pistol which he pointed at the Texan. 'Or does your refusal come because you are "Cap" Fog?'

As soon as the old man produced his weapon, the Gambel brothers and Kinch drew theirs. All of them displayed their pleasure at the situation.

'Somebody snitched,' drawled the man who had called himself '*Rapido* Clint', bitterly aware that for once he had been taken unawares. He had allowed himself to be distracted by Flack's gestures with the right hand. 'Blast the radio. Word gets passed around too quickly on it.'

'As you say,' the old man answered, but his voice was growing brittle and his hands shook a little. 'Receiving information from even so far away as your homeland is not a lengthy process with one.'

'It takes a right smart *hombre* to set up something like that,' Alvin Dustine 'Cap' Fog praised, playing for time and an opportunity to utilize his speed in drawing the big Colt holstered against his left side.

'True,' Flack replied, noticing how the Texan's respect for his brilliance did not appear to have diminished. 'Establishing a secret radio receiver and transmitter of such power was very expensive, but worth every penny it cost. Not even that old swine Reeder learned of its existence.'

'Keeping *him* from learning about it must have taken some doing,' 'Cap' Fog conceded, throwing a quick glance over his shoulder. Much to his relief, he found that – although pale and tense – Beryl was showing no sign of panicking. 'And, talking about him, I wonder where's he's at right now?'

'He's dead, father!' Olga almost screeched, as the old man's gaze stabbed at her. 'I saw the dust fly from his clothes as he was hit!'

'Wax bullets do that, ma'am,' the Texan pointed out, still watching the women.

'*Wax* bullets?' Olga gasped.

'Wax bullets,' repeated 'Cap' Fog, returning his scrutiny to the old man. 'Ordinary blank cartridges don't always feed properly in an automatic, so you make a hard wax head shaped like a regular metal bullet. It'll feed from the magazine to the chamber without jamming, but softens as it's being shoved along the barrel. Happen it comes up against something – like a real thick cloak, say – it'll kick out dust, but won't go through to the feller who's wearing it. I was real surprised, though, at Stivvins' Wharf when good old J. G. said he'd got some "waxies" we could use to make folks reckon he'd been gunned down by "*Rapido* Clint".'

Never had Beryl Snowhill needed to draw so deeply upon her reserves of inner strength. It took every fragment of will power she possessed to stand motionless with the cold twin muzzles of Olga's Remington touching the side of her head. Yet she knew that she must continue to do so. While she could not see any way out of their desperate predicament, she was confident that the Texan was doing all he could to produce one. She also realized that any mistake, or untimely and ill-conceived action, on her part, could ruin whatever slender chance they might have.

Once they had been in the safety of his room, while she had been on the point of defending her honour by any means possible, '*Rapido* Clint' had told her his true identity and purpose. He was Alvin Dustine 'Cap' Fog, commander of a special Company of the Texas Rangers. Posing as outlaws, he and his men infiltrated criminal organizations and, by causing dissension among the members, brought about their downfall. Hearing from 'Bucky Borofin' that something unusual was taking place in England, but not where, 'Cap' had been allowed to follow in case the Federal agent required assistance.

Being unable to contact Mr. Reeder the previous night, 'Cap' had called the private telephone number of an English relative. Colonel Brian Besgrove-Woodstole – the relationship had come about through the marriage of 'Cap's' grandfather, Dusty Fog, to Lady Winifred Amelia Besgrove-Woodstole[1] – to ask for assistance. Although the Colonel was unavailable, his capable batman had provided 'Cap' with the transport and knowledge needed to circumvent the ambush. With this accomplished, other plans – including the story about the digression between Scotland Yard and the Public Prosecutor's Office – had been formulated.

Unfortunately, Beryl told herself, her impulsive inter-

1. How this came about is told in: THE MAKING OF A LAWMAN, THE TROUBLE BUSTERS, THE FORTUNE HUNTERS and GUNS IN THE NIGHT by J. T. Edson.

ference had created a serious hazard and was throwing 'Cap' into even greater danger.

'Reeder's still alive!' Maurice Gambel screeched, his face losing its triumphant leer as he realized what was implied.

'Alive and kicking,' 'Cap' Fog confirmed and hoped the girl would realize that the moment of climax was very close.

'That's more than you will be!' Flack howled and sent his chair flying as he thrust himself to his feet.

Immediately, displaying exultation, the Gambel brothers and Kinch started to raise their weapons.

Knowing there was not the slightest chance of dealing with all his assailants before he was killed, 'Cap' Fog commenced his draw.

A whistle shrilled outside the house!

With crashes, the dining room's three doors and French windows burst open. Through each came—

Mr. J. G. Reeder!

Apart from slight variations in height, the four newcomers were identical in their characteristically archaic attire, hirsute adornment and features. There was only one major difference in their appearances. The man who erupted through the French windows swung the barrel of his telescopic sighted Lee Enfield rifle into alignment on Cyril Gambel. His duplicate in the left side doorway pointed the Winchester trench gun towards Maurice. Showing an equal determination, the triplicate on the right side of the room covered Kinch with Mrs. Grible's double barrelled shotgun. Carried past Beryl and Olga by the impetus he had put into entering from the entrance hall, the quadruplicate was armed with a Colt Government Model automatic pistol.

Hearing the sounds of the forcible entries, the Gambels and Kinch stared about them. So amazed were they by the sights which confronted them, that each was frozen into immobility.

Not so old Mad John Flack!

However, the aged villain was in such a rage filled state that he had eyes only for the two men who were standing in front of him. He was not aware of the other three identical newcomers' presence. Nor could he select which of his enemies he wanted to kill first. Much as he hated the young

Texan who had so successfully outwitted him, his abhorrence of Mr. J. G. Reeder was of far longer standing. So the Mauser began to turn in the direction of his older enemy.

Neither Beryl nor Olga duplicated the Gambels' and Kinch's lack of action. Feeling the Remington move from her head as the quadruplicate Mr. Reeder dashed by, the girl showed remarkable presence of mind considering she had never been in such a desperate and dangerous situation. Snatching her arm free, she flung herself sideways and down. Ignoring her, realizing what the arrival of the four Mr. Reeders must mean, Olga thought only of escape. Turning, she darted out of the door through which they had entered.

Even as 'Cap' Fog's Colt emerged from beneath his jacket, the automatic in Mr. James Garfield Reeder's hand crashed. Aimed in the only manner appropriate under the circumstances, to ensure as near an instantaneous kill as possible, the .45 bullet punctured a hole between Flack's eyes. Spinning around, with the load from the Texan's weapon narrowly missing his head, the old man involuntarily discharged his Mauser. By the kind of coincidence no author would dare allow to happen in a work of fiction, the barrel had turned until it was pointing at Benner and the bullet that was emitted flew to strike him in the heart. Oblivious of what he had done, Flack tripped over the chair he had thrust away from him as he rose and went down. He did not feel the impact as his body struck the floor.

Mad John Flack was dead!

'My – um – bird, I think,' Mr. James Garfield Reeder said mildly to 'Cap' Fog.

'Yours,' the Texan confirmed and swung around to find out what had happened to Beryl.

With the sound of the shots ringing in her ears, Olga crossed the threshold. As she entered the entrance hall, she saw several obvious plainclothes policemen coming through the front door and was conscious of another person much closer. Before she could react to the sensation, a powerful hand grasped her right wrist and shook the Remington from her grasp. Then the trapped arm was deftly twisted behind her back. Looking over her shoulder, she found herself staring into the grim visage of Mr. Reeder's housekeeper.

'You won't get away *this* time, my beauty,' Mrs. Grible warned. 'I'm *not* Mr. Grant.'[2]

Finding themselves menaced by the firearms held by three obviously determined men – Mr. Jeremiah Golden's shotgun and the trench gun carried by Mr. Jason Grant being even more effective inducements than Captain John Gray's rifle under the circumstances – the Gambel brothers and Kinch flung aside their weapons. Raising their hands in the air, they loudly announced a mutual eagerness to surrender.

'It's all finished now, ma'am,' 'Cap' Fog said, going over and helping Beryl to her feet. 'You're not hurt, are you?'

'N – No,' the girl replied, after taking a few seconds to bring her emotions under control. Then her gaze went from one to another of the quartet who had arrived so fortuitously. Having seen photographs of the detective in newspapers, she identified him; but her eyes widened as she looked at the duplicates. 'Wh – Which of you *is* J. G. Reeder?'

'Confusing as it may – um – seem to you, young lady,' answered the man with the shotgun. 'We *all* are.'[3]

2. Neither Ms. Wallace nor the author have been able to find any explanation of why Olga Flack was not arrested at the conclusion of the 'Terror Keep' case. Ms. Wallace believes – and I am inclined to agree – that having suffered the traumatic experience of fearing the woman he loved had been killed and learning she was still alive, Mr. Jason Grant Reeder was more lenient with Olga than he should have been and allowed her to go free. J.T.E.

3. While building his reputation as an exceptionally competent detective and forming his organization, Jeremiah Golden Reeder had trained his three nephews, Jason Grant, John Gray – who also served as a captain in the Rifle Brigade seconded to M.I.5 – and, the youngest, James Garfield to carry on his work. Knowing the superstitious natures of the criminal classes, he had decided the organization could function more effectively if his nephews' connections with it were kept secret.

Using the family's chicken farm in Kent as his headquarters, Mr. Golden maintained the organization's main files and correlated the information from their multitude of sources. One of the nephews always acted as a focal point by posing as Mr. Golden in London. Whoever was currently in residence at Daffodil House dressed, spoke and employed Mr. Golden's mannerisms, even when in the company of the few people who shared the secret, using wigs and special make-up to emphasize the strong family resemblance of their features. As Mr. Garfield was in his early thirties, the resemblance had been overlooked by Asquith's watchers on Monday when he had gone to and left the Public Prosecutor's Office without his make-up and dressed in the fashion of an up-and-coming young barrister. Once inside, he had changed into the clothes and make-up kept on the premises and allowed himself to be seen as Mr. J. G. Reeder.

Contrary to Mr. Garfield's fears, Flack had not learned the organization's secret. Having heard of Captain Gray's participation with Mr. Golden in the 'Big Printer' the old master criminal had arranged for the booby trap to be installed in the flat in case Mr. J. G. Reeder should seek sanctuary there. J. T. E.

IN CONCLUSION

REALIZING that Mad John Flack would not assemble his subordinates until his hated enemy was dead and wanting to capture them all, Mr. James Garfield Reeder and Alvin Dustine 'Cap' Fog had hatched a plot following their meeting at Stivvins' Wharf. Having persuaded Olga Flack to arrange for the gang leaders to join her father on Tuesday, the Texan had signalled the information to Captain Gray's valet, Parker, who was at Paddington Station disguised as a porter.

Summoned from their vacations, Mr. Grant and Captain Gray had joined Mr. Golden and Mr. Garfield with the intention of ridding themselves of the malignant threat to their existence. Wanting to obtain the fullest dramatic effect, without exposing their true identities, it was decided that they would all dress as Mr. J. G. Reeder.

Knowing that the men they were up against were dangerous and would almost certainly be armed, the Reeders had laid a trap. Assembling their police helpers in hiding on a lonely stretch of road, Captain Gray had used the rifle equipped with a silencer and telescopic sight to puncture one of the horse-box's tyres. Doing so brought it to a halt without its occupants suspecting the truth. As the area had appeared to be deserted, the drivers told his passengers to alight. On leaving the vehicle, they found themselves surrounded by the armed officers – the Reeders remained concealed – and surrendered without a fight.

With the horse box carrying the raiding force following them, the Reeders and Mrs. Grible had made their way to Charles Wagon's training stables. They were in position around the building when the trainer came out to greet what he thought to be the arriving gang leaders. He was secured without raising the alarm and told where they could locate

Flack. Knowing that a large body of men could not move in silently and would endanger the lives of the prisoners, the Reeders and their housekeeper had entered with the results already described.

One of Flack's traits was that he always committed all of his plans to paper. So the Reeders found details of the proposed race course coup[1] and how he had intended to create his 'criminal empire' in England. In addition to supplying him with finances, the proposed bank holdups which were to have taken place simultaneously in several London suburbs and major cities throughout the country were to demonstrate to the rest of the underworld the full extent of his powers.[2]

There was sufficient evidence to prove that the Right Hon. Horatio Benner was a willing accomplice in Flack's scheme. However, wishing to avoid a scandal, the leaders of the three major political parties had asked that this aspect was suppressed and his death passed off as an accident. They were helped in the deception by the perception of the Reeders. Before any of the police officers entered the dining room, Benner's face was covered and none of them learned his identity. The Gambels, Wagon, his 'stablehands', Kinch and the rest of the domestic staff – no charges were brought against the imported jockeys, none of whom knew the M.P. – were persuaded it was in their best interests to remain silent on the subject. For some reason, despite her normally vindictive nature and being faced with a life sentence in prison, Olga also refrained from mentioning her father's connection with Benner.

In return for their part in the suppression, the Reeders insisted that there must be no mention of 'Cap' Fog's activities. So the true facts of the Richmond Terrace were distorted. It was claimed that the murder bid was genuine, but

1. The coup was so meticulously planned that, realizing it could have succeeded, the Stewards of the Jockey Club asked that the details of it be destroyed. As the Reeders honoured the request, only the facts related in this volume remain to supply a suggestion of what was to happen. J.T.E.

2. According to their records, the Reeders suspected that the reticence of Churgwin and Birkstone was partly caused by a desire to see whether Flack's scheme worked. J. T. E.

Mr. Reeder survived as he had been wearing a bulletproof vest under the cloak. In addition, it was stated that *Rapido* Clint had killed Joseph 'Joe the Actor' Steffens and his two associates – whose bodies were found in an abandoned stone quarry – during an argument over the division of spoils.

So 'Cap' Fog came to and left England without his presence receiving public attention. According to his records, he and Beryl Snowhill met again.[3] However, as yet no evidence is forthcoming that he and the Reeder organization were ever required to work together after having brought to an end the career of the brilliant, completely ruthless master criminal, old Mad John Flack.

3. Although 'Cap' Fog and Mr. J. G. Reeder are not involved, some details of Beryl Snowhill's later career are given in: SACRIFICE FOR THE QUAGGA GOD by J. T. Edson.

THE END

VIOLENCE AT SUNDOWN BY FRANK O'ROURKE

The town had been quiet for too long. Sooner or later there was bound to be violence in Olalla. A stray bullet and a dead cow-puncher were just the excuse two bitter men needed. The chance death gave them the reason to commit a vengeance killing . . . a reason to crush Marshal Bob Travis and the law he was pledged to uphold.

A tense Nebraska town splits wide open as a maddened range boss and his crafty foreman call the shots for VIOLENCE AT SUNDOWN.

0 552 10430 2 50p

LATIGO BY FRANK O'ROURKE

The idea was fool proof. Addis planned the action, Brotherton set the stage, and Ellington faked the holdup. They'd made the getaway at night after meeting at the river and splitting the haul. Then it would be lights out for the unsuspecting Ellington . . .

But they hadn't reckoned on the storm that flattened Ellington – and the money – and delivered both into the hands of Hester Johnson, who lived like a man, loved like a woman, and never forgot a grudge.

0 552 10407 8 50p

DOC LEROY, M.D. BY J. T. EDSON

Marvin Eldridge Leroy had been on the point of leaving home to attend medical college when bushwhack lead cut down his parents. Although he was forced to abandon his plans and take a job as a cowhand, he never forgot his ambition of following in his father's footsteps and becoming a qualified doctor. Working on ranches, or driving cattle over the northbound trails to the Kansas railheads, he took every opportunity to continue his medical studies – and gradually he earned a reputation as a doctor ... people even called him 'Doc'. There were men, women and children alive who would have been dead without his assistance. There were also men who had died at his hands – experience had made him lightning fast with a Colt ...

0 552 10406 X 50p

OLE DEVIL AT SAN JACINTO BY J. T. EDSON

In 1835, the oppressions of Presidente Antonio Lopez de Santa Anna had driven the colonists in Texas to rebellion. Major General Sam Houston, realizing that his small force could only hope to face the vast Mexican army when conditions were favourable had ordered a tactical withdrawal to the east.

At last, on Thursday, April 21st, 1836, Houston decided that the time had come to make a stand. The Mexican Army, fifteen hundred strong, was on the banks of the San Jacinto river: Houston, with half that number, launched the attack that would decide the future of Texas.

0 552 10505 8 60p